100

The Light of Lucinda

by Sherry Lazarus Ross

Color Illustrations by Fred Ross
Black and White Illustrations by Author
Photograph of the Author by Kara Ross

WELL FIRE
PUBLICATIONS
Port Reading, NJ

100 Markley Street
Port Reading, NJ 07064-1897
Website: www.sherryross.com

ISBN 0-9701912-0-0
Library of Congress Catalog LCCN 00-109676

For Fred, Gregory and Kara

"The Light of Lucinda, while directed to 8 to 11 year-olds, is a delicious novel combining fact-inspired fiction and whimsy. With her own experiences as a parent upon which to draw, Sherry L. Ross has created a story with insights and delights for all ages.
That Lucinda's world is brought to life with illustrations by both the author and her husband, adds an extra dimension of delight."

-----Christopher Forbes,
Author, Scholar, Philanthropist

"Lucinda and Sara are a delightful two-way bridge between childhood and adulthood, between fantasy and reality, between practicality and dreams. By weaving poetry and prose within and without these themes, Sherry L. Ross invites us to enter her world of promise made possible by responsibility. This is a book to be read aloud by the whole family."

-----Alexandra York
Author and lecturer, president of *The American Renaissance for the Twenty-first Century (ART)*, a nonprofit educational fine arts foundation, author of *From the Fountainhead to the Future*.

"*The Light of Lucinda* is a story full of magic and love, a celebration of family, home, and the natural world."

-----Robert Rosenheck
Author of *The Love Book*

"What luck that Lucinda found the human child, Sara, who up until then had been lonely and had no friend. What luck that Sara found the vine creature, Lucinda, who might have otherwise withered. And what luck for us all that Sherry L. Ross knows how to grow dreams of wonder."

-----Martha Burns
Author of *Reading Group Journal, Notes in the Margin*
by Martha Burns and Alice Dillon

The Light of Lucinda is a feast of arts—poetry, illustration, prose—melded seamlessly to tell a good story. Like the classics of children's literature, this story can be read and reread. In her book, Sherry Ross has planted a magic garden, inviting us to join her characters there.

-----Broeck Blumberg
U.S. Correspondent, Diamond Publications, Tokyo, Japan

ACKNOWLEDGEMENTS

This book was written with the encouragement, support and affection of many people.

Robert Rosenheck was the first person outside of the family to believe in *The Light of Lucinda* both professionally and personally. He enlisted for me professional editorial assistance in evaluating this project. He arranged for Cindy Capobianco and Diane Glickman to read the manuscript and give me their critiques and suggestions for improvement. Their editorial input was essential in my being able to make this book shine. Recently, Cindy and Robert were married. They met by way of this book, so it seems fitting that I wish them much happiness here in my acknowledgements. I want to also thank Alexandra York for her insightful recommendations and advice and Elena King for her impeccable detail in cleaning up the final galley. Also to Wolf Press for their beautiful job.

To my good friend Martha Burns, writer and kindred spirit, I owe much. She is also the founder of our reading group known to us as "Third Wednesday." She has generously shared with me tips of the business, contacts, and invaluable support. I would also like to thank all my friends in the reading group for their enthusiasm: Broeck Wahl Blumberg, Lynn Baletti, Claudia Ethridge, Charmion Rayburn, Linda Saltz, Andrea Van Kampen, Nancy Mendez, Roseanne Laucitica, and Rickie Morrison. My love and appreciation to Diana Levenstein-McGovern, Bernie McGovern, and their two wonderful children Elena and David. Thanks for always being there. I want to tell all my friends at *Rapture of Short Hills, NJ*, how much their interest and encouragement has meant to me. They have shared this journey with me. I give my appreciation for listening, sharing and artistic input to Penny and Carl Fink, Jamie Roberts, Michael Williams, Cheryl Fusco and Michelle Van Hooten. Special thanks to Jamie for his optimism and wisdom, to Michael for his humor and ability to get to the point, and to Cheryl for being a loyal confident. Dr. Martin S. Willick read this book both before and after its editorial process. His encouragement is much appreciated. He is also responsible for bringing my attention to digital processing and the trends in independent publishing. I have benefitted on both a personal level and professional level in a million ways because of the opportunity I have had to work with this man of high character, intelligence and compassion. I will also take a moment to thank Joyce Hall, who has been a mentor to my daughter and, if she doesn't know it already, an inspiration to me. She is a musical artist, a mentor, teacher, and a champion of all the arts. Her energy, enthusiasm, wisdom, and caring nature makes me feel fortunate to know her. Much appreciation goes to Maria Parreiral. Her help in running my home, affection for my family, and genuine support and enthusiasm for this book, have made it possible for me to have the time to concentrate and take charge of all the other details that occur around a creative project like this.

I haven't forgotten my family. I am just leaving them for last so that I can be especially attentive. My mom, Marjorie Olson Lazarus, and my dad Leon Lazarus, have always encouraged my creative pursuits and brought me up in a home where artistic endeavors were taken seriously. They have always taken the time to be supportive and have both helped with the editorial process. My sister, Rochelle Lazarus Saxena, my best girlfriend, loves to write and draw, read, decorate, visit museums—just like me—and we can talk for hours. I look forward to joint creative projects with her, as I have had with my husband Fred. I send my love here to my brother-in-law Sanjeet Saxena, who is always telling me to go for it, and to my most adorable niece, Kiara, whom I love dearly and whom I can't wait to read this book to! Or maybe I should let her mom? We'll see. Now for my two kids—Greg and Kara. I could brag here for half a day, but they've made me promise not to, so I will respect their request. I just want to thank them for all the joys and trials of being their mom.

ACKNOWLEDGEMENTS

They have made my life rich and meaningful and I have learned some of my most important lessons from raising them. As young adults, I take much pleasure in their creativity, dialogue and suggestions. Greg knows what words to cut out, and Kara suggested to me the idea of Lucinda planting the chocolate chips...a perfect mistake for Lucinda to make! I love you both so much. And Fred, what can I say? You have done everything to encourage me to write this story and to keep on writing. You are my best friend in the world, my comfort, confident, and forever love. Thank you for making these beautiful color illustrations for my book. We are both so fortunate to be sharing our lives together and to be sharing each other's dreams.

SLR

FOREWORD

When I was eleven I read George MacDonald's *At the Back of the North Wind.* It was then I knew I wanted to be a writer. Till then, being a writer was something my dad did for a living. But reading MacDonald's book made me want to do for another child what MacDonald had done for me. He had touched my emotions. He had made me think. I loved his character Diamond so much that Diamond had become a real person to me. The book had kept me spellbound. From there I went on to read MacDonald's more famous work, *The Princess and the Goblins*, and then later I discovered the authors Edward Eager, J.R.R. Tolkien, and C.S. Lewis. I had become a reader. In time I became a writer. So, if only a few children are delighted with *The Light of Lucinda*, I have had a dream realized.

SLR

CONTENTS

The Birth of Lucinda Vinetrope

Lucinda Vinetrope is half lady, half vine,
She grew in the garden beside the old pine,
Born in the autumn on a cool moonlit night,
She snapped off her stem and stepped into the light.

Lucinda looked up at a strange quiet home,
She recognized nothing and felt so alone,
She was born in a dress of pale orange and gold
And at twelve inches high she looked sixteen years old.

She's made of wise plant life with some blood of an elf—
The pulp from a pumpkin, the wood from a shelf.
Her face is quite pear-shaped like a gourd in a bowl,
And her legs are as slim as a newborn brown foal.

But her skin—it's amazing! It glows in the dark!
Just a little, like fireflies that blink in the park.
And she glows when she wants to, to light up her way,
To run a night's errand or to have a night's play.

For, you see, she believes she's the last of her kind,
There used to be thousands in a distant past time.
That's why she feels lonely, for she was born wise,
With the wisdom of Vinetrope in her almond shaped eyes.

She fears she is single, just one of a kind,
So she'll hide in the darkness behind the old pine.
On a bed made of nettles she'll lay down to think,
In the morning she'll venture for food and for drink.

But she'll have to be careful for the world seems so wrong.
Where are the bean trees and the Pools of Seedsong?
And the ground smells so dry like a stick of burnt wood,
So she fears that she'll vanish, she knows that she could.

Then a light in the house turns on with a flash,
Sara has to get up and get ready for class.
While Lucinda dreams on of her ancient lost pools,
Sara gets up and gets ready for school.

Sara's eleven with brown eyes that are quick,
She will notice a bird if its tail gives a flick.
Her hair is jet-black and flies over her face when
She hangs upside down or runs a good race.

Her family gets up with its usual fuss, with complaints
That they're late and she'll miss the school bus,
Her father makes coffee, her brother makes toast, and
Sara packs lunches and brings them their coats.

So she's made it on time and left for the day,
While her father and brother go on their way.
And Sara knows nothing of what is to come,
The trouble, excitement, the adventure, the fun.

It is just a plain day like a hundred before,
Where a teapot's a teapot and a door is a door.
The sun shines its yellow; the leaves have turned gold,
There is no simple clue as to what will unfold.

SLR

CHAPTER ONE

Sara's Amazing Discovery

Sara's school bus stopped right in front of her house. She came down the bus steps bent over with her heavy book bag on her back and made it down the walkway to her front door. Her house key was in the front pocket of the bag. Sara reached behind, deftly unzipped the pocket and retrieved the key. She let herself in, dropped the school bag in the front hall by the steps, and went straight to the den to feed her fish.

She picked up the can of fish food, flipped open the cover, and gave a shake into the tank. The three goldfish eagerly attacked the food. Then she went into the kitchen. Time to feed herself. It was two years since her mom had

died of breast cancer, and although the ache of loss was no longer the crushing, unrelenting pain it had been, life still did not seem right. Sara felt alone. She knew her dad loved her dearly, but he had thrown himself into his work since her mom's death. That was his way of coping. He was the head scientist of the biology research lab at WORTH LABORATORIES and he often had to work late, checking tests, collecting data. And Steven, her seventeen-year-old brother, had a life of his own. It didn't include much time for an eleven-year-old sister.

Sara went into the kitchen. First she rolled up her right pant leg which displayed a fresh scrape on her right knee. Beneath the new scrape was another partly healed wound and on her shin there were several other black and blue marks in various phases of recovery. She had a habit of falling down a lot and bumping into things. She washed the scrape with a wet paper towel and some dish detergent and patted it dry with another paper towel. Then she peeled and placed a Band-Aid® on the wound and rolled down her pant leg.

Next she took out a slice of bread from the bread box and got a butter knife from the drawer, took a jar of peanut butter from the refrigerator (smooth) and spread a thin coat on the slice of bread. Sara put the peanut butter back into the refrigerator and then dug around in the salad she had prepared for dinner that morning and collected six slices of cucumber. She arranged the slices neatly in two rows on the peanut butter, slammed the refrigerator shut and took a bite.

Remembering that she had told her dad she would do some leaf raking after school, she took a drink of water directly from the faucet, and went out the kitchen door with the rest of the bread in hand. Her long, shiny, black hair was clean, but in need of a combing, and it blew across her face as she stepped out into the cool October air.

Sara loved her house and garden. Here she had shared many wonderful hours with her mom. Her mom had been a painter and loved to paint outside in the garden, even on cold days. She also had loved to take care of the garden and in the spring and fall Sara would help her and they would have great talks. She liked raking in the fall because she could pretend that her mom was still alive and just out of sight, behind a bush or around the corner of the house. Sometimes she talked out loud to her.

The house was old, about 100 years old, and that was good. In so many of the really great stories about children there is an old house and often an old garden as well. Her mom had read her many such stories. In fact, Sara was quite certain that her house and garden were ideal for adventure. She particularly liked adventure stories that contained magic. You know, the kind of story in which everything goes crazy, but it all works out in the end. Of course, since it was her house, it made sense that she'd be the heroine!

She sat down on the upper garden wall facing in toward the lower garden with her feet dangling over the edge. The wall was made of large gray field stones. Below her was the space that used to be her mom's flower garden. It was like a sunken room. At this time of year, if her mom had still been alive, there would have been colorful chrysanthemums and a display of hay, gourds and Indian corn. Now there was just drying grass in need of cutting before winter arrived. Somehow Sara couldn't get herself to plant the flowers now that her mom was gone. Her dad and Steven couldn't do it either. They just kept up the basic maintenance—just barely.

Here Sara sat, daydreaming and finishing her snack. She needed a break before raking and then getting to her homework. She would order pizza and have a big salad with fat-free ranch dressing. Steve was having dinner at Lorraine's house and would be back around 9:00. Her dad was due home about the same time. She'd heat up some soup for her dad. Sara still did well in school. She liked to think her mom knew this and was proud of her. Also, she didn't want to give her dad any extra burdens. Her thoughts rambled on like this as she stared through the thinning trees into the clear autumn sky of late afternoon.

Right beneath Sara, busy at work underground and behind the wall that her legs dangled over, was Lucinda Vinetrope. Now, almost a day old, she was feeling strong and peppy. She had found a loose rock in the wall earlier that morning and was delighted to find that behind it was an open space in the ground. She had been hard at work smoothing the floor and had loosened and removed four large stones from the back inner wall of her new home. She was getting exhausted, as she had spent most the day digging up through the earth, with the plan of coming out above ground before nightfall. The earth in back of her room came up level with the top of the wall on which Sara sat. The tunnel she was digging would break out above ground, right alongside Sara. This tunnel would become her chimney chute and where she had removed the four large stones inside would be her fireplace. At least that was her plan. She was thrilled to have found such a perfect home so readily in this strange world she found herself in. Her positive nature was kicking in and all didn't seem so hopeless at this moment.

Tomorrow, she thought to herself, she would mix up a batch of sap tar and collect a couple hundred small stones and pebbles. Then, with the tar, she would line the whole length of the chute with small stones to prevent a cave-in. The tar would also make the chimney fireproof. She wanted this job done first, before the winter freeze. It was important to prioritize. She would have to come up with some kind of chimney cap as well.

Maybe, she thought, the giants who lived next door could be of some help. She realized by now that the big structure nearby must be the dwelling place of a family of giants. Giants, her built-in memory reservoir told her, were probably approachable, but she'd have to introduce herself carefully. Giants were unpredictable. Maybe she could do some work for them in exchange for some supplies. She knew she was a Master Rhymer, because she had invented twenty or thirty poems already in less than a day, and everyone knows that giants have a particular fondness for rhymes—especially when they're about giants. So as she finished her digging and reached the surface, she worked

on her rhyme for "influencing giants" out loud:

> *"Giants are known for*
> *Their kindness to others,*
> *They treat smaller creatures*
> *Like sisters and brothers.*
> *If you've got a problem*
> *Don't question a goblin*
> *A goblin will cheat you or*
> *even worse—eat you!*
> *But go to a giant,*
> *Just don't be defiant*
> *And I'm sure that you'll*
> *Get what you want!"*

With this, Lucinda burst into the sunlight, her fingers wiggling in the air—causing a shower of dirt to fall on her face and putting her into a coughing fit.

Sara flung herself around on her hands and knees, dropping the last bit of bread and cucumber, and the two met each other face-to-face. Sara was shocked speechless. The little being that met her gaze was beyond belief—beyond reason! Lucinda having an inner visual Vinetrope memory of giants was still not prepared for the real thing. The face that met her gaze was huge beyond huge and looked to be a different species altogether. Her mouth dropped open and her eyes popped wide with fear. Sara's eyes popped even wider, giving her a fierce look.

"Don't eat me, please," pleaded Lucinda. "I'll write

you a nice rhyme. Give me a chance!"

"Eat you?" said Sara, as though the words didn't mean anything. She was dazed. "You don't bite, do you?" To her Lucinda looked like a potentially threatening mutant.

Then Lucinda's quirky logic set in and she laughed. Her laughter was so natural that it worked like music and flowed right into Sara and Sara found herself laughing too.

"You're a child giant, aren't you?" guessed Lucinda.

"I'm not a giant."

"Well, you sure look like a giant to me! In fact, even larger than my memory shows me."

"Well, I never used to be a giant. But looking at you I do feel a bit like a giant."

"Maybe you're not feeling too well, dear. I could try and find a willow tree and make you some willow-bark tea with a little memory poem to go along with it. Maybe your memory is lost somewhere, in an arm or a leg perhaps, what with being so big and all!"

None of this conversation assisted Sara in making any sense out of what was going on. She moved closer and peered down into the hole from which the strange creature had just emerged. Lucinda was standing above ground next to the opening.

"This is my chimney chute," stated Lucinda matter-of-factly, as if this bit of information would clarify everything. "You don't happen to have a pie pan you could part with? I could write you a good memory poem in exchange for it. That might help you. You'd have to write it down of course. Do you know how to write?"

"A pie pan? Yes, I can write," Sara tried to answer the two part question, hoping she was handling the conversation satisfactorily.

"Then it's agreed!" said Lucinda excitedly. "This is going very well. You see, a giant's pie pan should make an excellent chimney cap for my chimney. Be back with the pie pan in ten minutes, and I'll have your memory poem ready. And don't forget," she added, a little worried. With that, she disappeared down the hole.

Sara was so flabbergasted that she just sat on the ground, listening to the rumbling noises coming from out of the hole. She called down, "Hello down there," just to make sure she hadn't daydreamed the whole thing. The little pear-shaped head popped up again.

"Did you get the pie pan already?"

"No, I didn't even go for it yet."

"Oh, dear. Poor thing, did you forget?"

"No, not at all. I was just checking."

"Checking what?"

"Checking on the size," said Sara, trying to seem casual, moving her hands around the opening.

"A six inch pan will do fine."

"Okay, I'm going. Don't run away."

"Why ever would I run away? I live here," confirmed Lucinda and she disappeared again, after shaking her head sympathetically.

Sara ran into the house at full speed and began to clatter around in the lower kitchen cabinets, looking for the pie pan. She pulled out a bunch of pots before she could get to the pans. They hadn't been used in two years. She found one big pan and two smaller ones that definitely looked larger than six-inches in diameter.

"Oh well, you will have to do," she spoke to one of the smaller pan. She closed the cabinet door and tore out of the house. In a moment she was leaning over the hole, a little out of breath.

"I've got the pan."

"Great! Just cover the hole with it and throw a few leaves on top to hide it. I'll punch a couple holes in it and tie it in place with a pulley after I line the chimney and make the ropes."

Sara covered the hole with the pan and scattered a few curled, brown leaves over the pan as instructed.

"Okay, come on down," said an instructive voice from a different place somewhere below.

Sara lifted the pie pan back up and called in, "I can't fit down here."

"No," laughed Lucinda, her voice loud again through the chimney chute. "I mean come to my front door at the bottom of the wall below you. I have your memory poem ready."

Sara put the pie pan back in place and threw on the leaves again. Then she leaned over the wall and looked below her. There was her new friend grinning up at her. She stood next to a piece of slate that covered a hole in the wall. She remembered her dad once telling her that the space behind the wall had once contained the main waterline into the house. The line had since been moved. The piece of slate was an old access point for getting to the pipe if it needed repair work. The little person waved at her to come down. Sara jumped down off the wall.

"How do you like my house? There's even a front door. It's pretty heavy for me to push, so I'll have to rig up some kind of pulley system to crank it open and shut. That will be trickier than the chimney cap."

"It's neat," said Sara, peeking in at the underground space. She was truly impressed at this being's energy and ingenuity.

"Let me formally introduce myself, I am Lucinda Vinetrope of the ancient people of Vinetrope, one of a kind and uniquely me," and she took a little bow. She held out her hand.

Sara gently shook her slender fingers (which felt a bit like peach fuzz) and introduced herself. "My name is Sara Umberland."

"A fine bold name, too. I really appreciate the pan. It's an enormous help to me. I've had to start from complete zero. No tools, utensils, or any familiar friend or foe. Not a single vinetrope in sight. It's such a strange land you have here. Where am I anyway?"

"Well, you're in Maplewood, NJ, in the United States."

"That doesn't help me one bit. Is this still during or after the Great Freezing?"

"I don't know."

"Well, we will work on these details later. Don't

pressure yourself. Not everyone has a gift for historical detail. But it's very important to try, and I can give you some rhymes for that too, once I have the facts straight. And now here's your poem in payment for the pan:

"If your arms are too big
And your legs are too long,
Your memories can drift
And get lost (or go wrong).
But don't be discouraged,
It's not that you're dumb,
Perk up and get ready to
Shine with a song,
Sing: Flow, flow
Let go, let go
Wherever you're stuck
Or you're hiding,
Just remember
It's easy,
Like summer then fall,
Your only shortcoming
Is that you're too tall!
But if you're determined
You'll learn to think small
And master your problems
With rhyming! That's all!"

"How do you like it?" finished Lucinda, satisfied with herself.

"I think it's just fine," responded Sara politely, completely at a loss for any other comment.

"Are you sure? You know, I've only been at these rhyming remedies for less than a day and I have so many other things to do."

"No, it's good, really, it's just that I don't see what it's for?"

"It's to help with your memory, dear. You'd better get a writing stick and board and write it down."

"I don't need to write it down."

"But my dear Sara, you have a bad memory. That's why I wrote you a memory poem to begin with. Remember?"

"I have a perfectly good memory," stated Sara firmly, wanting to have some control over these peculiar interactions.

"Now, now, don't be stubborn. How can I help you with your little memory problem if you won't even admit that you have one? No one's perfect."

"But I never said I had a memory problem."

"You most certainly did. Maybe you just don't remember."

"I do remember, and I never said it."

"You distinctly told me that you couldn't remember if you were a giant or not—and that, my dear, is a memory problem!"

"I was joking."

"Joking?"

"Yes, well sort of. I mean I never met a person like

you before. We don't have such small people here, you see. So when you asked if I was a giant, I felt like a giant—compared to you."

"I see, a joke. Oh. OOPS. Well, I like jokes, you know. There's nothing better than a good joke. We vinetropes like jokes a lot. I guess I messed up, didn't I?"

"Well, just a little. It's been confusing for both of us. But you're right about the child part. I'm eleven."

"Eleven? Eleven what?"

"Eleven years."

"What are years?"

"Well, like in spring, summer, fall and winter," Sara tried to think of a way to explain. "Like you said in your poem—summer then fall."

"Yes, yes, it's coming to me now. I'm still getting used to your language—so different than Vinetropese. Eleven years is an excellent age."

"How old are you?"

"I will be one earth rotation today at twelve o'clock midnight. I guess you could call me a newborn!"

"That's not possible. Not even one day old?" said Sara. "How can you be one day old and speak so much and know so much and do so much? It's impossible!"

"No, it's not impossible. Although I do speak too much and I am a bit bossy—a couple of my shortcomings. I guess I'll have to write myself some self-improvement poems."

"I don't understand."

"It's a joke," explained Lucinda.

Sara laughed. "No, I mean I don't understand how you could have just been born."

"Glowers are born full size. Come inside and I will try and explain. Just give me a hand with this door, will you?"

Sara and Lucinda pushed on the piece of slate and slid it open wide enough for Sara to fit through. As Sara entered the little chamber, the whole space began to light up with a warm, pleasant, orange glow. There was an interesting root growth on the ceiling, and Sara noticed a glow coming from the roots. The air smelt pungent but sweet—a bit like warm tangerines. They slid the door shut with some difficulty. Sara looked around. She could just stand, with her head brushing the ceiling. Now she really felt like a giant. The length of the room was about double her size. It had a dirt floor and not a thing in it except the exposed curve of the old waterline pipe no longer in use and a hole at the back with some loose dirt and stones spilling out.

"I'm sorry I have no rugs yet," Lucinda apologized.

"That's okay."

Sara took off her jacket, laid it over the pipe and sat down. Lucinda sat down on a stone that protruded from the earth in front of the opening that would be her fireplace. It was then, after they were seated, that Sara realized where most of the orange light was coming from. It was Lucinda herself glowing and giving off light.

"You glow!"

"Yes, glower vinetropes glow in the dark. That's what I was trying to explain. Very handy too. I can even

dim it down or turn it off."

With that she slowly dimmed herself down and then turned off completely so that for a moment they were in complete darkness. Then she turned herself on again.

"It's wonderful," said Sara completely delighted.

"Thank you. Even in my time it was singularly special. Only glower vinetropes have the power of light."

"In the summertime we have small bugs that fly and light up every few minutes—just a little blink—nothing like you can do."

"Really, how sad. They must be distant relatives of ours that have grown completely stupid over time."

"You keep talking about—in your time. What does that mean?"

"We were a race of intelligent beings that lived in this world such a long time ago. I think it must be this world? But it's changed so much."

"And what happened?"

"We died out—except for some of our seeds. At least that's what my memory tells me."

"How can you remember things from before you existed?"

"Well, that's what I'm trying to explain. A glower vinetrope is a special kind of vinetrope. There are two kinds of glowers—the Master Rhymer, who is always the keeper of history. We rhyme because a rhymed poem is an excellent way to pass on information to the young. I am obviously a Master Rhymer, or in other words, the Vinetrope Historian. That explains my inborn knowledge of the history of our people and also my advanced state of development for one so young. We also have a Master Healer who glows from birth too. The Healer and the Rhymer are necessary for our species survival. Unfortunately, from the way this world has changed and the lack of any signs of vinetrope life, I can only presume that I'm the only survivor of my race. My skills will not be needed." Lucinda's lovely smile vanished and she looked truly downhearted.

"Maybe not. You said you grew from seeds. Maybe there are more of these seeds. They just haven't sprouted yet."

"What a wonderful thought! You might be right. I should be more optimistic."

Sara found it hard to believe anyone could be more optimistic, but she had more questions to ask. "Why did your race die out, Lucinda, and what do you mean by special seeds?"

"We died out because the planet changed. There was a terrible storm from the sky that showered the world with millions of burning stones. The sky grew black, day and night, and it did not seem that things would ever go back to the way it had been. Our world got colder and colder. We are used to warmth. We can create our own warmth, but this was a cold that couldn't be warmed. First, the giants died. They were like us, but much larger. Many huge animals disappeared as well. We who were small did better than the others for awhile. We dug deeper into the earth, hiding pockets of our seeds for the future, preparing for the worse to come. For several generations our root systems warmed us and we managed."

"You mean like these roots above us now that are glowing?"

"Yes, they take some time to establish. That is why I need a fireplace for this winter. The root system won't be developed enough to sustain heat until next winter."

"How fantastic! How do they work? What makes them grow?"

"I water them with this tube." Lucinda pulled a piece of her green vine-like hair and a tube emerged. She pressed it lightly and a spray of clear liquid came out. It looked like water.

"And this spray makes the roots give off warmth?"

"Oh yes, eventually. When mature, the roots can work in reverse as well. They will remove heat in my home if it gets too hot inside. Some of the roots send the unwanted heat up and out into the air."

"It's like air-conditioning!" said Sara in amazement. "Where do the roots come from?"

"Oh, they're just the normal roots of whatever grows above our homes. We tend to them with our hoses. They increase in size and then become our heating and cooling system. We can even get them to grow in decorative patterns. Some of us were great artists with roots. But it takes awhile to get it all going in a new home like this. In fact, this spray is the same liquid we feed our babies with during the first few weeks of their lives. Mothers and fathers feed their young with this liquid to give them a good start. It's nourishing and seems to make them hardy and strong."

"But you said vinetropes were born full size and advanced."

"No, just the glowers—pay attention! You see, our young are born small and helpless and none of our people glow except glowers. We grow on a vine. The babies come from buds that become pods. When they are ready the pods open and their parents receive them. Glowers grow on the vine too. But a flower appears first, before the pod develops. Most of our young must learn as they mature."

"That's how it is for all human beings," Sara explained. "We have no glowers. But this means you have no parents to help you, Lucinda. No mother or father. That seems sad."

"It's not sad because it is natural for me to become self-sufficient very quickly. What is sad is not to be able to use my skills and be useful to my people. To be without your own kind is very lonely and frightening."

"I do understand, Lucinda. I mean about being lonely. My mother died two years ago and nothing has felt normal since. I have to be strong for my father because he is sad too and has so much to do. I don't want to worry him. And my brother Steven is older and off with his girlfriend a lot. I have friends, but none of my friends have had a mother or father die, and I feel like they don't understand — can't understand, really. So I pretend that everything is normal, like it's just the same pretty much as before, but it's not."

"Sara, how painful for you. I have great sympathy. I can imagine how terrible it would be for one of our little

vinetropes to lose a parent. I am in a way like a mother to all my vinetropes and I have no children to mother—young or old. I think we have both suffered great losses for beings so young. I'm sure this means we were meant to meet and be friends!"

"You must be right. This is all so amazing and magical. I was longing for an adventure and here you are Lucinda. Right here in my garden. I wonder if I'm dreaming."

"That's what I've been thinking since I snapped off my stem last night. But now that we've met, I'm pretty sure that this is really happening."

"And we will help each other. I want to help you find out if there are any more of your kind coming back into the world. How exciting! We have legends about a time when little people existed in the world—we call them fairies, elves, and the wicked ones goblins—but they're just children's stories. Now it may really be coming true."

"Did you say goblins?"

"Yes, real troublemakers."

"I have a memory of goblins. A wicked group of creatures. We didn't call them goblins in our ancient tongue, but when I wrote my giant poem earlier I had this memory of such a creature and used the word that your soil imparted to me. That word was goblin. They too were vegetable of course, but, as you say, troublemakers. Very interesting."

"It certainly is. Maybe the legends are first coming true. Or maybe they are reappearing. This is incredible.

Tell me more. I still don't understand why you became extinct," continued Sara. "With all your abilities, couldn't you have kept yourselves alive?"

"No. The cold became impossible. We were covered in layers of ice and snow so deep—it was beyond belief. Our green world was gone. You see, even though our homes are underground, we need sunlight. Where do you think our roots come from? From plants above ground! They need the sun, we need the sun. We are all plants, of course."

"I'm not a plant. Human beings, my kind, are not plants."

"You're not? How this world has changed! In our time, only the stupid beasts were not plants. All intelligent life was flora—plant life. Of course there was non-sentient plant life too."

"How amazing. We see the world the other way around. And so you died out, but some of your seeds remained buried deep beneath the snow and ice. We know about that time. Our scientists call it the Ice Age! Those piles of ice, we call glaciers. I wonder how your seed got here? Glaciers are far from here."

"That's a real mystery. I only have access to those things that happened before my seed was formed. Anything that has happened since, while I was dormant, is unknown to me. The only access I have to the present occurs during my sprouting and ripening period when I'm reemerging into the flora. I acquire the languages of the dominant creatures surrounding me as I grow in the soil of a particular geographic area."

"Then that's why you speak English! Oh Lucinda, this is incredible. And maybe your world hasn't ended," said Sara reassuringly. "Maybe it's blossoming again."

"Maybe," answered Lucinda hopefully.

"How do you think you were planted here in my garden? Do you think it was long ago?" Sara questioned.

"Doubtfully. If that were the case I would have sprouted long ago. It's warm enough here for me to have taken root. But I arrived here somehow—probably fairly recently. Within one of your years. If these glacier areas are so far away, it will take some explaining as to how I wound up here."

"Wow, it's awesome."

"Awesome, a perfect word."

"And you're born knowing almost everything. How to take care of yourself—like a newborn grown-up!"

"Yes. Almost everything. At least that would be true if my world had remained essentially the same. But under these unforeseen conditions, I certainly can't say I know everything. In fact, I know very little."

"Lucinda, I will help you. But you must stay out of sight as much as possible for the time being. You can't just pop up and talk to everyone, the way you did with me."

"I understand. Different beings respond differently."

"Yes."

"Don't worry. I'm a tough little gourd. I'll see you again then, Sara Umberland?"

"Of, course. Tomorrow afternoon when I get back

from school."

"Great! Friendship is highly valued by vinetropes. I'll try and have a friendship poem ready for you."

"You're terrific, Lucinda."

"I know," she confirmed the compliment and smiled her glorious smile. They slid the door open far enough for Sara to push through and step out into the garden. Lucinda handed Sara her jacket.

"I'm counting on you to teach me all about this world of yours," said Lucinda through the crack in the door.

"I will," she assured her, smiling a natural happy smile for the first time in two years.

Sara then returned to her house with a lot to think about.

CHAPTER TWO

Lucinda Meets Two Friends and Receives a Clue

Sara had a lot of trouble holding in her excitement. Should she tell her Dad and brother about Lucinda or not? Maybe just Steven? He was seventeen and pretty cool. Sometimes he'd drop her off at a movie with a couple of friends and then pick her up later. But usually he didn't have time. She couldn't make up her mind. She decided not to tell either of them till she could get Lucinda's opinion on it. Lucinda had to play a role in this. It was her life. She could hardly eat any dinner that evening. She kissed her dad goodnight. Steven wasn't home yet.

Once in bed, she could concentrate better. Lucinda

needed so many things. I must have some stuff around here that she can use, she thought to herself. What about a doll blanket? That would be useful. What about food? What does she eat, anyway? I'll have to ask her tomorrow. And clothes, that's it, she definitely had some doll clothes that would fit Lucinda. But did Lucinda's dress come off or was it part of her? It seemed so custom-made to her skin tones, except for the flecks of gold. What other special talents did Lucinda have that she didn't know about yet? There were so many questions to ask. She wished she didn't have to go to school the next day, but at least it was Friday.

As sleep began to take over, Sara's thoughts became less sensible. Lucinda was sitting at a spinning wheel and furniture was popping out of the wheel instead of cloth. Fruit was growing out of her vine-like hair. A grass rug was growing up under her feet with glowing mushrooms in it that looked like floor lamps. Then she was asleep.

Lucinda sat on the edge of the chimney entrance, her legs dangling into the chute, with the pie pan pushed to the side. She looked up at the moon. It was exactly twenty-four hours since she had first stepped into the moonlight. She was tired. She had been working almost since she was born. Next to her were three large piles of small stones and pebbles that she had been gathering since sundown. She would drop them down the shoot and then call it a night.

The air was cool and pleasant. Although quite a few trees had lost their leaves, some were at the height of their autumn glory. The wind rustled their leaves. The moon was full and bright. It was at quiet moments like this, after a hard day's work, when the body is tired, that a Master Rhymer writes the best poetry. Lucinda knew this. She could feel the poem growing inside of her. Then it came to her like water pouring from a jug:

"Here's a new world
a world still unknown,
to some it is ancient,
for me—a new home.
I look at each tree tip,
a life gone to sleep
means the coming of winter
but its life it will keep.
I'm just like a leaf bud
that's had its long sleep
and into this world
I've planted my feet.
And how will I change it?
For I know that I will.
And how will it change me?
For nothing stays still.
Oh world, you are ancient
yet as new as each day,
I claim you as mine,
till I'm old I will stay.
And between now and then
I will do what I can,
and we'll both grow together
in this ancient new land."

Lucinda felt content. It had been a good first day. She got up and went over to the first pile of stones and with her weary arms began pushing them, a few at a time, down the shoot. She worked until she was done with all three piles. She slid the pie pan back on top and then jumped off the garden wall, landing gracefully like a cat. She entered her home through the front door. The room was dusty, from all the fallen stones, but dust didn't bother Lucinda at all. In fact, she breathed just fine when there was dust in the air. This made her think of mud biscuits. She loved a good mud biscuit, her thoughts told her, and would bake some as soon as she got her fireplace working. The recipe was stored inside her mind and ready to be put to use.

Lucinda looked at the pile of stones that had gathered at the bottom of the chute and they looked pretty comfortable. She had an idea. She went outside and gathered up some dried leaves and brought them inside where she scattered them over the pile of stones. After two more trips she had a fluffy bed of leaves on top of a nice stone mattress—the perfect bed for a vinetrope. Exhausted by now, she lay down on her bed and was asleep instantly.

Lucinda woke up so hungry that it hurt. She had slept hard and long after so much work. Sara and her family had already left on their daily schedule. She got up and brushed off the dried leaves from her pumpkin colored dress and slipped out into the morning light. It was cold and drizzling, so she made her way back up through the yard under a line of bushes till she was back at the pine tree near where she was born. This was where she had slept that first night after her birth and she remembered that a delicious crop of tree fungi was growing on this tree.

Sure enough, here it was—a moist stepladder of nourishment climbing up the north side of the tree. Some of the ears of fungi were as large as Lucinda's head. She picked off three of the largest ears she could reach and checked their backs. Yes, there were the spores she was looking for. These were the spores from which more fungi could be grown. She tucked these large pieces into a huge pocket hidden in her dress. Her dress was designed with several hidden pockets that were useful for gathering. She would plant the spores into one of the earth walls in her home so that she could farm these delicious morsels all winter long. She would try to find other kinds of fungi and mushrooms to add to her in-house crop. Now she eagerly snapped off a small ear and ate it. It took five more ears to satisfy her hunger.

As she ate, a roaring noise whooshed by and startled her. Between the trees she made out a large pathway and the roaring object was now almost out of sight and moving with amazing speed down a hill. In a moment another one approached and this time she observed more carefully. There were humans inside this moving thing. It looked like a moving house. It was probably some incredible structure made by humans. A moving house that could take you places at great speed. Remarkable!

She sat down on a broken branch and looked around her. Not too far away, out in a cleared spot of land directly in front of her, she observed two furry reddish brown creatures, about her size, with bushy tails. They seemed very busy gathering little round things and stuffing them into their mouths. This might be some other possible food source. She would have to check it out. The two creatures seemed intent on their work despite the drizzle. They would fill their mouths, run up a tree for a moment, come back down and then start filling up their mouths again. They must be gathering food for the winter, just like me, thought Lucinda. I'll try and talk to them.

As she stood up to walk towards them, they noticed her. She stepped a little closer. They turned and ran half way up a tree trunk, stopped and looked back at her from a safe distance.

Mighty nervous, aren't they? Lucinda thought. But I can speak their language. There must be a lot of these creatures living here. It's a simple tongue and has grown into me quite completely.

"Greetings, friends," she called up to them. "You have no reason to be afraid of me."

"You look a bit strange," said the smaller of the two animals.

"And you look a bit strange to me. But I do envy your beautiful warm fur with the coming of winter."

"Thank you, it serves us well enough. My name is Ekle and this is my brother Apkin. He speaks only a few necessary words."

"Glad to meet you both. My name is Lucinda Vinetrope and I come from a far away place. But due to circumstances out of my control, I have come to live in this land of yours. It's strange and different to me." This was close enough to the truth.

"We don't want to share our acorns," spoke the larger fellow, Apkin, in greeting.

"Oh, I doubt they would agree with me," said Lucinda protectively. "I don't even know what acorns are."

"Please excuse my brother," continued Ekle with a whirl of his tail. "No manners. These are acorns," and from his mouth he dropped two of the round things Lucinda had noticed them collecting. "They are tasty and last well through the winter. There is enough to share, unless you have a large family?"

"No, no family at all. It's just me."

"Good," said Apkin.

"Would you like to come to our home and get out of this drizzle? We were just going to take a break and have a few acorns. That is, if you can climb," invited Ekle.

"I can climb
much like a vine
but I haven't done it
in a very long time," answered Lucinda in rhyme. Of course, it was in squirrel rhyme, so that the squirrel brothers could enjoy it.

"Ah, a rhymer ... I've always liked a good rhyme," said Ekle. "Are you coming?"

Lucinda read between the words of their language and decided it was safe. The more she learned about this world the better.

"I'm coming," she said and her hands and arms

clung to the surface of the tree trunk just like a vine. So did her foot tips.

The brothers made their way to the first branch and waited for her. By alternating her grip between her arms and feet, she was able to make her way up the trunk much like an inchworm does. She swung her arms over the branch and pulled herself up into a sitting position on the limb.

Ekle and Apkin nodded their approval. A good climber deserved respect, wherever she came from and however odd she looked.

Right next to Lucinda, where the branch met the tree trunk, was a small opening.

"Please enter our home," said Ekle. "Just climb in."

Lucinda peeked in and turned up her glow. She found a simple dry nest lined with nettles and bits of fur. Pleasant enough, she thought and moved to the back corner near a pile of acorns to make room for her hosts. Ekle and Apkin entered immediately.

"Ah, a glower." said Ekle, impressed again.

"You know of glowers?" said Lucinda astounded.

"Oh yes, before the misfortune of our "misplacement" there were odd stories about the coming of a new kind of creature. It was said that some of them glowed. Glowers. They supposedly all lived beneath the earth. I didn't believe the stories. But then I met one myself, eight seasons ago, before our unwanted adventure."

"Did this glower look like me?" Lucinda asked getting excited.

"Well, now that you mention it, there was some resemblance."

"Boy," said Apkin.

"What?" said Ekle, annoyed at his brother's interruption.

"Boy, boy, was a boy."

"I think my brother might be right. This glower was male. I guess that's the difference. I'm not really sure. His face was thin, I would say, and he glowed a blue/white glow, not orange/yellow like you."

"Eyes were rounder," added Apkin.

"Yes, and he played a pipe of some kind. A lovely music—it sounded like crickets and water and clouds moving."

"Where was it that you saw him? Can you take me to him?" Lucinda felt overjoyed at this piece of information.

"Too far," said Apkin in his flat voice.

"Yes, much too far," agreed Ekle. "It was before the terrible misfortune that befell us two autumns ago."

"What misfortune?" Lucinda questioned, concentrating now on this reference made several times by the squirrels.

"The wagon accident," explained Ekle. "You see, two autumns ago we lived very far from here with our mates. We each had our own place in a grove of oak trees."

"Terrible accident," repeated Apkin with more emotion in his voice.

"We were gathering as usual, Apkin and I together,

and we came across what we thought was a great find—a whole barrel of pecans. There were several of these barrels standing around. We thought, great luck, because the cover was off of one of them. We jumped inside and filled our cheeks. We were going to jump out and get our mates so that we could empty the barrel out more quickly."

"Very bad plan," grumbled Apkin shaking his head.

"Just then," continued Ekle, "we heard human voices. Before we knew it a huge bag of nuts was dumped on top of us. Then the cover went down and everything went black."

"Terrible cover."

"Before we knew it, we were being loaded onto one of those fast moving human wagons. The kind that moves itself."

"I've seen them," confirmed Lucinda. "But I think one of the humans controls them somehow."

"Whatever," said Ekle, annoyed at the interruption. "And then we were moving, fast, and we couldn't get out. We went on and on, far away from our mates, our home, our father's home. We just kept going until we got near here. A human took us down off the wagon and opened up the barrel to show another human the nuts. We jumped out and ran for our lives. Those humans were sure surprised!" and Ekle giggled here for the first time.

"How long did you travel?" asked Lucinda, trying to get some idea of the distance between here and the male vinetrope. She knew the glower Apkin had seen was a male. Males always glowed blue/white.

"Long, long time. Terrible dark time." said Apkin.

"A whole night, a long stop, and then part of the next day," Ekle tried to be more specific.

"Yes, that sounds like it's far from here," agreed Lucinda in a disappointed voice, "considering the speed of those wagons. Do you know what direction you were traveling in?"

"Don't know, too dark, too terrible," said Apkin.

"Well, let me think," said Ekle. "When we left home it was a pleasant enough autumn day, but when we arrived here it was a bit on the chilly side, felt more like winter, so I'd say we were moving north." He seemed pleased with himself. "I know it gets colder earlier as you go north because my brother-in-law was from the north. He hitched a ride down on a long line of wagons with cows in them."

"Cold, yes, cold. And we had no nuts gathered and no place to live," said Apkin in his longest sentence so far.

"And it gets a lot colder here than it ever did where we came from. I can tell you that!" said Apkin with great force.

"I understand," said Lucinda. "It's all a bit of a shock for me right now. I've just arrived myself quite suddenly and I need to do so much before the winter arrives."

"We'll help if we can," said Ekle in a friendly voice.

"Then tell me please, if you can, whatever you know about this other glower. What did he say?"

"Didn't say much. Just said he was practicing his flute. He played that beautiful song for us and left."

Lucinda was thrilled to the core to hear this. She was

not alone! She was not the only vinetrope in this transformed world. Wait till she told Sara. But it wasn't going to be an easy task to find this other glower. With winter almost here, there was no chance of travel until the spring thaw. She would just have to be patient. All and all, it was a fantastic piece of data.

"Here, try an acorn," suggested Ekle. "You bite it like this," he demonstrated, "and you eat out the meat from inside," and he demonstrated again.

Lucinda decided to give it a try. It was time to be practical. It was important to know about any possible new food source. She bit the shell off and popped a piece of nut into her mouth. To her delight it was delicious.

"These are terrific," she exclaimed.

"Too bad," said Apkin, shaking his head.

"I won't be greedy," assured Lucinda. "I'll just take a couple of piles about the size you've got here and use them in my mud biscuits to make them more nutritional."

"Oh, there's plenty," said Ekle graciously, "don't mind my brother. He's a grumbler and always will be. He talks the same way to me."

He laughed again. It seemed Ekle had a sense of humor.

Lucinda joined them in a few more acorns and then decided it was time to get back to work.

"Do you know where I might find some tall grasses?" she asked. "I need to weave a great deal of rope over the next few days."

"Oh yes," said Ekle. "No problem. The yard next

door. It is sunnier over there. It's more like a field. Along the back wall you will find plenty of tall grass. They don't chop it down as carefully as some humans do," he explained.

"Strange habits," said Apkin.

"They're not dangerous?" Lucinda asked. She was curious to get their opinion.

"Well, usually they leave us alone. But you never can tell for sure. They can go for months ignoring your existence and then suddenly they'll take an interest in you. They'll stand around watching you like they've got nothing better to do. Even feed you special nuts! And then, without any warning and for no reason I can ever figure out, they'll turn against you—setting traps and even trying to poison you. They've even gone as far as cutting down the trees. I suggest you be very careful in your dealings with humans. Keep out of their way, that's what I suggest."

"Keep away," repeated Apkin.

"The girl Sara seemed very nice," said Lucinda, thinking out loud.

"These humans do have some pretty strange ways," insisted Ekle.

"Keep away," said Apkin again.

"It's up to you," said Ekle. "I'm just saying to be careful."

"Well, thank you for your advice. I'd better get going now. I have so much to do. But I'll tell you what. Why don't you join me tonight in my home for some refreshments and a few good poems."

"That would be very nice," said Ekle.

"Good," said Apkin, surprisingly, in a friendly tone.

"But where is your home?" asked Ekle.

"Down in the lower garden at the end of the wall—behind the stone door."

"That's a house?" said Ekle.

"It is now," confirmed Lucinda.

"Okay, we'll be there after sunset. Good-bye."

Lucinda made her way back down the tree by doing a reverse crawl. The drizzle had stopped and it was just a gray, chilly day. She made her way into the next yard to gather tall grasses, but the amazing discovery never left her mind. There was another vinetrope somewhere. She would have to find him.

CHAPTER THREE

In Which Sara Meets Ekle and Apkin

Sara came home from school filled with expectation. Lucinda and a whole weekend lay ahead of her. The rain had stopped and although the sky was still gray, it no longer was dull and gloomy. Instead, the atmosphere had the charged excitement of a blustery autumn day. This was the kind of day that made you think of things like what costume you wanted to wear for Halloween, what you wanted for the holidays, and what you wanted to give. For a moment she felt the pleasure and anticipation of these events the way she used to. It used to be such a happy time when her mom was alive. But now this bright autumn mood fell back into sadness along with the memories of her mom and the things they used to do together. Her mom was very artistic and had made her the most wonderful costumes. She often helped out with her friends' costumes as well. Her mom had had a playful streak in her and a wonderful sense of humor that permeated the whole family. Her family had lost its sense of humor. Everything was down to business now. And thinking of the holidays brought her up against a dark wall. She didn't even like to think about it. How could she have let herself feel that happy feeling again for even a moment? But maybe Lucinda would change that. That is if she really existed and she hadn't imagined meeting her.

Sara let herself into the quiet house and went upstairs to her bedroom and shut the door. She wanted to savor the belief in Lucinda's existence, in case she had been dreaming while awake. She had a good size room with a bay window that offered a spectacular view of the front entrance to their driveway and well beyond down the road. It was the perfect place to sit if you were waiting for someone to arrive. It gave her a bird's-eye view of the world. It was her nest. When she was little she used to sit here on special days and wait for relatives and friends. She could see when they arrived from her nest. Her mom used to have Thanksgiving dinner every year and birthday parties and anniversaries for the family. Now they always went to Aunt Laura's house for these occasions. She missed the smells of her mom's cooking and the paints and varnishes she used every day. Most of all she missed the smell of her mom, a scent so subtle it could not be described. It just smelled like Mom. They had a standing joke between them. Whenever Sara was sad or worried she'd curl up by her mom and her mom's presence had such a calming affect on her that she'd start to fall asleep. Sara used to tease her mom and say that she gave off a sleeping aroma.

Sara went to her wicker toy chest and started to rummage around for things that Lucinda might find useful. She discovered two suitable doll blankets that she used to use for her baby dolls when she was five or six. It pleased her to think that she could do something for Lucinda that would make her life more comfortable.

One blanket was a solid baby blue with satin edging. The other was a blue and green flannel plaid. Two blankets are better than one, she thought to herself. She quickly stuffed the doll blankets into her school bag, and went downstairs taking the bag with her. She went straight to Lucinda's front door.

"Lucinda," she called. There was no answer.

"Lucinda." Still no answer.

I guess she's not home, maybe she never was, Sara thought to herself.

Her whole body took on a slumped posture.

"What's wrong?" said a familiar voice from behind her.

Sara turned around to see Lucinda standing at the edge of the neighbor's yard with her arms full of long grass.

"You look like you lost your best friend," teased Lucinda with a sweeping grin.

"I almost thought I did."

"Well here I am. Come in a minute, and then you can help me get some more grass."

They pushed inside and Lucinda turned up her glow. The entire room was filled with grass, reminding Sara of a scene from the fairy tale, Rumplestilkskin, in which the king ordered the farmer's daughter to spin mountains of straw into gold. There was also a pungent smell Sara hadn't noticed the last time she was here. It smelt like a road being tarred—only nicer—a lot like pine cones.

"What's all this for?" asked Sara.

"I've got to braid all this into rope. Several small braids tied together make a strong rope. I can tie the finished pieces together to make a longer piece."

"What do you need all the rope for?"

"Very important," she said as she plopped down on a pile of grass. Sara followed her lead and sat down too.

"Ouch!" she screamed as she hit the floor, her school bag landing next to her.

"Oh, sorry, that's my bed. It's all covered up with grass."

"Your bed? It feels like a pile of stones!"

"It is a pile of stones. Vinetropes like a very firm mattress."

"It's more than firm. It's lumpy and sharp. You don't like soft things?" asked Sara, settling herself into a more comfortable position.

"Well yes and no. We do pile a nice layer of dried leaves and grass on top of the stones. If you had realized the bed was there and sat down more carefully, I think you

would have found it pretty comfortable. I'm sorry if there was a sharp edge or two. I should have warned you."

"That's okay, I'm pretty comfortable now," confirmed Sara, wiggling a little to show she was.

"Where were we? Oh yes, the ropes. I need ropes to make a pulley for my chimney cap and the front door. Then I can open and close the chimney cap from down here depending on the weather. I'll rig up some kind of crank and pulley system for the front door as well, to make it easier to handle. I found this incredibly strong piece of wood that I can probably use for the crank. I'll need wheels. That will be a tough find." She held up an old crow bar that must have been left outside.

"You think of everything," said Sara. "By the way, that's not a stick. It's made of iron. And I can probably get you some wheels. I think I've got an old wagon in the basement from when I was little."

"Terrific. That will simplify things a lot. There are so many new materials to work with. In the old days, everything vinetropes built was made from what you found around you, mostly plant life, much of it self grown to suit our needs. We used some minerals too, like rocks and shells."

"Everything?" questioned Sara. "All your dishes, pots, clothing—everything?"

"Well, we did have clay, but it crumbled a lot. Sometimes we used animal bones, which gave added strength. We didn't like to, though. It kind of gave us the creeps. Everything else was vegetable."

"Maybe you can explain to me one of the things I've been thinking about. I've been wondering why none of our scientists have ever found the remains of your culture. I mean, we've been exploring in the regions of the world that vinetropes must have lived in. Why haven't we come across signs of your existence?"

"I guess, except for our seeds, which are very small and clearer than a tear drop, there's nothing left of us. We have no bones like animals."

"No bones!"

"No. Our inner structure, like our outer structure, is made of plant life. Of course the inner support system is a much tougher kind. It's very stiff."

"Maybe it's something like celery. You probably have a skeletal system made of very hard cellulose. My dad's a research botanist, so I know something about this. His lab team is working on cures for illnesses that might be found in plant life. They're also working on new food sources—especially rich in protein. Oh dear, I hope I haven't upset you by talking about eating plants!"

"Not at all. That's all that vinetropes eat! Just not in its intelligent form. It's meat we never eat. We harvest a whole variety of what I think you call fungi and mushrooms in our underground homes—right off the walls. It's very rich in nutrients to us."

"But what about the cold. I still don't understand. Wouldn't the extreme cold have preserved something from your world?"

"Well, remember, we had to live fairly near the sur-

face in order to harvest roots from existing plants. We would have died out and turned to dust way before the full force of what you called the Ice Age was on us. We knew that in the cold, they would not sprout and would be preserved. The clear seed cases are even tougher than what you call our skeletons. We hoped the seeds would survive and it seems we were right."

"I understand. You left no skeletons, and any animal bones found in the area would be just that—bones of animals."

"Exactly. And most of our furniture, clothing, even our art, was created out of root growth that we controlled and altered."

"Things are beginning to make some sense."

"And now I have some exciting news for you. I have made friends with two brothers, animals you call squirrels."

"You communicated with them?"

"Of course. Quite a few live in the area. Remember, we pick up the languages of creatures who live in the same area we sprout in. If a new kind of creature were to move in, now that I'm sprouted, I would not be able to speak their tongue. Squirrel talk is much easier than yours. The brothers call themselves Ekle and Apkin."

"They have names?"

"Yes, be patient. I'm getting to the exciting part. Ekle has met another glower. A male."

"What? That's fantastic. Oh, Lucinda, I'm so happy for you! When can we meet him? Where is he?"

"Well, that's the big problem. He's far from here and

we're not quite sure exactly where that 'here' is."

Then Lucinda went on to explain her conversation with Ekle and Apkin.

"Lucinda, this is the best news. We'll find him. We've got to."

"I hope so. It will take some planning. I'll need to talk to the squirrels more. They may remember more than they think. But now I need to attend to a few practical matters. You know me. I'm not sure when or where I'll meet up with this other vinetrope, so I must carry on as if I never will and plan for the winter. I can use all the help I can get."

"Of course. What can I do? I could sneak you in with me, maybe?"

"No, nothing that dramatic. It's best if I live as close to my original habitat as I can. That means under the ground. But I could use another pie pan. I'm digging a well in here and I need another cover. I don't want anyone falling in. I'm sure there's water under here. Your pie pans are so durable, although a bit shiny for my taste."

"No problem. Oh, I almost forgot. I brought you a present."

"I love presents. Let's see."

Sara unzipped her school bag and took out the two blankets.

"Here."

"Blankets, beautiful blankets! Thank you so much Sara." She jumped right into Sara's lap, put her velvety arms around Sara's neck and gave her a little kiss on the cheek that felt as light as cotton candy.

"I could keep warm enough with my fireplace, but the pleasure of having real blankets, soft warm blankets, is more than I could have hoped for. They're wonderful over a bed of stones and grass." She rubbed a blanket on each cheek.

"I'm so pleased you like them. I wasn't sure if you used blankets. Especially after I sat down on your bed before. I might be able to get you some clothes too, if you could use some," continued Sara, enjoying her own usefulness immensely.

"That would be wonderful. I never, ever, could possibly have grown enough cloth root or gathered enough plants, to weave cloth and sew clothing before winter. It will save me so much work. All I really need is a nightgown to sleep in and some kind of old work clothes. Shoes would be great, too. Then I would only have to use my special birth clothes for entertaining and holidays. We glowers are born with our best clothes on, you know. They're especially grown and custom-made for each one of us."

"That must be why your dress looks so beautiful on you," said Sara, paying Lucinda a compliment. "In fact, I was wondering if your dress came off or if it was grown right onto you."

"A reasonable question, considering what you know about me so far. But my dress does come off."

The dress did seem perfect. The fabric was almost the same shade as Lucinda's skin, only darker, a rich pumpkin color. There were golden threads woven throughout the dress, which gave the fabric the impression of being dusted with gold.

"I have a couple of dolls just about your size," continued Sara. "I don't play with them any more. I'm sure they can spare a few pieces of clothing."

"Sara, you are such a good friend."

Sara slid back a bit on the bed and adjusted her position.

"Oh, watch out for the tree bark trays right behind you, Sara. They're filled with sticky tree tar."

Sara looked behind her and saw three large pieces of bark filled with some gooey yellow stuff. She realized that the tar was causing the pungent smell she had noticed when she first stepped in. Her nose had become accustomed to it.

"What's it for?" she asked.

"Tarring the stones in the chimney chute. It fireproofs it. Very useful stuff. But I stopped tarring to get the grass, just in case the giants in the house next door decide to mow it down. Ekle and Apkin told me that giants, I mean humans, are very unpredictable about things like that."

Sara laughed. "Yes, we like to keep our grass short. The Carlsons next door take their time getting around to it. I won't even try to explain it now. But let's go, I'll help you with the grass."

They went outside and pushed between the two holly bushes into the neighbor's yard.

"There doesn't seem to be anyone home just now," explained Lucinda.

"They're both at work," said Sara.

"Lucky for me."

Sara could carry ten times as much grass as Lucinda. In no time they had all the grass Lucinda could manage.

They were heading back to Lucinda's house on their last trip, when Lucinda heard a "psssst" coming from the bushes along the garden wall.

"Pssst. Pssssst."

"What is that?" said Lucinda.

"I didn't hear anything."

"Psssssssssiiit!"

Lucinda peered under the bush. There were Ekle and Apkin. Sara stopped and watched to see what Lucinda was doing. She was making funny squeaky sounds under the bush.

"What's all the secrecy?" asked Lucinda in squirrel talk.

"What are you doing?" asked Ekle. "I thought we warned you about humans and we've been watching from our tree. We came to remind you before it's too late."

"Too late, too late," confirmed Apkin.

"Oh nonsense," said Lucinda. "Sara is a true friend. In fact, I even wrote her a friendship poem," she affimed as if that proved the point.

"I don't know," continued Ekle. "She may be fine, but you risk drawing the attention of the others when you hang out with one of them. Best not to associate with their kind at all."

Apkin just shook his head in disapproval.

"What's going on in there?" asked Sara.

"I'm talking to Ekle and Apkin," explained Lucinda.

"Really?" Sara knelt down with her bouquet of grass and looked under the bush. Sure enough, there were two squirrels. One was large, one a bit smaller, both reddish-brown and trembling lightly.

"Hi there," said Sara in her most cheerful voice. "Lucinda told me all about you."

"Oh dear, this is bad, bad, bad!" said Apkin.

Sara misunderstood the squeaks to be a friendly greeting and felt encouraged. "She told me you have a fine home in that big oak tree over there—up at the first branch," she pointed to their oak tree.

"Terrible, terrible, terrible," said Apkin.

"How could you?" asked Ekle. "She knows where we live now."

"Big teeth," said Apkin looking at Sara's smile, and he trembled even more.

"They seem a little nervous," said Sara, noticing their shivers.

"Well, that's because they're terrified of you."

"Yikes. I'm sorry to hear that. Try and explain to them that I won't hurt them."

"I did already. They're angry I told you where they live."

"Well tell them that I make a solemn vow never to tell anyone where they live."

"I'll do my best."

Lucinda passed on Sara's message.

Ekle was mad. "You don't know anything. You just got here. Didn't even know what acorns were, let alone

squirrels. What do you know of humans? Did you know that sometimes humans eat squirrels? Did you know that!?"

"Oh dear, oh dear," was all Apkin could say in response to his brother's tirade.

"I'll ask her what she knows of this," said Lucinda.

"Sara, they insist that humans eat squirrels."

"Oh no, no one in my family has ever eaten a squirrel. We eat a lot of chicken. But never squirrel."

"She swears she and her family never eat squirrels," explained Lucinda.

"That may be true," agreed Ekle, "but her parents could decide to poison us or cut down our trees at any moment. And all humans have eaten squirrel in the past. You can be certain that one of her ancestors ate squirrel."

"Well, there seems to be nothing I can say to change your mind, boys. But I won't give up my friendship with Sara. I know she's a friend."

"What's happening?" asked Sara.

"They won't accept you," said Lucinda sadly, "but I told them that I would be your friend no matter how they felt."

"Thank you, Lucinda. I would be so heartbroken if you didn't like me any more."

"Does this mean no poems tonight?" asked Ekle, suddenly acting disappointed.

"No, I'll still be glad to visit with you this evening. But just know, there may come a time when you come visiting and Sara will be visiting too. You'll have to be nice to her or leave."

The two squirrels seemed uncertain.

"What to do? I like rhymes," said Apkin.

"Maybe we'll come and maybe we won't," said Ekle. "We'll think about it."

The two squirrels then turned and ran across the lawn to their tree without even saying good-bye.

"I told them that I'd still see them. They may know something more of that other vinetrope that they haven't remembered yet. You have to be very encouraging with them. They're a nervous sort and may yet come around to you."

"I understand," said Sara. "No need for explanations."

"I guess this would be the perfect time for me to recite your friendship poem. Let's go inside."

They settled back inside Lucinda's home. Sara piled her armful of grass on top of one of the many heaps already filling up the space.

Lucinda began: "A Friendship Poem, for Sara

"When a friend is a friend
like you are to me,
you see joy in their eyes when
you do splendidly and
you feel quite the same
when they're doing grand,
it makes you feel useful
to give them a hand...
A slap on the back

an encouraging phrase
can keep you full charged
for several days and
pull you right through
to the light at the end—
well that's what I get
from Sara, my friend."

Lucinda concluded her rhyme with a flourish of her hands.

"I'm going to memorize it, Lucinda, so it will always be inside of me."

"I'm so glad you liked it. I meant every word. I would really feel lost here in this strange world of yours if you hadn't shown up."

Just then they heard a car pull into the driveway overhead. The driveway ran parallel to the flower bed on top of Lucinda's home. Often Sara's dad or brother parked the car right there, next to the flower bed, instead of going into the garage. Especially when they knew they'd being going out again in a little while.

"What is that wooshing thing you humans travel in, anyway?"

"Oh, you mean a car. It's called a car. My brother Steven just turned seventeen and got his license to drive. Kids can't drive cars."

"They certainly move quickly!"

"Yes, a great invention."

Sara looked at her wrist watch. "Oh no! It's 5:20!

I'm supposed be ready. I'm going to Aunt Laura's tonight for dinner. Stevie's bringing me over."

"Don't panic. Just slip out now and we'll talk more tomorrow."

"Okay."

Sara grabbed her bag, gave Lucinda a kiss on her vine-like hair, and left.

Lucinda heard the car pull away a little while later. She was pretty sure those two worrywart squirrels would show up for their rhymes later that evening. She liked them. A few good rhymes would win them over. She wanted to get the stone work done and scatter grass all over the living room floor—nice and thick—to make the room warm and cozy for her and her guests.

She worked non-stop till 10:00 P.M. Tomorrow she would start work on her well. The brothers hadn't shown up as expected, so she fell asleep.

CHAPTER FOUR

Lucinda Is Introduced to Someone Important

About an hour later she was awakened by the sound of small squeaks. She rubbed her eyes and sat up.

"Who's there?" she called out, but of course she was pretty sure who it was.

"It's us," said Ekle in his now familiar voice.

"Come in," called Lucinda, happy to have company and quickly straightening out her dress. "I thought you weren't coming after our talk this morning. It's quite late."

"We came," was Apkin's explanation.

"Smells good in here," said Ekle.

"Grass and pine tar," explained Lucinda.

"Good smelling," approved Apkin.

To Lucinda's surprise, in came a third figure behind Ekle.

"We brought a friend," said Ekle. "Someone we thought you should meet and who wants to meet you. This is Owletta. She is very important. She knows a lot about the world. Owletta, this is Lucinda Vinetrope—Glower and Rhymer."

"Welcome," said Lucinda graciously.

"I'm glad to meet you," said Owletta in a rich earthy voice. A voice like wind riding through a hollow log. "Owls have legends about glowers, you know. My mother told me some. Of course the glowers in her stories were owls. I always believed that glowers were make-believe characters invented to instruct the young. I didn't know they really existed. Then Ekle arrived in the neighborhood and told me of his meeting with one two years ago. Then yesterday, he told me of you. I had to come and meet you."

"You are more than welcome here," smiled Lucinda. "It is important for me to learn all I can, and by your beautiful language, I'm sure I have much that I can learn from you. I have the feeling our meeting will enrich our lives."

"I couldn't agree more. Your arrival is remarkable and must be noted and observed."

"And I'm interested in these legends of glowers you spoke of," added Lucinda. "They may hold clues to the whereabouts of others like me."

"I will be glad to share them with you."

"Please everyone, sit down."

"You've made it comfortable in here," acknowledged Ekle.

"A lovely home," confirmed Owletta, "and in such a short time! You must be a hard worker."

"Very busy," said Apkin, a friendly tone back in his voice.

"As busy as a squirrel," joked Ekle.

Everyone laughed. Things were going well and no one brought up the subject of humans.

"I have some acorns here," offered Lucinda, "and a few ears of tree fruit. My first crop hasn't grown in yet. I'm sorry I don't have much to offer."

"We're fine," said Ekle. "We had a big dinner."

"I only eat once a day," assured Owletta.

"I like acorns," added Apkin.

"Help yourself," Lucinda said with a smile and pointed to the little pile at the side of her bed.

"Now, Owletta, please tell me what your legends say about glowers. This news excites my curiosity," explained Lucinda.

Owletta had a lovely round face and her coloring was a mosaic blend of beige, brown, black and white feathers packed smooth and tight like little feather tiles. Her most amazing characteristic was of course her eyes. They were traditional, large and round, but what made them so unusual was their color, or I should say colors, for one was azure blue and the other was gold with little spots of green. She was perched on the pipe that protruded from the earth in front of the fireplace.

"Well, as I said, the glowers in our owl legends were always owls. They were usually great teachers and keepers of the history of owls. They also sometimes had the power to heal. Now I don't know if it's possible that just a few of your kind survived into the same period as the birth of owls. That's my guess. You influenced us in some way and then disappeared. It would only be natural for us to then credit your good influence to the wisdom of some special owl—a Glower Owl."

"I see what you are saying," thought Lucinda out loud. "Maybe, although most of our seeds were frozen underground. Maybe a few scattered vinetropes persisted through the Ice Age into yours."

Then Lucinda had to explain to her friends what she had already told Sara about the extinction of vinetropes and what Sara had told her about the Ice Age.

"Then why are you here now, Lucinda?" asked Ekle in his first truly thoughtful question.

"Yes, why?" copied Apkin.

"And the other one too," remembered Ekle.

Apkin looked back and forth waiting for someone to come up with the answer.

"Maybe there is some special need in the world now," suggested Owletta.

"And the glowers have returned," said Ekle.

"Danger," added Apkin, showing that he was following the conversation.

"Yes," picked up Owletta, "some danger or need in the world that has brought you back either by fate or acci-

dent. After all, your kind were great teachers and healers."

"Oh my," said Lucinda in a bewildered tone. "That's an awful lot of responsibility! I'm having enough trouble just figuring out how to make it through the winter, let alone solving the problems of this world."

"I wouldn't worry about it," said Owletta in her philosophical voice. "You are here and that is enough. If there is some special purpose, it will be known in time. For now, you are warmly welcomed by all of us."

"Yes, yes," agreed Ekle and Apkin, showing Lucinda respect after Owletta's explanations.

"But why do you have to be friends with that human child?" remembered Ekle.

"Is this true?" asked Owletta.

"Yes, there's a girl child, Sara, in the big house. She is very special to me. She is a very fine being."

"There must be some good reason that you trust her," said Owletta. "You are a glower and you must trust your instincts."

"You look like her," said Apkin, much to everyone's surprise.

"Like who?" asked Lucinda.

"Like humans," explained Apkin.

"You know what," said Owletta, "I believe Apkin's right. There is something about you that seems very human, other qualities that seem more like us, and yet you claim you are a plant."

"Yes. That's it," cheered Apkin, "you're everything!" and he squeaked at his own wisdom.

"There's so much to think about," said Lucinda.

"But now, my dear, I think it is time to be going. We arrived late and I know you must get your sleep. We'll ask for rhymes another time. I on the other hand, have a couple of mice to catch."

The squirrel brothers flinched.

"Never fear, my dear friends," reassured Owletta. "I dine on insects and mice, but I no longer have any interest in squirrel for my dinner."

With that, Owletta waved her wing in a graceful arch as a farewell gesture, and was the first to leave.

"We'll see you tomorrow," said Ekle. "Maybe there will be time to hear a rhyme!" he chuckled.

"Of course," said Lucinda, getting up to see her guests to the door.

The brothers gave a little nod and were gone.

Lucinda fluffed up the dried grass on her bed and laid out one of the blankets from Sara on top—the solid blue one. She lay down and pulled the plaid one over her and gave a little sigh of satisfaction. She thought to herself—interesting, Apkin and Ekle don't trust humans, yet they're friends with an owl who used to eat squirrels all the time till he became friendly with them. This is quite peculiar. But she was too tired to work on this new puzzle. "Good night," she whispered out loud to no one in particular and fell asleep.

Chapter Four

Sara didn't knock on Lucinda's door till about 2:00 Sunday afternoon. Her dad was working on his laptop and since it was such a nice day he had taken a seat at the patio table. He called this outdoor activity. But today it was very annoying. Sara kept herself busy raking leaves. This was an endless job during the month of October because their property was basically in the middle of a piece of deciduous woods. Lots of old oak trees. She had another school bag full of goodies for Lucinda, and she couldn't wait to present them. Finally her dad went in. She was alone. Sara knew Lucinda was home because she saw her orange head pop out a couple of times from the corner of her eye. She grabbed her bag, which she had tossed to the side of the back door, and made her way to Lucinda's door.

The door slid open gracefully as she approached.

"That's terrific," said Sara as she came through and watched Lucinda crank the door shut again.

"Yes, I had a real find this morning. Wheels. I just had to unscrew them from some kind of hollow thing."

Sara checked them out. They looked like they came off a child's doll carriage. Sara decided not to bother Lucinda about where she had found them. Whoever owned the carriage would just have to wonder.

"I guess you won't be needing any wheels from me," said Sara. "You've done a first rate job with your door. This will make your life much easier."

"You haven't seen anything yet. Wait till I get to my

interior decorating. I think I'm going to have some artistic flare. I can't wait till I'm able to work with a fully developed root system and can cover all my walls with lovely glowing designs. Please sit down," Lucinda gestured and took a seat on the pipe.

Sara settled down carefully this time on Lucinda's bed.

"That's what my mom was. An artist."

"Really? What kind of artist, Sara?"

"She was a painter. She also made pottery. I'll show you sometime."

"I'd love to see her work. But paintings? Are paintings picture illusions or three-dimensional illusions?"

"I guess picture illusions would be the right answer. She painted three-dimensional illusions on a flat surface. We call that painting. We call the three-dimensional kind of art sculpture. My mom used to poke fun at a lot of the art in fashion today. She used to say that a lot of people who called themselves artists didn't even know how to hold a pencil or paintbrush, let alone know how to draw. She said that the more knowledge and skill you had as an artist, the more freedom of expression it gave you—not the other way around. That it was stupid to throw out all the knowledge of the past."

"Your mom was wise. In a way that's what I will be for my vinetropes if I find them—their knowledge of the past. But why have your artists thrown out this knowledge?"

"I'm not sure. My mom used to talk about it, but I

didn't really understand. She'd get all worked up about it. She definitely didn't approve of calling blue, yellow, and green squares on a rectangular canvas a work of original art. Especially if it cost $400,000 dollars. It made her mad. One of the things she admired most in my dad was his pursuit of knowledge. He has endless patience. He never takes any shortcuts. Right now he's heading a team of scientists who are working with certain microbes that might be able to eat up the toxins in our environment."

"And that would be a good thing, I presume?"

"Yes, of course. But they have to be sure that the microbes don't have any secondary side effects that could be dangerous to the environment. My dad keeps very strict controls on all his testing and is extremely responsible. Since mom died he spends almost 100 percent of his time being a scientist. When the husband role died the father role got pretty thin."

Sara was surprised at her own anger and disappointment in her dad. She had not vented these feelings to anyone. Lucinda didn't seem taken back by this at all.

"Well, my dear friend, grief takes the joy out of us. It's not that easy to get you to smile either. I can experience grief enough through my memories to understand your dad's pain and yours too. But since I have not actually lost someone I've loved in my own personal lifetime, I'm sure I can't completely know how it feels. I do know that your dad's work sounds important and that you are both proud of him and angry with him. If you've been silent about your sadness, maybe he doesn't see your pain because he's lost inside his own. He and your mom must have been very close."

"They were. He laughed a lot with us then."

"Well, we will have to find some distractions for him that give him time with you. I might have some useful knowledge for him as well—as a scientist. I mean, after all, plant life is my specialty and there's still plenty of that in your world. But what are toxins and why do they need cleaning up? And what are dollars? So much information to learn. I wish I could put a strand of my vines on your forehead and drink up your world."

"Lucinda, you haven't even been here three full days. You're a living miracle to me. You're so full of surprises, newness, courage."

"I'm glad I bring you some happiness. I see you the same way. You are brave too, being so strong for yourself and your dad. And you are a fine thinker, a deep thinker, and a kind being. That's the best part. I would be very proud to be your mother if I was human and wasn't just a newborn."

They both laughed at this and Lucinda climbed on Sara's shoulder and put her arms around Sara's neck.

"Now tell me about toxins and dollars."

Sara explained as well as she could, and Lucinda caught on quite easily.

"We had many of the same things in our time as you humans have now. We had trade and many vinetropes specialized in different skills. We bartered a lot. You know—I make the root lights for your ceiling and you make the

root tapestries for my dining room—but we used coins as well for everyday needs such as food and clothing. There were coin makers. They often made what you call buttons and buckles as well. Our coins were made of Fregwood seeds which were large enough to imprint designs on, but small enough to carry in your pockets. The Fregwood trees grew around pools of water we called the Pools of Seedsong. That's because the leaves of the trees, when moved by the wind, sounded like humming or singing in the distance. You could hear it and yet not quite make it out. Our buttons were also made of these seeds and our buckles of Sharwood bark, which was quite durable. We had artists too. Some were famous and others were just family members who had a flare at making their homes beautiful. The sculptors worked with the roots, creating beautiful three-dimensional pictures and patterns on the ceilings and walls. Our painters used the stains of many kinds of berries and grasses, mixed with pine and nut oils, to make their paints. What did you mother paint?"

"Well, her specialty was landscape painting. Pictures of fields, gardens, forests, mountains, you know."

"You mean plant life in all its glory!"

"Yes." Sara laughed.

"I think your mother and I would have gotten along just fine. And your brother? Tell me a little about him."

"He's very funny. He's also a great storyteller and a whiz on the computer. Mostly he spends time with his girlfriend Lorraine these days. Next year he leaves for college."

"College?"

"Further education."

"Ah! And computers?"

"The only way I can begin to explain that one is to sneak you into my room and show you."

"Maybe we will do that. I can use all the experience with your world that I can get. I would love to see how you live. But what about toxins? I still don't have a clue to that one."

"Another hard one. Toxins are like poisons that are harmful to life. They are often unstable compounds that come from many of the amazing things we do as humans. We call these poisonous by-products of our inventions and busy world of making things—pollutants. Our air is getting polluted and our earth and water as well."

"Why would you do this?"

"Well, most of us aren't doing it on purpose. It's the way our inventions and human world came about. We didn't know that the effects of these new things, like cars, would have a polluting side effect. And then there are those who are careless or greedy and don't care. But most of us do. We just don't know what to do. We can't undo our whole world. That's why my dad is so hard at work. If he can create microbes that eat the poison and then disappear when they're done, it would be a great help. Others are working on cleaner fuels."

"This is quite a shock to me. Maybe that's the odd smell I've been smelling. Something a bit off, but not out-and-out dangerous. A warning smell that something is not

quite right. It shocks me because in my ancient world these things were better balanced. But then we did not have things like cars and whatever else you have."

"I'll try to teach you more."

"And I'll try to problem-solve as well. Anything to do with the earth is in my territory."

They both became pensive for a time.

"I almost forgot, Lucinda. I've got some more supplies for you," said Sara, opening her school bag.

"Here's some clothes." She pulled out two white nightgowns, two pair of knit pull-on doll pants in blue, a dark red sweater, a royal blue blouse and a little dress in a brown flowery print that came with a white apron attached.

"This is great," said Lucinda. "They look like a perfect fit!"

"They're from my old Madame Alexander doll," explained Sara. "Oh, and wait, I almost forgot the best part." Sara pulled out a pair of long miniature black leather boots.

Lucinda tried them on right away. Because they were made of soft, pliable, leather, they fit like a glove on her feet.

"This is too good to be true!" Lucinda chirped and literally jumped for joy. "You can't imagine how much this means to me Sara, how much work you have saved me."

She danced around and gave Sara a kiss. Then she pulled off her golden-orange dress. Her body glowed with a light orange glow and looked a bit like young birch bark in the early spring. She pulled on the pants and sweater and squealed with delight, dancing around some more.

Sara was equally delighted to see this unusual "being" dressed in something that looked like a jogging suit.

"Well, you certainly look very up-to-date in that outfit!"

"Do you think so? It fits perfectly and it's nice and warm."

"All I need to find you now is a good winter coat, hat, and gloves and you'll be pretty well set."

"I certainly will."

"I have a few more things." Sara pulled out two plastic pails.

"Here's some pails for your well, and I also found a set of doll dishes and a little sauce pot from the kitchen. You already found yourself some wheels."

Sara took out several white porcelain dishes with blue flowers on them. There were six cups and saucers, six dishes, and a teapot, creamer and sugar bowl. Sara had filled the sugar bowl with sugar and held it shut with a piece of tape that she now removed. She took out the saucepan as well.

"They're beautiful," said Lucinda. She picked each piece up lovingly and looked them over. She dipped her finger in the sugar and took a lick. "Delicious," she approved. Then she placed them carefully on her mantle and they gave the room a real "homey" look.

She put the saucepan in the fireplace and the little pot looked as big as a large soup kettle in the small opening.

"Just perfect. I can make all my vegetable stews and soups in here and keep them simmering. I'm sure it will take

the heat. It makes me hungry just thinking about it. In the old days, we had root ovens. They got as hot as fire, but didn't leave any dirty ash like wood-burning fire does. We had vents to the outside that let out the steam. Very efficient. But twigs will have to do for now. It takes time to nurture enough roots for all the things we can make with them."

"A root oven. It sounds like a mysterious way to cook."

"To us, of course, it was just the usual. It's like so many of the fantastic things I see in this world that probably seem ordinary to you. Like those cars of yours and huge homes. I can understand why you can't undo what you've created. It just needs some sensible adjustments."

"Yes, I see your point. Now, if you want to try something from our world that is really fantastic—try this." She handed Lucinda a whole bag of chocolate chip cookies.

"What do I do with it?"

"Open the bag and eat one of the round objects in it. It's food and we call them cookies."

Lucinda opened the bag and took out a cookie. It was nearly as big as her face. She took a bite. Her face began to glow so bright that Sara was afraid it was going to catch on fire. She was afraid that she had poisoned Lucinda by accident.

"Are you all right?" asked Sara with alarm.

But Lucinda's smile should have been explanation enough.

"This is delicious beyond delicious! You call them cookies?"

"Yes, chocolate chip cookies. You see, these little brown pieces are the chocolate."

"They are fantastic. Here, have one."

Sara helped herself to a cookie.

"Now sit down," instructed Lucinda between bites. "Let me show you how to braid this grass and while we braid I've got more news for you."

Soon Sara had the hang of it and while they braided, Lucinda told Sara of her visit from Ekle, Apkin and Owletta the night before. She did not miss a word.

"We have just got to find that other vinetrope," said Sara decidedly. "Somehow I will get you there."

"Right now we're not really sure where 'there' is. We have to be on the lookout for clues. It will take some real serious detective work. There is a plan somewhere in all of this. If I could only pinpoint where Ekle's and Apkin's home was before they got stranded up here."

"Maybe this Owletta can be of more help. She sounds smart and more worldly."

"Yes, and get me inside your house. I will definitely take you up on that. The more I learn about your world, the easier it will be for me to communicate with it."

"I'll try and arrange it as soon as I can. And Lucinda, if you run into trouble with anything, you just ring the doorbell and ask for me! My family will just have to meet you without any warning if it comes to your safety."

"That will be a scene to remember."

"I'd better get going now, I've got a lot of homework to do and Steven said he might take me with him and

Lorraine to a movie later."

"A movie?"

"Don't even ask. My brain is too worn-out for now."

They both laughed again.

"Okay, next time."

Sara left and Lucinda cranked her door shut.

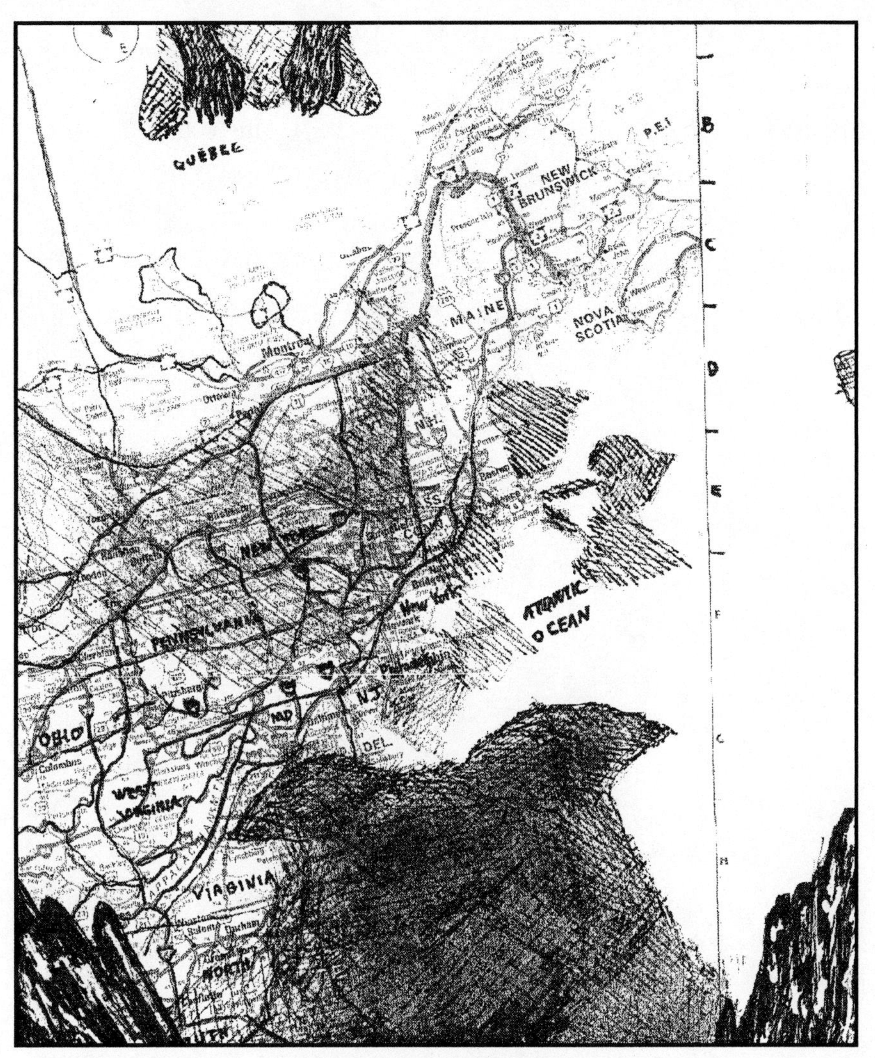

CHAPTER FIVE

Owletta Makes a Brave Offer

The night turned cold, but Lucinda had her first fire going and was snug and content. She had wheeled an old stump into the living room earlier that evening to serve as a table. Then she set the table with her new dishes and a generous pile of chocolate chip cookies. Water was boiling

in the kettle for dandelion tea. She had made a permanent bed in the room with the stones tarred into place. At the end of the bed was a hole in which she could drop hot stones from the fire. The room was small and the heated stones would keep a chamber this small warm for quite some time after the fire was put out. This method of heating wasn't as clean or safe as using a well developed root system, but this was the method used when vintropes were establishing themselves in a new territory. She sat on her bed with her legs crossed and her elbows on her knee wearing one of her new white nightgowns. She had just draped the plaid blanket over her shoulders when her guests arrived.

"Who's there?" she asked to make sure.

"It's us," came Owletta's distinctive voice.

She cranked the door open.

"Splendid job," approved Owletta of Lucinda's door system. "You're very clever with your human-like hands."

"Hey, look at all this," added Ekle as they came in. Lucinda cranked the door shut and they all took places around the tree stump table quite naturally.

"This is very beautiful," said Owletta and the brothers nodded.

"Where did you get all these things?"

"I know," said Apkin. "Human girl. Sara girl."

"That's right," confirmed Lucinda. "Sara brought me all these dishes and some new clothes and these delicious chocolate chip cookies. Please try some."

She stood up and took the teapot over to the kettle of

hot water and carefully tipped the kettle forward by the handle and filled the teapot. The bottom of the teapot was already prepared with dried dandelion leaves and flowers.

"The tea will be ready in a few minutes."

Her guests were impressed with all the added luxuries and Lucinda was enjoying being the hostess of her comfortable home.

"I've had a real brain storm," started Owletta. "I'm excited to tell you my plan."

"Please do," Lucinda encouraged as she poured tea for her friends and herself and then took her seat.

"Well, I'm going to take a trip for you down south and see what I can find out about this other glower."

"Really? You would do that for me? Would you really?" Lucinda could hardly believe her ears. "Is it on your way somewhere else?"

"No, it's not on my way anywhere else. I just feel it's something I want to do. Lucinda, there is a reason you are here. Imagine, glowers, like in the tales my mother used to tell me. I must help you. It will be an honor. I am convinced it is something I am meant to do."

"I can't believe you're doing this for me. I'm so appreciative," answered Lucinda, teary-eyed.

"I know that," said Owletta leaning over from her spot at the table to tap Lucinda gently on her shoulder with her wing tip.

"When would you leave?"

"I will leave in two nights on a full moon. I haven't been out flying in a long time and need the extra light. My

eyes aren't quite as good as they used to be."

"Two nights is soon," said Apkin. Then, he began to squeak excitedly, "Mate! Mate! You find our mate!"

"Yes, of course, our mates," Ekle picked up on Apkin's excitement. "Helping Lucinda means possibly finding our mates. If you find them, you must tell them we're alive. Tell them we want to get back to them. Now there's a chance."

Ekle was beside himself with joy. Apkin was whirling around on the floor.

"Oh dear, so much to accomplish on one trip," Owletta responded.

"You must try," said Lucinda, "and I feel a plan of my own growing. Now listen to this."

Ekle and Apkin leaned down to their teacups and lapped up a little tea. Apkin eyed the cookies and then stepped briefly on the table, took a cookie in his mouth, and returned to his seat. All three looked up at Lucinda and waited for her to continue.

"When I spoke with Sara this morning, she said she would help me too."

"Mates, mates! Watch out for Sara," squeaked Apkin.

Lucinda ignored this outburst. "So maybe Sara could somehow arrange for us to use that car of theirs. It travels quickly and we would all easily fit."

"Risky. Dangerous!" Apkin returned to his old worries.

"Are you nuts?" asked Ekle, popping an acorn into his mouth.

Apkin started to laugh.

"Maybe, but if Owletta can pinpoint the exact location of both the glower and your mates, don't you see? Then Sara could drive us straight there."

"Wonderful!" shouted Ekle.

"Sounds nutty to me," squeaked Apkin. His love of poor jokes seemed to be increasing.

"This is a pretty wild plan," Owletta said bluntly. "First of all, Sara is too young to drive. She would have to get her father or brother to do the driving. Second, you are expecting me to find two pins in two haystacks anyway. But let's just say I can do it. I find out where the other glower is and where Ekle's and Apkin's mates are. Then you're telling me you're just going to go up to two large humans, introduce yourselves and ask them to take us—us meaning two squirrels and a glowing possibly extinct species they've never seen before, in fact no one has ever seen before, along with them on a family excursion to reunite you, the strange sort of human-looking one, with your lost tribe and also to reunite two lost squirrels with there heartbroken mates? This would be a chance to witness a miracle."

"Well, it's an event you'll see for yourself," laughed Lucinda, "because you'll have to introduce yourself to them too. We'll need you along to give directions!"

Ekle and Apkins eyes were bulging. They'd never heard so many words spoken at one time. Apkin pushed a whole chocolate chip cookie into his mouth at once without thinking and started to cough.

Owletta shook her head, made little clucking noises, dipped her beak into the tea, shook her head some more and then said, "Okay, let's try it."

"Hurray!" said the brothers. No longer worried about humans, a surprising change in viewpoint. They lapped up some more tea and really seemed to like using china.

"Thank you," said Lucinda, grinning wide like a crescent moon.

"I can't believe I'm agreeing to this, but everything about you is so amazing, Lucinda, that I just can't say no. When you speak, everything seems possible and if you can convince me and these two brothers to ride with humans in a car, then you can probably get the humans to agree to your plan as well."

"I know I can. I didn't know it until tonight, but now I'm as sure of it as I am that you're all my friends. I will have to plan a means of introduction, but Sara will help me with that. I feel great," and with that Lucinda broke into a poem:

"Tonight is the night
We've made a great plan,
So stick out your paws
Your wing tips and hands
And shake on the promise
To do what we can
To make a success
Of our joyful, great plan.
It's risky, it's wild,

Why, it's never been done!
Which adds to the challenge,
The adventure, the fun.
So what if we tremble
So dizzy we spin?
Let's lift up our teacups
And let it begin!"

With that, the little group cheered and everyone seemed as merry as at a holiday feast. The cookies disappeared, a second pot of tea was made, and many stories of courage were told.

*****

Tonight was the night Owletta was to leave. Lucinda decided to make her friends a going away feast for Owletta. She had spent time with Sara the past two afternoons, but hadn't broached the subject of using her family's car. Maybe an opportunity would arise when she spent some time in Sara's house. Right now she was busy preparing acorn and mushroom stew. It was simmering in her kettle, flavored with some dried wild chive. There was spearmint berry tea and steamed crocus bulbs. The bulbs were plentiful. She would slice the bulbs thinly just before serving. For dessert Lucinda would serve the remaining chocolate chip cookies. They had been a big hit with everyone.

To make sure she had a new crop of cookies by the time Owletta returned from her journey, Lucinda reserved one cookie and was in the process of removing all the little pieces of brown chocolate to plant in the crevices of her interior stone wall. She was sure the dark, luscious morsels were the seeds that would sprout in the rich earth between the stones. She planted them on the wall opposite her fungus and mushroom crop so that they would not interfere with each other's nutriments. Just enough light was emanating from the fuzz of new root growth to plant a crop. By keeping her own glow turned up each day she could supplement the light source of the young roots.

Lucinda also spent time decorating the room. The table center was enhanced with a lovely bunch of bright orange bittersweet. On the mantle, she arranged holly branches with their red berries and several milkweed pods, spilling their white silk and brown seeds. The chimney cap worked fine and the well was almost done. She dug the well in the far corner of the room and built a small stone wall around it so no one could trip and fall in. Lucinda surveyed her home with pride and then stirred her stew with a large stick from which she had removed all the bark.

There was a sound of wings and then Lucinda heard the familiar hoot at her door. She cranked her door open and in came Owletta.

"Yum, smells good in here."

"It's a little meal I've prepared to celebrate your leaving tonight," explained Lucinda.

"How lovely everything is, but I'm not sure if owls can eat the same things as vinetropes. I have to say it certainly does smell good."

"Well, it's an acorn and mushroom stew and I have the sugar bowl filled with worms for you."

"Very thoughtful."

Ekle and Apkin scurried in. They each had a rust colored mum in their mouth and offered the flowers to Lucinda.

"Why thank you Ekle and Apkin," she said, taking the flowers and tucking them into the bundle of bittersweet on the table.

"You're welcome," said Ekle while Apkin checked out the stew.

"Good food. I smell acorns in here!" said Apkin.

"Yes, acorn stew," confirmed Lucinda. "Please, everyone, sit down." She cranked the door shut and went back to the kettle to give it another stir.

"This is a little going away party for Owletta. Tonight she leaves on her trip. A journey that is important to all of us."

"Yes," said Apkin, "an important trip!"

"And I think this evening, while we visit and dine, you brothers should try to remember as much about your old home as possible. Talking about it might uncover clues that will be helpful to Owletta on her quest."

"A very good idea," agreed Owletta.

"We'll try and remember what we can," said Ekle.

Apkin sat at his place with his paws on the table. "Haw, haw" he said.

"What's so funny?" asked Ekle as everyone took their places.

"Haw, haw," repeated Apkin.

"I don't know what you are talking about," said Ekle getting annoyed. "Can't you do any better than haw?"

"Now don't get so angry with your brother," said Lucinda in a soothing voice.

"Yes, let's keep calm," chimed in Owletta. "Maybe Apkin is remembering something. It just takes him a little longer with words. He doesn't have your knack for it, Ekle."

Apkin became excited. "Yes, remember—water—big water. Remember Ekle? Our tree near the water!"

"Yes, that's true. Our tree was near a river."

"That's grand!" said Owletta. "Now we're on to something. You lived near a river?"

"Yes, we lived near a river. But I don't know what river. We squirrels simply called it the Long Water Path."

"That's fine," said Lucinda. "It's a clue. Just keep talking. Remember whatever you can."

"Haw," said Apkin again in a calm voice that contained a touch of disdain.

And then easily, as if he'd been saying it all along. "Haw River. We live on the Haw River." He tapped his paws on the tabletop, quite pleased with himself.

"The Haw River," repeated Ekle. "That does sound a bit familiar."

"Farmers said Haw all the time," continued Apkin. "Up Haw, down Haw River. Haw, Haw, Haw."

"This is just the clue we've been looking for, Apkin," said Lucinda. "I think we've been underestimating you. Your language abilities are growing stronger by the moment. I only wish we had a map. Vinetropes were very good map makers."

"I've seen maps before," Owletta announced. "Humans are very fond of making them. I could easily follow one if I could get my wing tips on the right one. I've observed the humans looking at a map in their car. All we'd need to do would be to find out where the Haw River is in relationship to where we are now and I could fly straight there. Then I would have to make my way along the river and ask the local owls if they'd had any sightings of glowing creatures that fit your description, Lucinda. Since I speak Squirrel, I can ask the squirrel population as well. Oh, by the way, what are the names of your mates, boys? That would be helpful too. I could ask about for them by name and mention yours. That might bring me to them."

Ekle piped right up. "My mate's name is Regata and Apkin's is Selena."

"Regata and Selena," repeated Owletta, making a mental note. "And now that I think of it, how is it that I can now understand squirrel talk, when two years ago it would not have been possible? In fact, it would have been more likely I was eating squirrel than talking to one. I've never really thought about it as being strange till now. It's crept up so slowly, along with our friendship!"

"Yes. How is it that we talk to each other?" picked up Ekle. "Even Apkin is going at it with no trouble now. This is weird. Why hadn't we even realized it? What's going on? It's kind of spooky."

"It's Lucinda!" said Apkin.

"But Lucinda has only been here a short while,

Apkin, and we've been friends for nearly four seasons," said Owletta, confused.

"Maybe it was her seed," said Apkin.

"The seed?" said Ekle.

"Remember you complained something was pricking your foot all the way here?" said Owletta.

"Yes, till after we were here a couple of days and then it stopped bothering me. What does a vinetrope seed look like, Lucinda?"

"Well, it's as clear as pure water, very small, and has little spikes on it that can easily hook onto moss, or earth, or fur. Fur!"

"That's it!" said Ekle. "Lucinda, your seed traveled up here on my fur when we were locked in the barrels. It was stuck in my foot. That's how you got here. Your seed came with us. You came from where we came from! And from where the other glower is. We all came up here by accident!"

"This makes perfect sense. I'm so pleased with your detective work," said Lucinda. "It might mean that there are other seeds, other vinetropes down south, besides the one glower you saw!"

"And it might explain why Ekle speaks so well and has a flair for owl talk," picked up Owletta. "With your seed pricked in his foot on the way up here, he probably absorbed some of your talent for language, Lucinda. It kind of sprouted in him."

"How wonderful. And this talent I've unknowingly gifted to Ekle seems to be contagious!"

"And that explains why I know what a map is," concluded Owletta. "I think I'm beginning to understand something of human speech as well as squirrels."

"You must have a real knack for language," said Ekle, "if now that you've caught this talking condition you can understand humans. Because I'm speaking owl well enough and humans still make no sense to me at all!"

"But wait a minute," said Lucinda. "Does it sound like I'm speaking two distinctly different languages? I don't feel like I am. I'm just talking."

"That is really weird," confirmed Owletta. "Maybe we're speaking some universal language and don't know it?"

"Too weird," said Apkin, returning to a short phrase.

"But that's the only explanation," added Ekle. "We must all be speaking what we think and saying it in a way that is understood by all…"

"Even though we aren't aware of "hearing" a new language," concluded Lucinda. "Yes, that's it. When you think of it, do you feel like you're using new words, or do you just find yourself easily saying what you want and now for some reason we all understand each other?"

"That's it," said Ekle. "That's just how it feels."

"And now it's happening with humans for me," said Owletta. "That's how I know Sara is too young to drive. I heard her talking to her brother about getting his driver's license and how it will be six years before she gets hers."

"Does that mean we will start to understand humans too?" questioned Ekle.

"Of course," said Apkin. "It's only logical."

"Which brings us back to the map," said Lucinda. "How do we get hold of one?"

There was a buzz around the room.

"We could check out the car," Ekle interjected.

"Yes," said Owletta. "Remember, I was saying I've noticed humans looking at maps in their cars."

"Great idea!" said Lucinda.

"Do you think the doors of the car are locked?" asked Owletta. "If they are we're out of luck."

"Let's go find out," said Ekle.

"Sara's dad and brother rarely lock the car doors," Owletta said with certainty. "They just slam them shut and carry things in and out. But even if it's not locked, how will we get the door open?"

"Easy," said Lucinda. "We'll just bring some of my grass braid along, tie it around the door handle and then we'll all pull!"

"Who will read?" asked Apkin. "There's no Sara late at night."

"I think I can read English," said Lucinda. "I can certainly speak it well enough. In any case, I'm willing to give it a try."

"Okay. Then, let's get going," said Owletta.

" Our dinner?" complained Apkin.

"It will be here when we get back," said Lucinda, "and we'll be even hungrier for it."

The friends slipped out into the night. Lucinda held several feet of her homemade rope gathered in her hand.

She turned her glow off completely. Owletta flew directly to the garage and waited while the other three made their way up the few stone steps to the upper garden and across the driveway to the garage. The garage was open.

"We're in luck," said Owletta from the hood of the car, "the door's not locked. The button's up."

Lucinda turned up her glow just a bit. "Okay, Owletta, we're going to need your help here. None of us can reach the handle. Take the end of this rope and fly back up on the hood."

Owletta did as she was instructed. She sat on the hood with the end of the rope in her beak.

"Now," continued Lucinda, "edge your way closer till you're directly over the door handle. Then see if you can drop the rope through the opening in the handle. It's like threading a needle."

"What's a needle?"

"Never mind," said Lucinda. "Just lower it slowly, the opening between the handle and the side of the door is pretty generous."

Owletta grasped the rope with one claw and slowly lowered it down the side of the door using her beak to assist in the process. It almost slipped in place but then it hit the handle and flopped over it instead of through the opening.

"Pull it back and try again," encouraged Lucinda.

Owletta pulled the rope back up and once again positioned herself directly above the handle. She carefully lowered the rope and this time it slipped right through without any trouble.

"Yeah!" everyone cheered a bit too loudly and Lucinda quickly grasped the end of the rope with both hands.

"Now keep hold of your end, Owletta, and come on down."

Owletta secured the rope firmly in her beak and flew down to the garage floor.

"Great job!" congratulated Lucinda.

The squirrels leaped around with excitement.

"Now comes the big test," announced Lucinda as she took hold of Owletta's end and tied the two ends together. "Let's all take hold of this rope and pull like our lives depended on it!"

Lucinda took the position closest to the car and tied a slipknot around the end. Then she pulled it tightly against the handle and left a long length of rope hanging behind her. The brothers each grabbed a piece with their teeth and front claws and Owletta took the end piece in her beak.

"At the count of three, pull," ordered Lucinda.

"One-two-three-PULL!"

The four friends held firm with their feet and pulled with all their might. The door did not open. They relaxed a moment.

"Okay. Let's try again. One-two-three-PULL!"

Again they gave it their all until they felt like they were going to burst.

"It's not working," said Owletta, dropping the rope. They all rested for a moment, catching their breath.

"I think it's because we're not getting enough leverage against the handle to release the door." Lucinda thought out loud. "Humans are higher up when they pull the handle. We could pull all night like this and get nowhere. We have to pull from a higher position."

"Let's stand on these small barrels!" squeaked Ekle as both Ekle and Apkin circled around three paint cans at the side of the garage.

"Great idea," said Lucinda. "Give me a hand."

One of the cans was taller than the others and looked as if it might give them the height they needed. With all four pushing, they were able to slide the can directly opposite the car door. Lucinda picked up the rope and climbed to the top of the can.

"Here," she said, throwing a length of slack rope behind her so her friends could take hold.

"Ready!" she cried, "One-two-three-PULL!"

The door flew open, tossing Lucinda to the ground and toppling the paint can as well. The squirrels rolled on the floor and Owletta paddled the air, feathers flying, as the rope released altogether. Fortunately the can was sealed tight.

"We did it!" shouted Lucinda joyfully, getting to her feet.

"Shhhhhhh!" said Owletta, reminding them to keep it down.

Lucinda took a look outside. Everything was dark and silent.

"We're all right," she reported.

They all climbed into the car and began to look

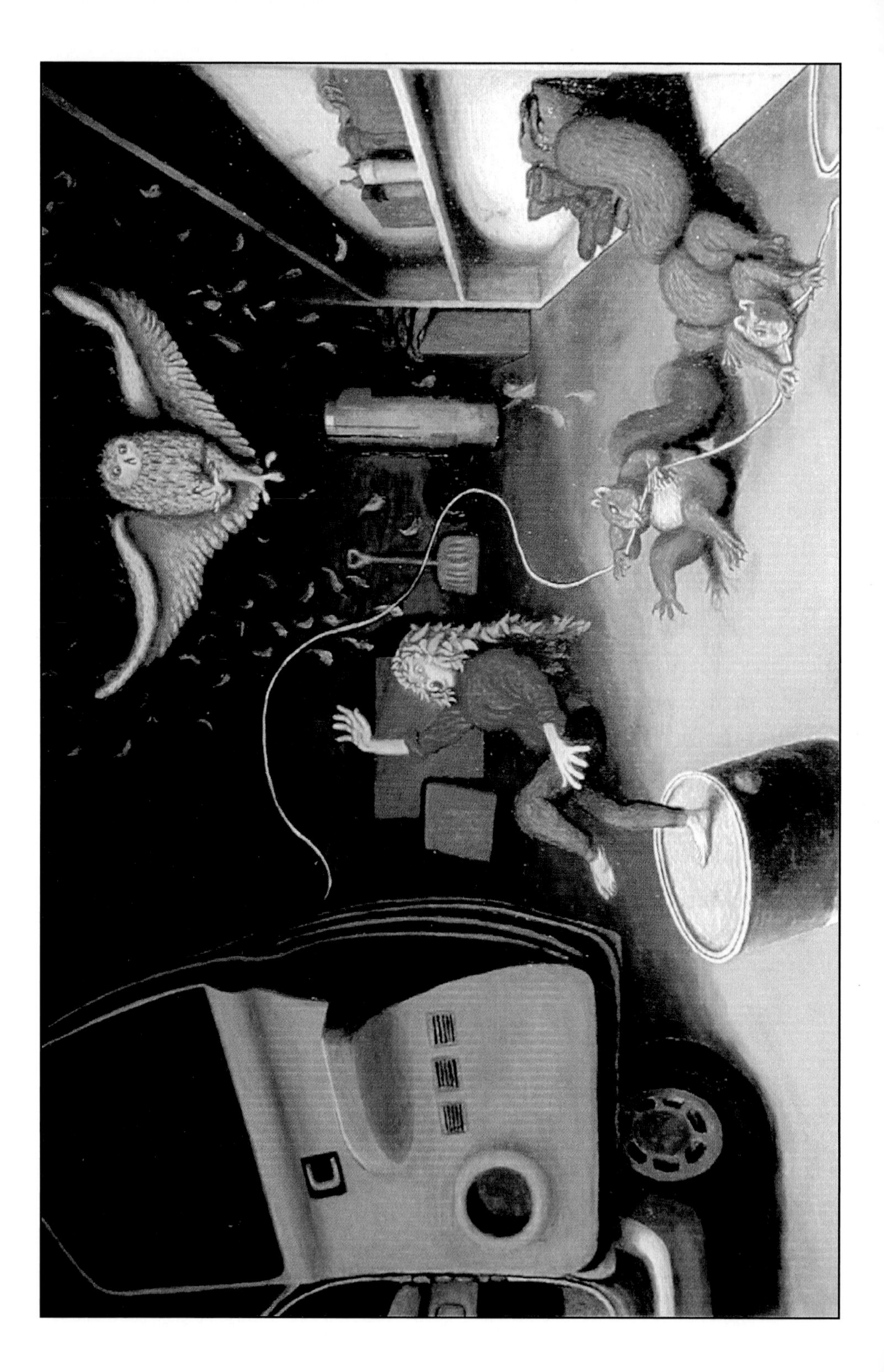

around. A little light had come on automatically so Lucinda kept her glow off.

"Where's the map?" said Apkin.

"It's here somewhere," whispered Owletta.

"Was it a book of some sort?" questioned Lucinda.

"Here's something," said Ekle and he tapped on an object in the side door pocket of the driver's seat.

Lucinda took hold of the book with both hands, but couldn't pull it out of the pocket.

"Give me a hand," she said to Ekle.

He took hold with his teeth and front claws and together they were able to slide the book out and lay it on the seat. It was a large red book, bigger than Ekle's body, and its cover now displayed a few fresh teeth and claw marks.

"Oh, dear," said Lucinda, seeing the scrape marks.

"What does it say?" asked Owletta as she and Apkin joined them on the front seat.

"Let me see," said Lucinda, placing herself in front of the book. "It says, Road Atlas-Maps of the United States."

"That's it!" said Ekle in a loud whisper. "We're in luck!"

"And you can read!" added Owletta.

"Yes, I guess I can. Now what do I do?"

"Open it up," said Ekle.

"Yes, of course. All right. I know we are in New Jersey," said Lucinda. "Sara mentioned that to me. And we know we need to go south. So what we need is to see a big picture of that whole area. Then we can decide what details we should look at." She was thinking out loud again.

"A map of the whole country. Look in the front," suggested Owletta.

Lucinda flipped through a number of pages with writing on them. Then, sure enough, there was a map of the whole country. The United States, as Sara had explained in one of their conversations.

"Are we on the east side of this country or the west?" questioned Owletta.

"Well here's New York," said Lucinda, pointing to it with her long index finger. So that means we're on the east side. Now we move down slowly looking for the Haw River."

"Everything is too detailed to find it," explained Owletta as though she had been using maps all her life. "If it's a small river it may not even be listed on this map. What we need to do is look at the detailed map for each of the states that move south from here. You see, here are places all south of New Jersey—Georgia, South Carolina, then North Carolina, Virginia, Maryland, Delaware and some place called Washington, D.C. Here we are back up at New Jersey. Let's try those maps first. You want to look for blue lines like this," she pointed with her wing tip. "They represent rivers. Isn't this exciting!"

"It is. Now let's get to work," said Ekle. "The Haw River must be in one of those places."

"Yes," agreed Lucinda. "Lets' start in the middle

between the most southern, called Florida, and New Jersey. Here at North Carolina or Virginia. We'll check those places first."

Lucinda opened to the map of Virginia. "Help me find rivers, everyone. The red ones are roads."

They looked carefully. No luck.

Lucinda moved to the map of North Carolina. She and the others checked every square inch of it. Ekle pointed to the rivers he found and Lucinda read the names. "Pee Dee River, Cape Fear River, South River, Neuse River, Haw River—Haw River! That's it! We've found it!"

She pointed to it and everyone took a look.

"It's west of this large city called Raleigh."

"I can find it," said Owletta with confidence. "I now have a picture in my head of the direction I must fly and I have an idea of distances as well from this distance chart. I also have three names to help me—North Carolina, Raleigh, and then west to the Haw River. It's when I get to the river that it will become tricky. There's a lot of miles of river to cover. That's where my investigating skills will really come into play. But I promise to give it my best try."

"We can't ask for anything more," said Lucinda.

The squirrels nodded their agreement.

"Then I will leave tonight. Let's finish up here and go back to your place, Lucinda. I'll leave at midnight."

They were able to get the Road Atlas back into the door pocket. They all got out and pushed the car door shut. Lucinda picked up her braided rope and wound it up again

around her arm. The four friends left the garage and went back to Lucinda's home to feast and to celebrate.

CHAPTER SIX

Time to Sneak Inside

The Friday of that following week an opportunity showed itself. When Sara got back from school her dad was already home and Steven was home too. There was a science convention going on in Chicago and her Dad had been asked to give a lecture on the potential use of common microbes for both fuel and clean-up potentials in a holistic system of energy. Her dad had explained it as a system of energy based on the way our bodies work—like burning calories—with microbes speeding up the breakdown of biodegradable waste. Some theorists felt that adding a robotics component to the microbes might be necessary. They'd be giving lectures too. She'd forgotten about this speech. Her dad was often asked to give lectures, and she knew he was a well-known and respected scientist, but to her he was just Dad. Also, she had been preoccupied with Lucinda and she and her dad hadn't been on the same wavelength in some time. Sara was to stay home with Steven. Steven was to make sure that he slept home Friday and Saturday night and to touch base with Sara during the day. Her dad suggested that it might be nice if he did something with his sister.

"You mean like drop her off at the Delaware Water Gap to do some white-water rafting," he teased.

"Sounds like fun," Sara came back. "Especially if you joined me."

"You'll probably have to settle for another movie."

"With Lorraine?"

"What's wrong with Lorraine?"

"Nothing. I like her. I had fun the last time."

"Why don't you have a friend over or arrange for a sleep over," suggested her dad.

Sara had friends, and was social enough at school not to draw attention to herself, but since her mom's death she hadn't pursued these friendships much after school. At first the grief was too much, and she wanted to be alone. Then it became a habit. Now she wanted to be alone with

Lucinda.

"I might call Jennifer," she answered cheerfully. "Steven can drop me off if I need a lift. I've also got two reports due next week that I can get a jump on."

"Okay." Her dad readily accepted his daughter's good cheer because it was too difficult to do otherwise.

"The cab will be here any minute. Which jacket do you think I should take for the lecture?" he asked his kids. "The tweedy one or the solid navy?"

"Tweedy," the kids answered in unison.

"Okay, I'm just about packed. Where did I put my briefcase?"

"It's downstairs by the front door," reminded Steven.

"That's right."

They heard the cab honk.

"Okay, kids, I'm off. Wish me luck. This is a big one for me."

"You'll do fine," said Sara and kissed her dad on the cheek.

He gave them both a hug and descended the stairs with them behind him. In a moment the cab pulled away and Steven and Sara were alone in the center hall.

"Don't get mad," said Steven in preparation, "but I've got tickets for a show with Lorraine tonight for her birthday. I only bought two because it was weeks ago and I didn't remember that dad was going to be away this weekend."

"No problem, I'll be fine."

"I'll be back by midnight, promise. Dad left money in the dresser box. I promise tomorrow Lorraine and I will take you with us."

"Have fun. I'm fine," and she gave him a hug.

She loved her brother. There was a pretty big age difference, and even if things hadn't changed so drastically, he would have been going his separate way by now.

"Okay, Sara. I'm going to get ready and be out of here by 5:00, or we'll never make it to the city in time."

Steven rushed upstairs leaving Sara thinking to herself, *"This is it. Lucinda comes inside today."*

A half-hour later Steven was in the family car and gone.

Sara took a brown shopping bag out of the broom closet and went out the back door. She raced to the upper edge of their property to a cluster of pine trees and in short order had the bag half-filled with cones. Then she hurried back down the outer edge of her yard to the lower garden and turned in along the wall to Lucinda's home.

"Where have you been?" Lucinda asked dramatically.

"It took me awhile. I had to wait to say good-bye to my dad and Steven. Dad's off to a science conference for the weekend and Steve's on a date with Lorraine. We have the house to ourselves till the magic hour of midnight."

"You mean I'm going into your home?"

"Yup."

"Fantastic! And I've got some exciting news for you."

"Hop in this bag."

Lucinda peeked in. "Pine cones."

"Yes, thought it would be a good way to transport you around—inside and out. You can duck under the cones if necessary."

"Nice," said Lucinda hopping in and wiggling into the cones.

Sara cranked Lucinda's door shut except for a crack and headed for her house. She opened the back door into the kitchen and placed the bag on the floor.

"Okay, the coast is clear."

Lucinda jumped out onto the earth colored tile floor.

"Wow, everything's so big. I feel dizzy. Look at this floor. How did you get your dirt so even and clean and shiny?"

"It's not dirt. It's tile colored like earth."

Lucinda sat down and stroked the floor with her hand. "Beautiful. It's something like polished stone. Very attractive and practical. I bet it keeps the bugs and worms out."

"Yes, it does. Mom would have had a fit with a living floor. Dad would probably have us all studying it and taking notes."

"Where does all this wood go?"

"Those are cabinets for storage." Sara opened a door to demonstrate.

"Of course, I know what cabinets are. We had them too—lined with dense moss, doors made of woven bark. These are so huge I didn't recognize their function."

Sara lifted Lucinda to her shoulder and took her around the kitchen. She showed her the refrigerator, oven, dishwasher, and sink.

"I love this well you call a sink. Imagine, running water. I could fill this and use it as a swimming pond. I can't

believe the size of these pots. You could cook three vinetropes in this one," she pointed to a pasta pot in the drainer.

Sara took her from room to room and everything was a marvel to Lucinda. Lucinda had to see everything. When they got to the toilets Lucinda was puzzled.

"This seems a little low for a human sink or bathtub. Do you use it for some kind of recreation?"

Sara giggled and then explained.

"By the way Lucinda, you must have a need for something like this too. What do vinetropes do?"

"Well, my friend, since you ask, much of our liquid waste is recycled as the nutritional liquid I showed you when we first met. The source of our spray that we use to water our roots with. The liquid waste comes out as a morning sweat you call dew. It just evaporates. As for the solid waste, it is close to being rich top soil, but it is a bit strong to keep indoors. We build another chamber near our homes to "deposite" it in. In short order it becomes topsoil to use in farming. We used to farm indoors and outdoors in our time."

"So you use what we call an outhouse, and it is also your compost heap. Interesting."

"I think you have a bit of the scientist in you Sara, like your dad."

"I guess so," Sara chuckled. "But meeting you would pique anyone's curiosity. So where's your outhouse?"

"It's further down inside the wall. I found another smaller hollow and cleared it out a bit. I don't need a door for my outhouse. I just slip through a space I loosened between the stones."

Finally they made it to Sara's room. Sara plopped Lucinda on her bed.

"I have so much more to show you, my computer, television, music. I'll order out for dinner. I'm sure we can find something on the menu you'll love."

"We're going to have a splendid time. But sit here first next to me on this royal bed of yours. I want to tell you the news first."

Sara took off her shoes and sat cross-legged next to Lucinda.

"Okay, shoot."

"Owletta left last night on a trip to a place you call North Carolina to investigate for me. She will be looking for the other glower, signs of other vinetropes, and to possibly locate Ekle's and Apkin's mates."

"She left last night? Does she have any idea where she's going? I might have been able to help with that."

"She has a pretty good idea of where she's going!" Lucinda answered with confidence. "It may take her a few weeks, but she's going to give it a real try."

Then Lucinda explained the whole episode of the map in the car and the Haw River as well as the logical explanation of how Lucinda was transported on Ekle's back as a seed spur caught in Ekle's foot. She also explained their hypothesis of how language was transmitted from her seed into Ekle, then on to the others after exposure to him.

"This is all too fantastic! It's starting to sound like a science fiction story. You mean exposure to you enables animals to learn to talk to one another?"

"It seems so. And it's not language in the usual sense. It's like they all just talk in a way that seems natural to them and we just seem to understand each other. It is quite astounding."

"You sound like you're speaking English to me."

"Well I am, that is true. I can experience the difference as I speak it. It's not an effort, but distinctly different from squirrel or ancient Vinetrope. As a glower I can actually speak several languages as naturally as my own tongue. It's what's happening to Owletta and the squirrels that is the really astounding part."

"Was this always true? Does your built-in memory tell you anything about this?"

"No, it doesn't. I find no memory of different species communicating like this. We were the world's highest intelligence in those days. But Owletta told me that owls have legends of glowers. Glower owls that were master teachers in the beginning of owl history who then went extinct."

"What could this mean?"

"It sounds like some of our kind might have survived longer than I realized. That they may have gained additional survival abilities and for awhile lived and worked with the creatures that came after the Ice Age. But these vinetropes were probably few in number, and eventually died out. The owls, over time, naturally made the stories of glowers into Glower Owls. It's possible that now, under such different conditions, my abilities may be somewhat different then in ancient times."

"Exactly. Excellent thinking. But this would probably be a result of chemical interactions going on now, not evolution, since your seed would be genetically coded in the deep past." Sara was remembering what her dad had taught her about evolution.

"Or I might be a descendant of these later vinetropes. But then I would have to explain why my historical memory doesn't have a record of these later vinetropes."

"That probably means you are from a more ancient seed. But I suppose it could mean that the memory process of glowers had changed in the new vinetropes. If this were true it might mean that your memory abilities are not identical to the ancient ones, but you are not aware of anything being different."

"Are you telling me that I have faulty memory? That's ridiculous."

Sara started laughing. "Remember when you wrote me my memory poem."

"Well that's before I knew anything about you or people. But a vinetrope glower does not have poor memory."

"I wasn't suggesting poor memory. I just meant that in adapting, during and after the Ice Age, the way in which glowers store memories may have altered. Other traits may have altered too. You remember everything you need to know, but you may not remember everything that ever happened to vinetropes. And your current memories and access to past knowledge is incredible."

"Yes, but I don't like to think of myself as having damaged memories."

"Well then don't. It would be a different, not damaged memory. Compared to the way our memory works yours is perfect. People are always forgetting things. I think you're overreacting. Anyway, this is all just guesswork. We don't know any of this for sure. We probably never will have a full answer for you. What we can do is try and find the other glower and maybe some clue as to where your particular seed came from."

"But how do I have the ability to stimulate language between animals?"

"That's a hard one. Maybe there's something different in the atmosphere or environment. The soil and air are certainly different. It may have added to your abilities in some ways and reduced other abilities. Who knows."

"You're right Sara, and as you said we're mostly guessing. I think you're going to be a scientist like your dad. You can put together a good sounding theory!"

"Thanks. None of this explains how you and that other glower got to North Carolina."

"This is quite a piece of detective work. Let's hope Owletta can do her job. Her increased language skills should make her task easier to accomplish. She may even be able to speak with other animals besides squirrels and not know it yet. She said she was beginning to understand people."

"Amazing. Lucinda, this investigation plan could really work. If you'd asked, I could have helped with a map."

"We did pretty well. Just left a few scratches on the cover. Where you could help is later. If Owletta can prove for a fact that this glower exists, than maybe you could drive me and the squirrels there. Owletta could join and give us directions to the exact location once we're there."

"I'm not old enough to drive."

"I realize that. Owletta explained that to me. She said she heard you and your brother talking about driving. It would mean introducing me to your dad and brother and getting them to help."

"You've got to be joking!"

"I'm very serious. Anyway, we said we needed reasons to get your family to spend some time together."

"Yes, but Steven wouldn't believe in you even while he was looking right at you and it might push my dad over the edge."

"I think you should give them more credit than that. Especially your dad. He'd probably find me very interesting."

"You're right about that."

"Does that mean maybe? You'll think about it? I'll help you with a means of presentation. We don't have to do anything till we hear from Owletta, so we've got some time to make plans."

"Yes, Lucinda, of course I will ask. I was wondering about telling them myself and planned to talk to you about it. If Owletta actually finds this other glower I will do whatever I can to get you there."

This caused Lucinda to break into a poem:

Chapter Six

"The famous five
Are faithful friends
Who sealed a plan
When at wits end.

They found a map
And marked the spot,
To find the place
Is Owletta's lot.

They'll wait until
The first snowfall
To learn if they'll
Succeed at all.

And then stage two
They'll usher in
On owl's return
Plan B begins.

They'll need some wheels
To travel far,
They hope to use
Smart Sara's car.

And then the five
Shall add two more
And all the plans
Will surely soar."

Sara and Lucinda joined hands with Sara on her knees on the bed and Lucinda hopping up and down. They sang through the poem together.

"This bed of yours is quite a jumping enhancement," appraised Lucinda taking a couple more leaps.

"Shall I order dinner now?" asked Sara.

"Yes, I'm hungry."

"I looked over the delivery menu and I thought you might like one of the vegetable wraps. I could get a cold one and a grilled one. I'm going to get a pizza too with mushrooms and extra cheese. You can try it, but I don't know if you can digest cheese."

"I'd better stick with the vegetables and experiment slowly. I don't want to spend the next two days making compost."

Sara and Lucinda laughed at that one. They were having fun and Sara didn't think to stop herself. It had been a long time since she had fun like this. Lucinda explored Sara's room while Sara called the delivery service to place their dinner order.

Like many kids, Sara's room displayed a large collection of toy animals in many shapes, colors and sizes. She could also boast an old-fashioned, four-poster bed and of course the bay window with the view. Lucinda admired the view from the window. When Sara returned, Lucinda stood in the middle of the bed, turning around and around like a music box ballerina, taking it all in.

"Your room is so artistic!" remarked Lucinda, who seemed to be dazzled by the size and array of colors and

shapes that met her eyes. "I've never seen anything like this."

"Of course, you haven't," Sara chuckled.

"You never told me you collected sculpture," continued Lucinda, as she pet a toy fox that was as big as she was. "I've never imagined there could be so many sculptures in one place. Did your mom make any of these?" Now Lucinda was stroking a Kermit the Frog that Sara had sitting on one of her pillows.

"Oh, that's not sculpture."

"It must be. Look at all these three-dimensional creatures all over your room!"

"They're just toys."

"Pretty fancy toys," said Lucinda, impressed. "This is quite a huge sleeping room for one person!"

Lucinda jumped off the bed and approached a green creature perched on the wicker toy trunk under the window. "This guy looks just like an Ezak."

"What's an Ezak?" asked Sara.

"I don't know how to explain. But I know they looked a lot like this. It was a creature that lived at the same time as vinetropes when we were plentiful. They were huge creatures. Really huge. But they were pretty stupid and we managed to keep out of their way most of the time. There were some disasters, though."

"Well, we call this guy a dragon. Dragons are just legends to us, but they do look a lot like dinosaurs. Dinosaurs were gigantic creatures that went extinct with the Ice Age."

"So dragons are to dinosaurs what owl glowers are to real glowers? Then maybe dinosaurs are Ezaks!" Lucinda laughed.

"Maybe so. Legends sometimes have a bit of truth to them. And they died out during the Ice Age. Again, some more logical data for our hypothesis. But I sure hope dinosaurs don't make a come back the way you have."

"I hope not too."

"Actually we have a movie about just that. It's called *"Jurassic Park."* You should see that one! You could tell me if the movie looks anything like your old world did; if our science and imagination is at all accurate."

"I can't keep up with all this. What's a movie?"

"Lucinda, you've got so much to learn about us. I don't know where to begin: television, computers, pizza, the problems in our world? Where do I even begin? I don't understand so much myself."

"Just pick something and we'll get started. One thing is going to be just as new to me as the next. It will hook up in my brain somehow. At least I hope so! Here in your house I feel like I've left one planet and arrived on another and I haven't even gotten used to the first one!"

"All right, then. Let's start with TV and movies. I guess that's the American thing to do. And it will give you a lot of information to chew on. I'll go order dinner."

"This clear stuff is amazing," said Lucinda. She was stroking the window.

"It's glass. We call it a window."

"Yes, I understand it's a window. It's the glass that's

intriguing me. It's beautiful. Lets in the outside, yet keeps you protected from the weather."

"Exactly."

"We had root roofs in the old days as well as earth roofs. The root roofs were in the rooms closer to the surface. When the weather was good, a part of the roof made only of roots—like a window, I guess—would pull open and let in air and sunlight. The weave of the roots would collapse or contract, revealing the outside. But much of the time they were kept shut. This glass is especially beautiful. Vinetrope seeds are clear like this, you know, but so small."

Lucinda seemed dreamy with wonder. There was so much to absorb. Sara was concerned about how much they should try and accomplish at one time.

"Maybe we should skip the TV?"

"Oh no, I'm ready for more. Don't hold back," Lucinda reassured.

Sara opened two cabinet doors in a piece of furniture across from her bed. She had managed to talk her parents into a TV in her room. She was a good student and did not choose to spend all her time in front of the set. So when they got a new set for the family, she inherited the old one.

"This is it, a TV," said Sara. "That's short for television."

She did her best to explain, before turning the set on. Finally she gave up. The only thing to do was turn it on. She put in "Jurassic Park" first because she thought a story would be easier to get the hang of than all the jumping around of regular television, with its advertisements coming and going. Also, maybe some of the visual images would be familiar to Lucinda.

The movie began and Lucinda was entranced. At first she was confused by the changes of images and movement. But then the natural story line took over, and her mind quickly adapted to this new process of visual storytelling. She cuddled up to Sara and at the exciting spots clutched onto Sara's arm. "Yykes! Wow! Uh-oh!" she called out at the right moments.

"This is a thrilling way to tell a story," said Lucinda. "Of course you've got a lot of stuff wrong about dinosaurs, but that doesn't stop it from being exciting. Very imaginative!"

"What do we have wrong?" questioned Sara, putting the movie on hold.

"Oh, don't stop. Well, the skin color is wrong. Brighter greens, blue green, and the brown ones had a rusty color mixed in. Also, these Raptors, as you call them, weren't as fierce as you make them. It's those long neck plant eaters that were the vicious ones."

"Well, obviously, that's because you're a plant," Sara asserted.

"Of course!" Lucinda laughed. "Okay, get it going again."

The food arrived. Sara went downstairs for it and returned with a tray holding pizza, two veggie wraps and a couple of Cokes.

Lucinda tried the pizza anyway and loved it except for the cheese. Sara helped her peel off the cheese and she

dabbed the crust into the tomato sauce. She tried the coke and at first the bubbles put her into a coughing fit and burned her throat and nose. But when she got used to it, and took small sips, she loved it. The wraps were a big hit, but one wrap was nearly half the weight and the size of Lucinda herself. Sara cut off a one-inch round from each wrap and Lucinda "pigged-out".

Now came the hard part. The first movie done, Sara thought it was time to expose Lucinda to the news. She had to understand this world of humans for better and worse, if she was going to survive in it. There was nothing Sara could do to prepare Lucinda. Lucinda grew very quiet and gave her full concentration. The knowledge of the kind of weapons humans possessed staggered her. Sara had never seen Lucinda so quiet.

"Maybe this is enough for one day," Sara suggested.

"Oh no," Lucinda waved her hand, "this is very important for me to watch."

Then a documentary came on that discussed current research into forms of clean energy. It even mentioned the convention that Sara's dad was at and about his work.

Lucinda became excited, and burst into one of her winning grins.

"I can help solve that one!"

"Solve what?" said Sara, getting a bit sleepy.

"The energy problem!"

"You can solve our energy problem?" she woke right up.

"Well, at least point your scientists in the right

direction."

"How?"

"Vinetropes have always made clean energy, as you call it. I explained that to you already, didn't I?"

"Explain it again. I must have missed something."

"When we change sun light into energy inside us, we produce our special watering system that I told you about. Glowers have this liquid in their systems in even greater concentration than other vinetropes. This water is sprayed and passes on the energy to our root systems, changing the plants that grow above our homes into a new kind of plant. It uses the sunlight to enable itself to create much more energy than it normally would. Not only does it produce enough energy for its own needs, but it gives off extra energy that we use to warm and cool our environment. These are the same plants we harvest for food and this all becomes a self-sustaining clean energy system for maintaining a comfortable environment and growing food. The system can last a long time, even if we're not around to water it for a few months. It takes about three seasons for all the roots to whither or return to their original chemical status. We've always done this, and it never occurred to us that there was any other way. Of course, the chemical process, this process you call photosynthesis, is natural to us. And it's obvious that our kind of photosynthesis is very unique in your present world."

"This is incredible. This is the very kind of stuff my dad's been working on. How can we steer him in the right direction? I'm afraid if we make you available to people, with all that you have to give, they might just take you away somewhere and use you for experiments. You would become a treasured prisoner."

"Yes. I've glimpsed into your world a bit more and I know this could happen. Even if I can trust your father, once I was in the open, things might get out of his control."

"Yes, exactly."

"Truthfully, if I was certain that I was indeed the last of my kind, I would volunteer for the job. It would give my life purpose. But if there is any chance that my kind may be re-emerging in the world, I have a responsibility to my own kind first."

"I understand. This is a serious issue and we have to move carefully. Lucinda, you learn so quickly. Every hour you seem older than the hour before. When I first met you, you seemed about my age and unsure of everything around you. Today you are talking like you are a thirty-year-old woman."

"My situation requires it, and as you know, glowers mature very quickly. You seem older too, Sara."

"Older, but more interested in things than I've been in a long time."

"We have work to do together."

"Important work. Finding more vinetropes, helping Apkin and Ekle, and now guiding my dad's research on energy. How can we go about that and still keep you invisible?"

"Let me harvest my crop of roots. It will take till spring before there is enough to work with. The chemical process is in them. Then no one need know of vinetropes, except for your family. By then I will know what Owletta has found and will have also met your dad and brother. I will give your dad samples of the roots. Your dad can study the process, create the glower liquid, feed more roots and create the fuel. He may be able to find a way to harvest it in abundance. Everything you humans do seems to be on a large scale—for better or worse. He can claim it as his own discovery."

"But that seems unfair."

"It's not. He will have to do a lot of work, so the discovery will certainly be partly his. I can make it, but I don't understand it. He will have to understand it so that he can make it. What would be truly unfair would be keeping this knowledge from being used and keeping me from my own kind. Eventually I may be able to come into your world. But I need time to mature. I need to find out if there are more of my kind. And if there are, what do we need for survival? It's obvious the world needs better energy—vinetrope energy. And if vinetropes are again in the world, then the planet belongs to us as well."

"Everything you're saying makes sense," Sara agreed. "It's almost like you were brought back to help save the world."

"Let's don't go haywire! All it may be is a fortunate accident that we need to take responsibility for."

"That my dad's a scientist working on trying to find clean energy and you get carried on a squirrel's back to grow in my garden?"

"A very fortunate accident!" Lucinda laughed.

"Tomorrow I will introduce you to the computer. We can access a lot of information for you there."

"We will get to it. But to tell the truth, I am finally exhausted."

"Then we'll go to sleep. I'm bushed too."

Sara went to the bathroom and when she returned she couldn't find Lucinda. She looked under the bed but she wasn't there. She had a moment's panic. Then Lucinda whispered, "I'm over here." She had climbed into Sara's old doll cradle and pulled the blankets around herself.

"Cozy in here!" said Lucinda. "But it could use a few stones. I think I'll make this a sleep over. That's what you call it, right?"

"Right."

They both giggled.

"This has been quite a day!" said Sara.

But Lucinda didn't answer. She was asleep.

Sara and Lucinda reconfirmed the decision to hold off telling Steven and her dad about her existence until Owletta returned from her journey. Then they would hopefully have all the information they needed to make a proper presentation to Sara's family. Meanwhile, Sara continued to teach Lucinda about the world of humans. She was able to sneak her in three more times over the next week, and showed her how the computer worked. Lucinda was enthralled and learned quickly. While Sara did homework, Lucinda surfed the net and absorbed as much knowledge as she could.

"In some ways, the way these chips store memory, is like the way I store memory in the precoded part of my brain," she told Sara after her second session on-line. "I've been studying like crazy—about computers, human biology and botany."

"What do you mean—like the way you store memory?" Sara questioned.

"Well, the memory I am born with is not like living memory. It's more like stored data. My living memory is really much closer to human memory. What I remember since I've been conscious, that is alive, is not as reliable as my coded memory. My living memory is influenced by my feelings and by my continuous exposure to new events. The "newness" of actually living. You know, new experiences, new interactions with others living creatures, new decision making. All these things make living memory imperfect, but it also make you feel alive. My coded memory is presented to me as fact. It works much the same way as explained in some of the reports I have been studying about robotics and computer theory."

"Excuse me," Sara interrupted, her eyes widening. "Did you say you'd read papers on robotics?"

"Yes, lots of reading. I read and comprehend about 500 pages an hour."

"This is extraordinary. Why didn't you tell me?"

"Well, that's what I'm getting to. I thought this was

normal for humans as well until I reached a certain level of comprehension. That's why I say part of my brain works like a computer. When I read, all the words and facts get stored immediately in my memory and I can access them any time I want. What I do with them, disagree, be creative, and so forth, is left to my conscious mind. But I can store all this data and retain it quickly, like a computer does."

"How can that be?"

"I suspect that my nervous system is built on a cellulose structure that functions a lot like a crystalline structure and that part of my brain functions like a large hard drive. I was born with this hard drive already downloaded with a ton of data."

"That's why you were able to function at such a high level right after you were born!"

"Yes, but without emotional maturity or any real experience with the world around me. In fact, now that I've reached a certain level of understanding, I can even say that some of the facts stored in my "old" brain could be wrong and I would have no way of knowing that. What counts, is that what I'm born with enables me to survive and then I can go on to learn. If I can't continue to learn I'd remain immature with a lot of knowledge going to waste."

"So that's why when we first met you made childish guesses at things. Like assuming I was a giant."

"Right. I was trying to make today's reality fit into a very different reality, a world view from eons ago that my "computer brain" was showing me. Even though you didn't look like anything I'd ever seen before my stored memory told me that you fit closest the image of a huge vinetrope-like being that existed in my time that was rather stupid and died out before the Ice Age. Your English word for something similar is "giant." That's why I assumed you weren't too bright, had a poor memory, and needed to be treated carefully, like a big child."

"Amazing. But how did you explain the huge house I lived in? A stupid being couldn't create something like that."

"True, but I was so new to the world that I wasn't putting two and two together yet. I was disoriented and trying to make sense out of information that didn't fit into the knowledge that I had been given. It was insufficient and I didn't always use logic in those first few days. I've come to learn in the last couple of weeks that the knowledge I get by living is more important than the knowledge I was born with, even though it was a lot. If I couldn't learn, even with all those facts and images floating around in my head, I wouldn't be able to survive. In fact, in many of the articles I've read on robotics, the thing the scientists keep talking about is "consciousness." They wonder at what point, if ever, a computer will be able to take its stored data and be creative with it or make decisions in a way that would mean it had become conscious—alive."

"So you're saying you're like an evolved computer?"

"No, not really. I am organic, plant life, not a robot. I'm just saying my brain is somewhat more like a computer than a human's is."

"And I think you're also saying that you can make mistakes like humans do, even though you can store more data more quickly than we can. And that making mistakes is part of learning."

"Exactly. I'm trying to understand how I fit into this world. In a way, I've come to see a little of myself in everything."

"In plant life, humans, animals and the new technologies that have evolved since your kind lived on this earth."

"Very well put, Sara."

They had many such conversations, in which they bounced thoughts and ideas off each other. Sara felt that Lucinda was the first "person" to take her seriously in a long time. She felt exhilarated by these conversations. It was like being a scientist, detective and a character in a magical adventure, all at the same time.

CHAPTER SEVEN

Trick-or-Treat?

It wasn't too long after this conversation that Sara decided Lucinda should have some more real life experience with the human world. One of Sara's favorite holidays was fast approaching, and she had an idea. It was two days before Halloween when she arrived at Lucinda's with her plan. Ekle and Apkin were visiting. They didn't run away, but actually bobbed their heads up and down in greeting. The relationship between Sara and the squirrels was coming along fine.

"Hello, Ekle, Apkin," Sara said in greeting.

The squirrels bobbed some more and sat back on their haunches.

"You're completely in with the squirrels, now," Lucinda reassured Sara. "Ever since after the map incident when I told them you would find a way to drive us to North Carolina if Owletta brought good news."

"It seems like they're happy to see me," Sara laughed as she pat each squirrel on their head.

"Lucinda, I want to make you an offer," began Sara as she rubbed the brothers behind their ears the way you would a cat. Apkin rolled over on his back and practically smiled. "This Friday," she continued, " is Halloween. How would you like to go trick-or-treating with me?"

"What's Halloween?" Lucinda asked.

Ekle and Apkin seemed to respond to the word. There was more head-bobbing and nodding.

Sara tried to explain how things went on Halloween in her town.

"You go out at night, dressed in costumes, to your neighbors' homes and say *trick-or-treat* and they give you candy. Really little kids do it during the day. You bring a bag along and try to load it up with as much candy as possible."

"What's a costume?"

"Oh, well, it's a disguise—so no one knows who you are. It can be funny or scary. Scary costumes are usually preferred because Halloween is supposed to be the night when the dead can come back and walk the earth."

"Yikes. This sounds weird."

"Not really, it's tons of fun. In our town, the neighbors who are home and want to give out candy, light up

their jack-o-lanterns with candles and put them out on their front steps."

"What's a jack-o-whatever?"

"A jack-o-lantern. Well, you clean out a pumpkin, which is like a big gourd, carve a face in it, and light a candle inside so the face glows in the dark. It makes a lovely orange glow."

"It sounds a bit like me!"

"Yes," laughed Sara, and the squirrels seemed amused too. "But I can promise you that a pumpkin is way down on the evolutionary scale of intelligence! Please, Lucinda, come along in my bag. It will be so much fun. You'll get lots of candy. Like the chocolate in the chocolate chip cookies."

"Chocolate?"

"Yes.

"Okay, you've talked me into it. I'm coming. I could do with a change of pace."

"It could be dangerous!" squeaked Apkin, using his favorite word in a full sentence.

"Did he say something?" asked Sara.

"He said it would be dangerous."

"Nonsense. It will be a blast." Sara got up and started to leave.

"Where are you off to so quickly?"

"To make my costume. Halloween is in two days. I'm going to be a giant jack-o-lantern, so we'll kind of match."

When Sara had gone, Apkin shook his head in disapproval and Ekle began to scold.

"Lucinda, you'll be out among so many people, mostly kids. I've seen this thing Sara calls Halloween. I never knew exactly what it was, but now I know why the kids are always checking their bags. They may want to check in on Sara's bag."

"How do you know? I didn't translate Sara's explanation to you."

"You're right. But I understood her! The costume part and the older humans putting candy in their bags. And I understood that candy was like those brown pieces in the cookies we tasted."

"Then you're starting to understand English."

"Me too," confirmed Apkin.

"But Sara didn't understand us," added Ekle.

"Not yet. And don't worry. Sara and I will make sure no one discovers me."

Before they knew it, Halloween had arrived. Sara had struggled with her own costume, but she had learned more from her mom than she had realized when it came to sewing and she was pretty pleased with the results. Sara decided not to go around with friends. She hadn't the year before and no one had asked her to go along anyway. If she hadn't met Lucinda she would have felt left out, but it would have been partly her own doing because of how unsocial she had been. But right now this suited the situation fine. She felt it would be pressing her luck, with Lucinda in her bag, if she was going out with a troop of kids. At the same time, she didn't want to roam around by herself. She convinced Steven to go with her. Next year he would be away at college so she talked him into it for old times sake. She knew she could keep him out of her bag pretty easily.

"I'll share my loot with you after we get home," she promised.

"Yeah, like usual, all the stuff you don't like anyway."

"Well, you like a lot of that gooey sour stuff. It works out pretty well."

"As long as you haven't chewed on it just to make sure you still don't like it."

"I never do that."

"Some of the pieces you gave me last year were a little wet."

"You're just making that up," and she poked him.

He chased her upstairs. Sara went to her room to get into her costume. Steven was still fun to be with. She was glad she had talked him into this. It was good to have some time alone with him.

The sun was setting and she and Steven were in the kitchen putting fresh batteries into their flashlights. They were lucky. It was a clear night and cool, but not freezing.

Last year it had rained. A sweater under the pumpkin costume would be enough to keep Sara warm.

"I'm going to run out back for a minute, Steve, to see if I'm warm enough like this," explained Sara.

"Okay, it's a little early yet to start out. Give me about fifteen minutes," Steven said picking up the kitchen phone. "I just want to make a quick phone call to Lorraine."

Great, thought Sara, that will give me more than enough time. She picked up her sturdy, thick, trick-or-treat bag and went to the front hall. By the front door on the hall table was a big old wooden bowl where her Mom always put the candy. Sara had placed it there herself and reminded her dad to pick up some candy. This year, there were chocolate Crackle Bars, small boxes of pretzels and packages of chewing gum. Also, a small plastic pumpkin pail with coins in it for UNICEF.

Sara threw four Crackle Bars into her bag. She was sure Lucinda would love them. She also dropped in a couple of boxes of pretzels. Then she went back to the kitchen and put two kitchen towels into the bag. That would give Lucinda a little coverage, a place to duck under. Steven was still on the phone, and the conversation sounded in full swing, so she went out the back door to pick up her friend. She had her pumpkin costume on and it was so wide she barely made it through the doorway.

"Lucinda, we're just about ready to leave. Are you ready?"

"Yes, come on in a minute."

"I can't fit. My costume is too wide.'

"I can't wait to see this!"

With that, Lucinda slipped out and looked up at Sara. She laughed so hard that her glow went out of control for a moment and lit up the whole corner of the garden.

"Watch what you're doing! You look like the New York skyline!" warned Sara.

"Okay, okay, I've just never seen anything like you before. If you looked like this when I first met you, I'd have fled so fast my vines would have dried out before I turned the corner."

She was still laughing, but she brought her glow back down to a light evening dim.

"Here's the trick-or-treat bag, jump in before my brother comes out."

"Can't wait to get a closer glimpse of him," added Lucinda with a mischievous lift to her voice. She climbed in.

"You sure seem in a good mood," noted Sara as Lucinda made herself comfortable at the bottom of the bag.

"I am feeling good. I'm going to see some more of this world of yours. We vinetropes like a bit of adventure, you know."

"That's fine," said Sara peering into the bag. "But please don't go haywire on me. I don't like that gleam in your eyes."

"Don't be such a worrywart. What's this?" questioned Lucinda holding up a box of pretzels in one hand and a candy bar in the other. "Chocolate," she read out loud and immediately ripped off the wrapper of the Crackle Bar. She started right on eating.

"Now don't get yourself sick on this stuff and for heaven's sake, eat more quietly!" Sara complained. "You sound like a nest full of mice in there."

"Well pardon me! I didn't know you'd become my mother!"

The back door opened and slammed.

"Sara, I'm ready. Let's get going," Steven announced.

Steven was zipping up his jacket and coming towards her at a clip with his flashlight on.

"I'm ready," smiled Sara as she picked up her bag and turned on her own flashlight.

"Are you warm enough like that?"

"Huh? Oh yes. I'm fine."

They went up the steps from the lower to the upper garden and onto the driveway. They cut across the lawn, through a patch of woods, and out to the street—Hilltop Way. They made a left on Hilltop, walked about 200 feet and crossed over to Rennselear Road.

"I thought we'd hit Rennselear first," explained Steven, "because we know half the people who live there."

"Sounds good," agreed Sara.

"What do you say we start on the left side and come back the other way. Then we can kind of play it by ear."

"Okay. But I don't want to miss Elena's house."

"Well, that's a bit of a walk. Maybe we'll save that for last and I can drive you over before we call it a night."

"Sounds good," repeated Sara.

Lucinda gave a little squeak of excitement, but only

Sara seemed to hear it. Within seconds they were walking up to the front door of the Sandersons' home. Three jack-o-lanterns greeted them along the front walkway, one for each of the three children who lived here. On the front porch was something quite unusual, the largest jack-o-lantern Steven or Sara had ever seen. It was the kind used for displays at roadside stands. But this pumpkin was very unique because it wasn't carved into a face, it was carved into a house with a front door and many little windows all lit up from the candles inside. On one side of the door was a tiny jack-o-lantern with a little face glowing and on the other side was a tiny scarecrow sitting on a miniature bench.

"Hey, this is fantastic," acknowledged Steven.

"It's wonderful," agreed Sara. "It's really magical!"

"Mrs. Sanderson is pretty creative," added Steven.

Sara felt some wiggling in the bag and then much to her concern she heard a little ripping sound. Then, as they stood on the front porch, she looked down and to her shock she saw two of Lucinda's fingers sticking out from the middle of the bag. Then the fingers quickly pulled back in. She looked in and Lucinda winked at her and then placed her two eyes against the two holes she had just punched into the bag.

"Oh well," thought Sara. "I guess there's not much point in her coming along if she can't see anything."

"Well, aren't you going to ring the bell?" asked Steven.

"Of course." She went to the door and pressed the

bell. It was one of those musical kind and she heard it chime throughout the house.

In a second, the door flew open and there stood the two youngest of the Sanderson kids (two- and three-years-old) and Mrs. Sanderson.

"Trick-or-treat," said Sara and the three-year-old dropped a bag of potato chips into her bag.

"Thank you," said Sara and she heard a little more ripping of the bag.

"That's quite a pumpkin house," commented Steven. "It's very creative. I bet you'll start a fashion trend with it. Next year every kid in town is going to want one of these instead of a traditional face." Steven was good with words. He knew how to make people feel good, if he was in the mood.

"Yes, it's beautiful," added Sara.

"Thank you very much," said Mrs. Sanderson. "But I can't take credit for it. Mr. Sanderson had the idea and did the carving. I'll tell him you liked it. He's out with Jimmy, our eldest."

"Please do," said Steven. "It's really great."

"Have fun," added Mrs. Sanderson as she closed the door.

Sara peeked into the bag again as they headed back down the path. Lucinda was eating a potato chip about half the size of her head. She gave another wink.

"Oh dear, I'm in trouble," said Sara under her breath.

"What's that?" asked Steven who was a little in front of her.

"Nothing, I just said I'm glad it's double."

"What's double?"

"My trick-or-treat bag. I made it extra sturdy. Two paper bags stapled together."

"Oh? Planning on a huge haul this year?" Steven laughed.

"Yup."

"I see. And how much of your loot do I get for going around an extra hour?" teased Steven.

"Oh, I was planning on giving everything a try and then leaving you a nice wet pile. Like you suggested I did last year," Sara teased back.

They both laughed. At this point they were approaching Rona's house. Rona was in Sara's class. She had a sheet ghost hanging from the front porch and a lot of fake spider webs all around the door with a few handfuls of plastic spiders thrown in for effect. There was one nice traditional jack-o-lantern glowing to the right of the door. Sara rang the bell. She hoped Rona would be out, because knowing Rona, she'd want to go through Sara's whole bag to see what she'd got so far. Rona opened the door.

"Hi Sara! How did you do so far?" She leaned right over to look in the bag.

Sara pulled back and put her own hand in the bag and pulled out a Crackle Bar to distract her.

"Here. I brought you a Crackle, just in case you miss my house. You're only my second stop so I haven't got much yet."

"Oh. Thanks. I'm going out in a few minutes, but

I've already got a full bag of loot."

"No kidding? How?"

"My Gram picked me up after school and took me around near where she lives. All her friends spoiled me and gave me handfuls of stuff. My bag was loaded in no time."

"Cool."

"And now you're going to do the evening shift," teased Steven.

"Yup! Oh here Sara. My Mom made these big popcorn balls to hand out to friends. Here's one for you, Steven. How come you're taking your sister around? Does she need baby-sitting still?" She tossed two large popcorn balls wrapped in orange cellophane into Sara's bag as she said this and giggled.

"No, she's baby-sitting me. I begged her to let me tag along. My last time around the old town before going off to college next year."

"That's cool. Hey, what's that glowing in there?" Rona questioned. The bag seemed to quiver with light for a moment and then stop.

"Glowing where?" answered Sara getting really nervous.

"In your trick-or-treat bag. I saw it light up."

"Oh, that's just an extra flashlight I brought along. I must have left it on. Yeah, that's it," explained Sara, pretending to turn off the light, while giving Lucinda a pinch. "Okay, we'd better get going or I won't even have one bag of loot," and she quickly spun around and headed down the steps to the walk, where Steven was waiting.

Bringing Lucinda along was more trouble than she had bargained for. Every stop was going to be another worry. They passed a group of kids coming from the other direction. Two Count Draculas, a werewolf and a Freddie Kruger.

"Don't miss the Capiellos' house," recommended the Freddie Kruger with enthusiasm.

The next two houses were dark, so they moved on. Soon they would be at Alexandria's house, another classmate. After that came the Capiellos' place. Jim Capiello was 13, and cute in Sara's opinion. He had two older sisters in high school. The Capiellos went all out on Halloween. They were also known as the wealthiest family in the neighborhood and didn't hold back on the decorating. They usually turned the front yard into a graveyard, lights, sound effects—a full theatrical event. There was an original theatrical surprise as well each year. No one in town missed this house on Halloween unless there was an emergency or they had absolutely no sense of play. It was a town tradition. As they got closer, the street grew busier and louder.

"Wait till you see Capiello's place this year," said a familiar voice. It was Danny's younger brother. Sara recognized his Dalmatian dog costume from the school party. Danny approached seconds later.

"Hi Dan," said Steven. "I hear Mr. Capiello has outdone himself this year."

"Pretty fantastic!" confirmed Danny.

"What's he done?" asked Sara.

"No clues," said Danny. "Let them find out for themselves, Wayne."

"You bet, bruth," Wayne grinned.

The next house was Alexandria's. Alex had her whole pathway lit up with little orange bags with sand and candles inside. The bags gleamed a friendly orange. She had two jack-o-lanterns lit on the steps and they both wore witch hats. The front door had a huge cardboard witch taped on it.

Sara rang the bell. Alexandria opened the door. She looked like Dorothy in the Wizard of OZ, except for her blue denim jacket with the red lining.

"Can I come along with you?" she asked.

"Fine by me," said Steven.

Sara made a face at her brother.

"Mom," Alex called into her house. "I'm going around with Sara and her brother Steven."

"Okay," answered her Mom coming halfway down the steps. "Thanks, Steven. I'm glad someone is going to be keeping an eye on them," said Mrs. Cohen. "I really hate this holiday for kids. I don't know how they came up with it, but all it does is make the kids sick on candy and the parents sick with worry. About how long do you expect to be out?"

"I figure till about 9:30 or 10:00. Depending on how we hold up. Don't worry. I'll have them back safe and not too sick either."

"Thanks so much Steven."

Alex picked up a large picnic basket from off the hall

bench. It had a brown toy poodle sticking out of it, to represent Toto, and would double as Alex's trick-or-treat basket.

"I'm ready," she said, and they left, closing the front door behind them.

"We'll get sick if we feel like it," whispered Sara to Steven halfway down the path.

Another group of kids approached.

"Don't miss the Capiellos' house," a Ninja Turtle called to them.

"We always get a ton of kids," explained Alex, "because we live right next to the Capiellos. "We don't try and compete. Dad said we'd have to start digging up our lawn over Labor Day Weekend if we were to even have a fighting chance."

Steven laughed.

"Well, let's go see it," said Sara.

"Naturally," said Alex. "Of course I've seen it, but it's different at night like this."

"And Mr. Capiello always has that last minute surprise!"

They turned left out of Alex's yard and in a few seconds were bombarded by mournful sounds, blue lights and a lot of kids and grown-ups mulling around, laughing and talking. The entire front yard had been turned into another graveyard. Many of the graves had spooky details such as a rubber hand coming out of the dirt or a full size skeleton leaning against a gravestone holding a bottle of whiskey in one hand and a glowing lantern in the other. The spooky blue light gleamed everywhere. That was a new detail this year. It seemed that Mr. Capiello had replaced every garden light on his property (and there were a lot) with a blue light bulb. In the huge old oak tree that graced his front yard with an impressive spread of branches, he had arranged an army of ghosts. He must have spent a whole weekend up in that tree to get everything just right, the fabrics draped to perfection. With the eerie blue lights aimed up into the tree, and the motion of the breeze, the stage was set for excitement. Everyone was delighted.

Rona popped up again.

"Hi, guys, guess what the deal is this year."

"What?" asked Steven.

"You see that coffin leaning up against the house on the porch?"

Everyone nodded.

"Well, in order to get your treat, you've got to go up and knock on the coffin. Then it opens and the headless horseman leans out and gives you a key. Then you've got to use the key to open the front door!"

"You're kidding?" said Sara and Alex in unison.

"Nope. You've got to go in by yourself. Then, when you get your treat and come out you've got to knock on the coffin again and return the key."

"Did you do it yet?" asked Sara.

"Yup!" and she pulled out a family size bag of nacho chips from her treat bag.

"Did they decorate inside too?" asked Alexandria.

"I'm not going to tell a thing."

Just then the door banged shut and out came a child

carrying a bag of Doritos.

"I might go for this one myself," said Steven, getting a kick out of the whole thing.

"Okay, then you first," said Sara, getting behind her brother and pushing him down the walk. There were about nine children lined up waiting their turn.

They waited as the next child in line walked up to the coffin and knocked three times (three seemed to be the magic number). The coffin opened very slowly with a lot of mechanical creaking. And there was the headless horseman —tall, with a black cape swirled around him with nothing coming out of the dark collar. In his left arm he held a glowing jack-o-lantern and in his right hand he must have held the key which he offered silently to the child. The child, dressed as the Easter Bunny, took the key, went up the cobweb-draped steps, and stood a moment in front of the door. Then he used the key and went inside. In about three long minutes, bang went the door and out came the Easter Bunny looking both happy and in a hurry, carrying his reward. He hurried right past the coffin.

"Hey, don't forget to return the key," said the child next in line.

The bunny returned to the coffin and knocked three times. Again the coffin door opened slowly. The headless horseman bowed graciously and retrieved the key. The children patiently waited their turn. This ritual of waiting was part of the excitement and fun. A couple of the kids screamed dramatically as they came out and said it was just horrible inside.

Sara and Alex argued who would go first and Alex won. All she said to Sara as she returned with her prize was: "That was really weird!" She stood to the side on the lawn with Steven as Sara went for it. Sara got the key from the headless horseman. He sounded a lot like Mr. Capiello in a hollow box. She marched up the steps and it was just as she approached the front door that she heard the ripping noise again.

"Hey, what are you doing in there?"

"The holes aren't big enough. I don't want to miss this."

"Okay, but keep quiet for heaven's sake."

Sara put the key in and turned it to the right. She stepped inside and pushed the door closed behind her, but it didn't click shut. The blue light from the hall chandelier glowed just enough to show off the cobwebs, bats and skeletons that decorated the hall and staircase. Then, suddenly, a dark shadow on the staircase stood up and a frightful witch (one of those hideous masks) in full costume came down the steps and approached Sara.

"Hello, my dear. Please help yourself to a little treat," said a cackling voice that sounded a lot like Mrs. Capiello with a sore throat.

She pointed to two black kettles at the bottom of the steps. One was filled with large bags of chips and the other with giant size Hershey bars.

"Help yourself my dear," continued the witch.

Sara set her bag down a moment and bent over the kettles to make her choice when a terrible thing happened.

The Capiellos' dog, Poncho, (a huge fellow with some German Shepherd in him) came up to Sara's treat bag and started sniffing. Sara had a hold of her chocolate bar and was turning around.

"Hey, Poncho. Leave my bag alone," Sara ordered.

With that, Poncho grabbed the handles of the bag with his teeth and ran to the front door, which was now ajar. He pushed with his nose, bag dangling from his mouth, and was out the front door before Sara could stop him. Mrs. Capiello called out in her normal voice, "Just give me the key, honey, and then go after him."

Sara handed her the key and took off after Poncho.

"Help! Help!" screamed Sara as she tore out the front door dropping the candy bar on the front porch.

"Stop Poncho. He's got my bag," she screamed coming down the front steps. She was terrified for Lucinda's life.

At first Steven thought Sara was just screaming like some of the other kids—for dramatics. Then he saw Poncho run by with a bag in his teeth, half dragging it on the ground, and what Sara was yelling registered.

"My bag, my bag!" she called again in desperation.

Steven broke into action and took off after Poncho, outstripping Sara and tearing on ahead. He tore around the back of the house after Poncho and into the border of trees and bushes between the Capiellos' house and their neighbor's.

"Poncho, you stop right now. Poncho! Come here, boy. Come on, fella."

Then he spotted Sara's bag on the ground, glowing.

Poncho must have gotten scared and dropped it during the chase.

Steven walked towards the bag, catching his breath. He figured the glow must be coming from the extra flashlight Sara had mentioned. It must have gotten knocked on during the bumpy ride. Then he heard it. The little voice.

"Help, help! Get me out of here. I'm so dizzy. I don't know up from down. I think I'm going to throw-up. What a ride. Sara, where are you?"

Just as Steven came up alongside the bag, a little pear-shaped face, glowing as bright as a jack-o-lantern, peered out of the bag. Steven gasped and stood there speechless.

"Oh, Steven, it's you," spoke the creature. "That was a close one! You'd better pick up this bag before that monster of an animal tries to make off with me again. Don't just stand there doing nothing, young man. You act like you've never seen a vinetrope before!" Then she smiled a smile that Steven would never forget as long as he lived.

Steven did as he was instructed and just in time. He turned around with the bag in his hand to see several kids quickly approaching. Sara and Alex were in the lead.

"I've got the bag," announced Steven. "Everything is fine. It didn't even rip. See?" He held the bag up for everyone to look at. The other kids, no harm done, turned back to the front yard.

"Here's your bag, Sara," and he handed it back to her.

Sara's small face, under the green stem of her pumpkin costume, looked as pale as a ghost. She took the bag and looked inside. There sat Lucinda as cozy as could be, surrounded by candy. She waved to Sara.

"Okay," said Steven calmly, looking a little drained himself, "let's get going again or we're going to miss out on the whole night."

Steven and Sara exchanged looks, but Sara couldn't tell for sure what the look meant. Had he seen Lucinda or not? It would have to wait until they were home. Alex stood right alongside them and then they headed back into the activities up front and along the street. So they continued their evening route of trick-or-treating as planned and ended it with the promised ride to Elena's house, dropping Alex off on the way home.

When they parked the car back in the garage, Sara jumped out with the bag and headed down the garden steps into the lower garden.

"Where are you going?" asked Steven.

"I'm just taking the long way around. I hate to see this great night come to an end. Wasn't it more exciting than usual?"

"It sure was. I guess your little friend got the biggest thrill of all. Dropping her off somewhere by any chance?"

"You saw her?"

"A vinetrope, I believe she said she was? But I can't say we were properly introduced. It was more one of those caught-up-in-the-situation kind of introductions."

"Yeah, I see what you mean."

By now Steven had followed Sara down into the

lower garden and was standing next to her near Lucinda's front door.

"Oh for Heaven's sake," said Lucinda hopping out of the bag with a chocolate bar in each hand. "You've seen me. Here I am. Lucinda Vinetrope. We've got a lot to catch up on, Steven."

"Seeing you is no problem. It's believing in what I'm seeing, that I'm having the problem with."

"And what about your hearing?" teased Lucinda. "Is that giving you a rough time too? Well, never mind about it, Steven. I talk a lot, as you'll soon find out, and your hearing will catch on fine. So will your eyes. I guess what you really need now is one of my poems. A believing in-what-you're-seeing-and-hearing poem would be very useful. What do you think, Sara?"

"Yes, very useful. Lucinda is a great poet," Sara confirmed.

"I'm ready," interrupted Lucinda.

"Ready?" said Steven.

"With the poem."

"Already?"

"She's real fast at this stuff," Sara explained.

Lucinda folded her arms behind her back and recited her poem:

> *"If what you see just isn't there,*
> *like seven moons up in the air,*
> *you're in a pool of trouble.*
> *But if a friend says: 'See that kite,*

it's way up high and shining bright
in wavy stripes of red and white'
and sure enough when you look up
you see the kite just fine,
that means you're seeing double
so there probably is no trouble.
Though it is true that sometimes two
can play the fool, if someone's out
to trick you. But most of the
time if what you see
is also seen by two or three,
it means it's really there,
even if it's seven moons
floating in the air."

Lucinda took a bow.

Steven, still incredulous, found himself laughing. "That was very funny."

"Thank you. You see, Sara, I knew your brother and I would hit it off just fine. But we'd better call it a night. I am utterly exhausted and my ears are ringing from all that tossing around. Unless you two hear the ringing, as well?"

"No ringing," said Steven.

"All right then, Sara," said Lucinda, waving the two candy bars about. "We've got time to fill Steven in on the plans. Good night Steven, it was nice to meet you."

"My pleasure, I think," he answered, for lack of knowing what to say.

With that, Lucinda bowed and slipped inside her

house. Steven and Sara stood motionless as Lucinda cranked her door shut.

"She lives in there?" asked Steven rather calmly.

He was surprised at his own calmness. It was the only way he could deal with it. He had come to the conclusion that there were three possible conditions which could explain what was happening to him right now: one, he was accepting the unbelievable; two, he was going nuts, or three, he was having hallucinations due to some major accident he couldn't remember because of the head trauma.

"It's quite nice inside," explained Sara. "I helped her out with a few things. She's got a fireplace, table, bed. It's quite cozy. The squirrel brothers and Owletta come to visit pretty often. But of course Owletta is away just now on an important mission."

"Sara, I can't deal with this right now. I'm just too bushed."

"Okay, let's go in and look at the candy," said Sara in her most matter-of-fact tone.

CHAPTER EIGHT

Owletta's Journey Part One

The night that Owletta left was clear, cool and perfect for travel. She circled over the yard several times, making a mental note of all the clues she and her friends had discovered: go south to North Carolina and find the Haw River, find a large human city called Raleigh and the brothers' mates, Selena and Regata. Her developing skill with languages gave her added confidence. She buzzed these clues around and around in her head as she circled, stalling a little before leaving her home. She hadn't taken a long trip like this in ages.

She thought about Lucinda. She remembered the legends of the glowers and the memory sparked her excitement. Maybe some day she would be an important part of a legend that others would tell. "Owletta's Journey" she thought to herself. "That sounds good." She felt her confidence rise, and with that, she pumped the air and lifted herself into the night.

She looked below and above, got her bearings and headed east. When she reached the great water she would turn south. In recent years, she had become content to stay at home. Her mate had died some time ago and she liked the company of those two squirrels very much. As she worked the air with her wings and looked out over the earth, she felt a sudden surge of energy. This was wonderful! Was it possible she was younger than she remembered? If her mate hadn't died, was it possible she would still be laying eggs in the spring?

She followed the path of lights that people traveled on in their cars. Now, since Lucinda's arrival, she understood that cars were a human form of transportation. She knew they flew in cars with wings because they had no wings of their own. She chose a wide and busy path to follow, one she knew was going east. It would lead her quickly to the water. Then, sure of her directions, she would turn south, choosing a less traveled route for most of the journey. She expected her wings to ache the first night out. She would have to build up her wing strength.

As she approached the big city, the night sky was lightened by the city lights and took away the stars, but the moon was still her guide.

"Follow the moon to the silver-black sea, then make a right turn to Haw River Valley," she hummed into the air.

She was starting to sound like Lucinda. She felt amused and chuckled to herself. Now she had to maneuver herself carefully through a maze of huge buildings. She took a path over the lowest rooftops. Many windows were lit up with human light, but then she approached an area where everything was dark. She glided and dipped over this patch of buildings. It looked like a low forest of brick, steel and wood. Owletta preferred the smaller homes of humans to these city buildings. The smaller homes were made mostly of wood and felt familiar. She knew of owls that lived in the high parts of wooden houses. Maybe owls lived in these bigger buildings too. She didn't know. She wondered why the other buildings were all lit and filled with people and these buildings were so dark.Then it appeared: the big water, the great silver-black sea.

In the day it had a different color. She had lived by the sea a long time ago, when she was young, with her parents. She had forgotten that. The sea made her feel both sad and happy at the same time. How strange! She settled on top of one of the dark buildings to rest a moment and just look. It had been so long since she had seen the big water.

"Nice night," said a shrill voice next to her.

Owletta jumped around and faced a strong but battered looking gull.

"I didn't hear you land," said Owletta, startled.

"I know, and very surprising for an owl. Usually you

owls hear something even before it's happened. Learn to listen like an owl, my dad used to say."

"I must have been deep in thought," answered Owletta.

"Yes, indeed. Or not used to having to be on your guard. You're not from around here, are you?"

"No. But not from so far away either."

"But you have a long way to go."

"You're very observant," said Owletta. "May I ask your name?"

"My name is Cobcaw. Cobcaw the Watcher."

"And you watch well. My name is Owletta. Owletta the Thoughtful," she teased back.

"In the city one must hear ahead of time and think on the wing."

"I'm fortunate you are a friend and not an enemy."

"You're right. And how is it that you speak seagull? I expected you to turn and fly away when I spoke to you."

"It seems to be a talent of mine—speaking with other animals. In fact, this talent seems to be growing all the time."

"In that you are fortunate, too! Are you hungry?"

"Yes, now that you mention it. Quite!"

"Then let me be your host. I can show you a place to find fish. And in return you may tell me your story. It must be a good one if it has given you the ability to speak seagull."

"I will gladly tell you. But by midnight, I must continue my journey. I want to be well past the city lights before dawn. Then I can rest during the day, hopefully in peace and safety."

"Agreed. Follow me."

Cobcaw glided off the roof and swooped down to the right. Owletta followed. The gull made several turns—mostly to the left—but still going east. All the while they were gradually descending. Finally they rested on a small roof that was very close to the big water. From the roof you could see many ships docked. Some had tall parts that reached into the sky like the huge bare bones of an ancient bird. Some looked like the big silent buildings of humans placed at a large distance out in the water. Owletta settled down next to Cobcaw and took in the view.

"Very impressive," said Owletta to her host.

"Just home to me."

"Where are we?"

"This is a fish building. In the daytime many humans come here to eat fish. Come, we'll go down in the back. No one is here. I always find fish. There are mice as well."

Again Owletta followed and in no time she was having dinner. She delighted in the small fish humans called sardines.

"It's very pleasant to be talking to a bird," said Owletta. "Even though I am so fond of Ekle and Apkin."

"Who are Ekle and Apkin?" asked Cobcaw as he tossed a fish bone behind him.

"Squirrels. They're my two best friends since my mate Ashbah died."

"Squirrels?!" Cobcaw was incredulous. "I thought owls ate squirrels."

"Oh, I used to, but since I became friends with Apkin

and Ekle, I wouldn't dream of it. I made a solemn vow to them I would never eat squirrel again. They'd have nothing to do with me if I did. It bothers them enough that I eat mice."

"You are the strangest owl I have ever met. My dad said owls were eccentric."

"It is a bit odd, I have to agree. I've never run across such a friendship in any of the owl legends or gossips from my childhood. But when my mate died, I was very lonely and those squirrels made me laugh. They were afraid of me at first, even though they could speak to me in owl talk. Especially Ekle. Amazing, isn't it? With time, I began to speak their language better than they spoke mine. It all happened so slowly and naturally that none of us thought of it as unusual till very recently. Until Lucinda came into our lives. That's when we realized that it was Lucinda who was causing all the changes. She gives the gift of languages! Anyway, those squirrels made home seem like home again, so a little modification in my diet seemed worth it."

"You must tell me the whole story. Especially about the creature you call Lucinda. Come with me to my home where we won't have to be on guard."

"Yes, I will. Lead the way."

Again Owletta played follow the leader and in a short time they entered Cobcaw's nest in the roof of a factory facing the water. They settled in and could see a piece of the sea and sky through the hole in the roof. Cobcaw explained that he too was alone. His mate had been killed by a truck not far from where they had just had their dinner.

Then Owletta told Cobcaw her whole story. She explained beautifully the coming of Lucinda and how a human child named Sara was going to help them all. How Lucinda glowed and seemed to have the power to inspire learning languages between animals. She explained her role in the story and how it was her job to find Ekle and Apkin's mates and investigate the whereabouts of the other glower.

Cobcaw listened very quietly and attentively. After Owletta had finished her story, he remained quiet for a while, deep in thought.

"Well then, Cobcaw, tell me then, what you think of my story?"

"I think it is a sign of great change—hopefully a good sign. I have decided to help you with your search. I have many relatives all along the seacoast—down south where it's warm all the time. Someone among them will have heard or seen these glowers if they exist. I will come with you and they will talk to me."

"Cobcaw, I am very grateful to you and furthermore, I appreciate the company."

"Then rest another hour here in my nest. I must tell a few gulls that I am off on a journey, so they won't worry about me. I will be back within the hour and then we will leave."

"Fine."

Cobcaw stretched his wings and prepared to leave.

"Cobcaw?" Owletta called out.

"Yes?"

"Have you ever heard of an owl and a seagull becoming good friends?"

Cobcaw stood shaking his head. "No, never. But then, I never had an owl understand me before. Very strange."

"Yes indeed."

Owletta got some much needed sleep. Her wings did ache a bit, but she felt ready to move on. Soon she and Cobcaw were on their way.

They flew south by night and rested in quiet places during the day. Nestled in some tree or hollow, they spoke of their lives, exchanged stories and slept. About eight days into the trip, Owletta awoke to the screeching of gulls. It was still day, but the sun was beginning to set. Where did Cobcaw say they were this time? Owletta blinked her eyes and looked around trying to get her bearings.

"Don't remember where you are?" said Cobcaw's familiar voice.

"Not too clearly," admitted Owletta, glad to hear her friend.

"This is my cousin Skitter's nest," explained Cobcaw. "These are his children Skeet, Pickit and Ditta. Skitter and his mate Tulla are out just now. We're gull-sitting, you might say. They had a fit when I brought you in. Then you spoke to them. Calmed them down. They went off to do a little investigating for us."

"That's right. I do remember some kind of introduction now. I must have been exhausted. I'm not used to all this flying. Hello there, little gulls. I'm glad to meet you."

The three little gulls were very excited to have such an unusual guest. Their screeches seemed friendly, but Owletta couldn't really make out what they were saying.

"They only know a little of their own language," explained Cobcaw.

"Very cute," complimented Owletta. "And they seem quite smart."

Ditta, who was female, brought the strange guest a little fish in her beak.

"Thank you very much," said Owletta and she ate it right away, which seemed to delight all three gulls.

"Well, how far south would you say we are now?" Owletta asked, eager for information.

"We're close to our destination," said Cobcaw, popping a fish into his own mouth.

"How are you so sure?"

"Because of what Skitter told me."

"What did he say?"

"Well, first he wanted to know why I brought you here."

"I can imagine."

"As I said, you spoke to him in seagull talk and he calmed down. Then you fell asleep and I filled him and Tulla in on our quest. He wasn't as surprised about the "glower" part as much as I thought he would be."

"He's seen glowers?"

"Not personally, but there's rumors of their existence all over the area. A whole village of some kind of new creatures with glowers in their midst. That's what Skitter and

Tulla are doing now. Trying to pinpoint a location along the Haw River."

"I can't believe it. We're there!"

"Almost."

Owletta helped entertain the gulls' children and she was wide awake by the time their parents returned.

"Good morning, Owletta," said Skitter.

"Good morning. Thank you for your hospitality."

"Have you eaten?" questioned Tulla.

"Yes, your delightful children fed me well."

"What did you find out?" said Cobcaw, impatient for Owletta and himself.

"We flew inland along the Haw River asking questions," explained Skitter. "I thought it might take several days of searching to accomplish, because the further you move away from the sea, the less seagulls you will find. But several birds told us of the coming of a new animal. They were not seagulls, but they spoke to us in seagull. Just like your owl friend here, Cobcaw. It was easy to communicate with almost any bird in the region and they were very willing to be helpful. That's why we had success so quickly."

"It gave me the creeps," added Tulla. "This is not natural at all."

"It's not really creepy when you think about it, Tulla. What could be more positive than improved communication? In fact this makes perfect sense," said Owletta. "If there are vinetropes in the area, they would be passing on the gift of language to many animals living in the area. This actually proves that we have found the right spot. We have found Lucinda's long lost world."

"It seems so," continued Tulla. "We were told their homes are underground like a mole's, but they spend a lot of time above ground as well, so they must like the light too. They are a busy kind, always building and making things, but they have kept to themselves pretty much."

"It's just a rumor of course," continued Skitter, "but it's said that some of them glow. They have some kind of inner light that they turn on and off at will. Everyone along the river is talking about them."

"But no one has actually been in their homes," added Tulla. "They've stopped to chat with some of the birds and animals in the area, but mostly they've been observed from a distance. They speak many bird and animal languages, you know, and are reported to be friendly, but very busy."

"That sounds a lot like Lucinda. Friendly and always busy. I'm sure it's no rumor. Where are they located?" asked Owletta.

"There's a whole village of them now. Out by Merry Elms," Skitter reported.

"And they wear clothes and work with their hands like humans," said Tulla. "It's most peculiar and causing some concern. No one knows what they're up to for sure."

"I wonder what it means?" thought Cobcaw out loud.

"I think we'd better have a look for ourselves," announced Owletta. "But if they're anything like Lucinda, then they're up to good things! Can you give us directions to Merry Elms?"

"No problem," said Skitter. "It's west of here, not far from the banks of the Haw River. I can take you there. I don't know the exact spot of their village, but I know where Merry Elms is and it's an easy flight."

"Terrific," said Owletta. "Near the Haw River. Just what we expected."

"Is it?" jumped in Tulla. "Cobcaw here said you met one of these glowers. Is that true?"

"It is. You might say I'm on a bit of a mission because of this glower that I know."

"What is a glower like?" asked Skitter. "Is it dangerous? What does it want of us?"

"The glower I know is very gentle and very smart. She means no harm and only wants to be with her kind. It's because of them that birds and animals are beginning to talk to each other."

"I guess we'll have to take your word for it," said Tulla, not fully convinced.

"When do you want to leave?" asked Skitter.

"Immediately," said Owletta. "I would fly day or night to finally reach my destination!"

"Let's rest awhile longer," said Cobcaw," and feed some more!" he added. "It will be better to travel by night."

"We will leave when the moon is up," concluded Skitter.

Owletta's Journey
Part Two

Owletta, Cobcaw and Skitter took flight shortly after the moon rose. They circled out over the water, made a U-turn and headed inland. They followed a great path of silver water for quite some time, but it wasn't the Haw River yet. The moon shimmered on the water's surface and its banks seemed soft and grassy from up above. There was a gentleness to the land below that made Owletta feel peaceful, despite the uncertainties of what lay ahead. To the right and left were farms, and deeper into the night, they left the water behind and moved out over what seemed endless farmland.

"Grow a lot of peanuts down here," explained Skitter

flying alongside Owletta.

"You grow peanuts?" asked Owletta, getting confused.

"No, don't be ridiculous! I mean the humans grow a lot of peanuts around here. Those are peanut farms down below."

"Oh, I see," acknowledged Owletta.

"Sorry I snapped at you. This whole experience is nerve-wracking," Skitter apologized.

"Soon, we'll turn south. Southwest, really," continued Skitter, who was positioned now between the other two birds. Cobcaw had moved up from a back position.

"Fine, you lead," said Cobcaw.

They traveled another hour.

"I think we're almost there," said Skitter.

"I don't know what's wrong with me," said Owletta. "I feel so exhausted. I want to arrive as soon as possible, but I feel if I don't rest for a few minutes, I'll crash."

"No problem," said Skitter. "Here's a nice stretch of woods. Let's drop down and take a little break."

As they closed in on the wood, Owletta noticed an old red beechnut tree with an amazing spread of branches. She felt drawn to it. It seemed to glow sweetly in the moonlight.

"Let's stop here," Owletta suggested.

As they settled into the branches, there was a bit of commotion. Several animals squeaked at them angrily, and much to Owletta's surprise, a large male tree owl spoke up in a commanding voice, from somewhere overhead.

"May I ask you what you are doing here? You make a most unusual and unexpected party in the middle of the night, so I think we are owed an explanation."

Owletta turned to her friends. "Let me try and do the explaining. I may have more success in communicating with this owl gentleman, who seems to be the protector of this tree."

Then Owletta flew to a higher branch, closer to the tree owl, and let herself be seen.

"Please excuse our unannounced arrival, but we are on a long and important journey with no idea of where to take some rest. The beauty of this tree called to our tired wings and we were drawn to it in our weariness. We mean no harm to you or any of the tree's residents."

The male tree owl seemed pleased with Owletta's formal language. "You need not be in such a hurry. We are a hospitable enough group, and welcome friendly guests when proper introductions have been made."

"This is understandable. Let me then introduce myself and my friends and tell you our tale."

"Please, Gracious Lady, your language is almost as lovely as you yourself, and I would be honored to hear your story and meet your friends."

Owletta felt her feathers ruffle. She was a bit embarrassed by the compliment, but also pleased. He was a handsome fellow indeed, and as good at speaking as she was.

"You are very kind. My name is Owletta and I come from the north. I live northwest of the Great City of Humans in the region once known as Dogwood Forest of

the Small Hills. The humans have built many homes in this region. I live in a lovely old oak, nearly as old as your beech. It is an old oak that goes back to a time before the towns were built."

"This sounds like a fine home. You have traveled far."

"And these are my two friends met in travel, who are helping me in my mission. This is Cobcaw of The Great City of Buildings and his cousin Skitter of the Great Water only an evening's flight east of here."

"I am pleased to meet you all. My name is Hool Beechum and this is my much beloved home. You are welcome to rest and take refreshment here. We all welcome you—Jip and Cep the chipmunks, and Selena squirrel."

"Selena squirrel!" hooted Owletta so loud that everyone nearly jumped off their branches. "Selena, did you lose your mate to the mischief of humans and is his name Apkin?!"

"Apkin! Apkin! Do you know my dear Apkin? Is he alive?!"

"Yes my dear, alive and well and looking for you. You and Regata are part of my mission."

"This is most incredible!" said Hool. "It seems we are already linked to the same history. Tell us everything!"

So Owletta told the tale, while Jip and Cep brought refreshments. Selena was beside herself with joy.

"And where is Regata?" asked Owletta.

"Regata remained at the old tree near the new land of the glowers. Their glowing made me nervous and Hool was kind enough to ask me to live in his tree."

"Then here too is an owl who befriended a squirrel!" remarked Owletta.

"Yes, relationships are changing between animals," acknowledged Hool. "I must admit to eating mice sometimes, but mostly I stick to bugs. I would never, ever, eat a squirrel or chipmunk again. These three who live in my tree are my dear friends."

"Most amazing," said Owletta. "You know my story, and my friendship with Ekle and Apkin has had the same effect on me. I adhere to the same diet as you, friend Hool."

"Ah! We have such things in common, Owletta, that I can't help but wonder if we were meant to meet."

"It must be so. Please, Hool, tell me what you know of these glowers and if you think it wise that I have befriended one and a human child as well. Only a few weeks ago I would have laughed in your face if you even suggested it, but one year ago I would not have believed that I would be friends with squirrels rather than eat them."

Cobcaw and Skitter said they had not been aware of any changes, but they could hardly deny it now. Selena was so delighted to know that Apkin was alive, and Ekle too, that she was even willing to risk dealings with humans and glowers.

"You see," explained Selena, "when I first came to live in Hool's beech tree, I wanted to avoid meeting a glower. But Hool has met with them many times since. He has even had conferences with them! He explained to us that some vinetropes glow and some don't. He says they are good creatures. And so I'm less fearful of seeing one now than I was when I first came here."

"Is this true Hool? You've actually had meetings with them?"

"Yes, many times, and I've been to their Councils on three occasions. They are hoping to regenerate a full Vine-trope Nation. They have all the members of their race but one. They need a Master Rhymer. The Master Rhymer, also a glower, always possesses the knowledge of their history. Often, much of their history is contained in rhymes. They are in desperate need of such a glower now. Having been reborn from an ancient time into this new world, they have no sense of their past history, of where they came from, so it is hard for them to plan their future. But unfortunately, there has been no sign of such a glower among their births."

"Until now!" said Owletta. "For Lucinda Vintrope is obviously the missing member of their new nation! Not only does she glow, but she is a natural rhymer and has already remembered some of their history."

"This is wonderful," cried Hool. "I must call a Council tonight, Owletta, and you must bring the good news yourself in person to the vinetropes."

"Then I gather from what you say that you also strongly approve of these glowers and what they do?"

"Indeed I do, Owletta. When you see what they have created, you will understand. Why, even the very land they live under seems richer and healthier than it has ever been in my time, and I am the oldest known animal in all these parts. That's why they sought me out for council."

"By all means then, arrange the Council," said Owletta.

"I will leave now, and return with news shortly. They live quite close to here."

With that, Hool spread his wide brown wings, an impressive three feet in diameter, and took to the sky as silently as a cloud.

"Good work, my good cousin," said Cobcaw to Skitter. "You've brought us to the right spot."

"And what unbelievable luck that we should have chosen this tree to take our rest in!" added Owletta. "It's too good to be true!"

"Maybe it isn't just luck," said Skitter. "Did you notice how the tree gave off a gentle glow? Or was it just me?"

"Well, I do believe you are getting caught up in our legend, Mr. Skitter," teased Owletta. "Yes, that's what drew me to it. I thought it was just the moonlight reflecting off its dark branches. But maybe the tree called to us. Hool has spent a lot of time with the vinetropes, and maybe that's had an affect on this old tree."

"Well, that's getting far-fetched," said Cobcaw. "But I will admit it's been quite a stroke of luck."

"Not necessarily. You heard Hool say the very ground seemed healthier where they lived."

Selena, overcome with excitement, began to ask Owletta a hundred questions. Owletta had to reassure her several times that Apkin had found no one else to replace her.

It only seemed moments later when Hool alighted in the beech tree and announced his return.

"Well?" asked Owletta eagerly.

"Great news! The vinetropes are overjoyed at your arrival, Owletta, and want to meet you as soon as possible. Tonight! Immediately!"

"That's wonderful!"

"But they asked that you come alone for this first meeting. They are protective, and the entrances to their town are a secret to most."

"I don't like being left out," said Skitter. "Came all this way to get an eyeful of them, too."

"That's just the point," said Hool. "They don't want to open their doors to anyone who wants to get an eyeful of them. They're just protecting themselves and their children, you know."

"I understand," said Cobcaw.

"It's only right that I go by myself, my friends," said Owletta. "After all, I am the messenger of their Master Rhymer. They would want to speak with me first. They have a million questions to ask and so do I."

"Those are the very words spoken by their Master Healer. Chantrek Wayforth Vinetrope is his name," explained Hool.

"Chantrek Wayforth," repeated Owletta. "When do we leave, Hool?"

"In a little while. Come with me to the top of the tree, Owletta. I need a few moments rest and would enjoy your company."

"Of course, Hool."

They flew to the top of the tree.

Here, at the top of the ancient tree, Owletta definitely noticed a light glow all around and below her. As though the tree itself was radiating a faint light.

"Beautiful, isn't it?" confirmed Hool. "This is what I wanted to talk to you about."

"Then I'm not imagining it?" asked Owletta.

"No. I have been watering the tree with a wonderful liquid that the vinetropes produce. I water the roots. I have been back and forth many times."

"And it is making the tree glow, like their root system? I know about this liquid. Lucinda has explained it to us."

"Yes, they instructed me how to go about it. It's a kind of experiment. You see, the earth had been a little damaged up around here near my tree—human pollution. Some trucks pulled up and dumped bad stuff here in the middle of the night some time back. Fortunately, they haven't returned. Well, the tree, now that it has the glowing power, drinks the bad material right out of the soil and destroys it. The soil is back to full health!"

"How fantastic! Then the vinetropes can actually help clean up the world? Clean up the strange areas of danger that humans have left in the ground," concluded Owletta. "Wait till the others hear about this! But why is the whole tree glowing, and not just its roots?"

"My fault. I wasn't watering deep enough at first. The glow will wear off with time, now that I don't have to water it anymore."

"Well, it's good that it was glowing. That's what made me land here."

"And that is the most wonderful event of all, Owletta, my dear, for I think I am completely in love with you!"

Owletta was thrilled to her heart. "And I know I love you too, Hool. From the moment we met. My mate died so long ago, and I never thought I would feel this way again."

They wrapped their wings around each other for a moment.

"Now," said Hool, "we must put our personal joys aside for the moment and carry out our historic duties. Shall we leave for Vinetrope Land?"

"Yes, my dear, lead the way."

Owletta and Hool swooped out into the night and headed west, further inland. Owletta praised the land below and Hool graciously accepted her compliments, obviously proud of his native country. The night air was pleasant against their wings, warmer than up north.

Soon they made out the silver ribbon of the Haw River glittering in the distance. Below, the land took on a rich, velvety quality that felt intense and lush in the bright, creamy, southern moonlight.

"Everything feels so soft and deep and dreamy down below," commented Owletta.

"Yes, we are nearly to the front entrance of their community," explained Hool. "What you see below is growing over the very center of their underground world."

"You can almost feel the life underneath. It's as though the grass and plants and trees are twice as alive as normal."

"Yes, exactly."

"What about humans? Haven't they noticed?"

"Not really. Not yet. The vinetrope village only covers about one square mile and it is not an area populated by humans. The glowing, unlike my tree, only occurs underground. We're here," said Hool beginning a descent.

Owletta glided down behind him, and in a moment they landed on the soft grass. It felt as lush and cushion-like as it looked and was even a bit warm against her feet.

"The grass feels warm," remarked Owletta.

"It's the root system at work underneath. The vinetropes explained it to me. The roots keep the halls of their world warm when it's cool outside. If it's hot outside they work in reverse. The roots remove the heat from the halls and release it into the outside air. The temperature is always kept constant inside. Of course the roots also glow and light their world as well."

"Yes, yes, Lucinda explained all of that to us. Her system is too young to warm her home yet, but a few of the roots are beginning to glow. I can't wait to see what a mature root system is like."

"Then let's enter."

Hool approached a tangle of vines that fell over a huge boulder at the foot of a small grassy hill. On top of the hill grew a weeping willow and the vines seemed to tumble down from the foot of the willow tree. The branches of the willow rustled for a moment as a night breeze caught them up. Hool lifted a few tendrils of the vine with his wing tip and leaned forward.

"Hool here, at the Willow Hollow, bringing the foretold messenger," whispered Hool into the vines.

There was a very familiar cranking noise. It sounded to Owletta like Lucinda's front door opening. A wonderful glow emerged around their feet, as if the autumn moon was held captive under the earth and was trying to escape. Hool merged into the light beyond the vines and Owletta quickly followed. As she adjusted to the strange light, she heard the door crank shut.

"Welcome," said a smiling face that could have been Lucinda's brother. "I am Klent Abo Rootroupe, your guide."

"Greetings," said both Hool and Owletta jointly.

"We're so excited that you're here with news of our missing glower. Chantrek has arranged for a MoonGlad Feast, and everyone is wide awake. Even the children."

"I'm very honored and thrilled," said Owletta. "This has been an adventure of a lifetime."

"Follow me, please. We will go directly to the banquet hall in the center of town. We have about a ten minute walk."

"No problem," said Hool. "We owls can walk even though we may prefer to fly."

Rootroupe was dressed in a rather plain brown outfit, pants and shirt, but as he led in front, Owletta noticed a subtle pattern of mushrooms on the back of his shirt.

In a short time the entrance hall widened into a much more spacious hall. It was about three times their height and almost four times their width. Owletta and Hool could walk side by side behind Klent Abo.

Owletta was overwhelmed by the beauty as she walked along. The root network overhead was as delicate as silk thread and woven into wonderful glowing patterns on the ceiling and down the walls. The designs changed every hundred feet or so. This created the impression of passing from one room to the next, each room decorated differently. Sometimes the patterns looked like snowflakes and draped the earth above them like a lace tablecloth. Other patterns were of flowers and leaves. And all the roots emitted the most wonderful light.

"The roots also have the practical value of keeping the earth from crumbling in on us," Klent Abo explained.

Then Owletta noticed that in some of the compartments the roots grew down in the center and formed shapes very much like crystal chandeliers. The light itself varied from room to room. One might glow in moonlight white, another might emit an orange-yellow light like Lucinda's, still another might radiate a silvery-blue. And some of the compartments had doors.

"Where do these doors lead?" asked Owletta.

"Homes, homes—different homes," explained Klent Abo.

The floors had a finished look as well. They were covered lavishly with a tight dense moss. On some of the walls, between the roots, a carpet of flowers grew, on others, mushrooms and plant fungi sprouted in endless varieties. The light from the roots allowed for such underground blooms. Just walking through these halls was an experience almost too rich to describe. And all the time the

air felt comfortable and fresh. It had a light herb-like scent carried in by breezes from hidden vents that reached outside into the night air.

"It is so beautiful in here," said Owletta.

"I know," said Hool. "Even though I've been here many times, it never ceases to amaze me. When I first came, the root system wasn't complete and I had two guides to lead the way. They turned themselves on like lanterns. But by the fourth season, the system was mature enough to give off all the light necessary."

"Why aren't there any vinetropes about?"

Klent overheard and answered.

"We're still a pretty small group. Only one-hundred and fifty. They're all gathered at the town center to meet you Owletta. This is an historic event for us."

"I'm very honored!" said Owletta.

"Yes, we're a small group, but we're growing. We've got the Vinetropes, the Rootroupes like myself, the Vineroots, the Fernfels, the Vineferns, the Fernroots, the Rootfels and the Ferntroupes!"

Owletta felt her head spinning. "Are they all different from each other?" she asked.

"Well yes," answered Klent. "Those are all the different family names. But we're all vinetropes, if that's what you mean."

"I guess that's what I mean."

"We're here," stated Klent Abo, and the hall opened into a huge dome-shaped room about 200 feet in diameter. There were thirty or so front doors in an array of colors all

around the circular room. A crowd was gathered at a beautiful fountain in the center which sprayed water into its many glowing tiers. As Hool, Owletta and Klent Abo entered, the crowd cheered at the top of their little lungs.

"Hurray for the messenger! Hurray for Owletta!"

"Thank you, thank you," said Owletta. "This is an amazing day for me. I'm almost bewildered beyond words at the sight of your beautiful town and your warm welcome."

Again a cheer went up on all sides.

"Welcome," said the slender figure of a young male vinetrope dressed in blue. "And may the stars be witness to the joyous message that you bring." He stepped forward, bowed and raised his arms upward.

Owletta followed the gesture of his arms, and as she looked up to the domed ceiling, she observed twelve circular windows slide open, revealing the autumn night sky.

Owletta gasped and so did Hool, who had not seen this latest invention of the vinetropes.

The blue dressed young vinetrope offered Owletta his hand. "I am Chantrek Wayforth, the Master Healer of my people, and our good friend Hool has informed me that you bring us the greatest news."

"Indeed I have. A most amazing being was born from the ground near my northern home. She is smart, industrious and cheerful by nature and possesses two extraordinary qualities. One: she glows at will." The crowd cheered. "And two: she makes up the most wonderful rhymes."

With this, the roar of the joyous vinetropes was

almost deafening. Owletta was lifted into the air to the tune of a wonderful song and the vinetropes pranced her all around the circular hall, while clusters of young vinetropes and their parents cheered from the sides.

Owletta was finally placed down by the central fountain in front of Chantrek Wayforth, who was grinning from ear to ear much the way Lucinda does.

"Let the MoonGlad Feast begin!" proclaimed Chantrek. The air filled with the watery music of wooden flutes and lovely singing as merry vinetropes busied themselves in every direction.

Tables and chairs were quickly set up and the front doors of many homes opened to reveal the smell of delicious preparations. Chantrek signaled to Hool and Owletta to sit down at one such table. Mugs and bowls of herb scented drinks were placed before them, as well as a plate piled high with something that looked like golden pancakes.

"Help yourself," said Chantrek. "These river cakes are nutritious and tasty to all animal life. And sip freely from your drink bowls my owl friends. Please make yourself comfortable and give me the great pleasure of hearing the whole story from the beginning, Owletta. Then we can decide how to have our Master Rhymer transported to us."

Owletta kept Chantrek spellbound with the full story and Chantrek made her tell it again later that night to all the vintropes. The vinetropes were aware that they inspired language in other animals. They had discovered this themselves through experience with the creatures who lived

around them. They also knew that their watering system destroyed pollution in the earth. They had some "bad" soil in their village that completely disappeared after their root system developed. That's why they gave the vinetrope water to Hool for his tree. Everyone agreed to Lucinda's plan of convincing the girl Sara to drive her and the squirrel brothers down. But Chantrek's advisors suggested that if Lucinda could convince her, they should only allow the child Sara to enter their new nation. No other humans for the time being.

"Let's take things one step at a time," said a female advisor by the name of Throna Fernroot. "We know we want to help this human world. By helping them clean the earth, it is obvious we help ourselves. But we should proceed slowly, and get to know their ways first."

Everyone could see the sense to this.

Chantrek agreed that this was a good plan. And so it was decided that night that Owletta would return with the news of a Vinetrope Nation in the making to Lucinda, and that the plan she had devised would go into effect, as long as only Sara was allowed to enter their world.

"But what if Sara can't convince her father and brother to help?" asked Klent.

"Then," said Hool, "I must accompany lovely Owletta home to the north so that if this happens, she and I can create some kind of transportation cradle for Lucinda and fly her here together. Sara would be able to help us construct it."

"Yes, Hool, that's a wonderful idea," confirmed

Owletta. "We'd just take our time, making as many stops as we needed."

"And I'm willing to do the same with Ekle and Apkin. We'd take one brother at a time. It might take months to complete the three journeys, but I am committed to doing it. The squirrels are as much a part of this story as I am."

"I agree," stated Owletta.

"I admire you both," said Chantrek. "You show the ability to be loyal and committed to what you believe to be right. You both will always be honored in the history of vinetropes."

The night turned into a double celebration, for somewhere in the midst of the merriment, Owletta and Hool announced their engagement. Cheers and toasts were made to Owletta and Hool's marriage plans and many more songs were sung.

CHAPTER NINE

A Catastrophy, Shocks, and Adjustments

It was Saturday morning, the morning after Halloween. Steven woke up convinced that he'd dreamt the Lucinda incident. He was feeling pretty much back in the "real" world. Pleased that he had his dad's car for the day, he got up to ready himself for a nice ride in the country

with Lorraine. Then Sara came in and knocked him back into "never-never" land.

"This is going to be a great day," she announced cheerfully.

"It is?"

"Of course. I'm going to go over everything with you and then we'll go out and visit with Lucinda. It's so great to be able to share this with you. I feel terrific."

"You mean it did happen?" he said foggily. "Can I use the bathroom first?"

"Sure, but hurry up. I can't wait to tell you everything."

Their dad had been picked up by one of the members of his lab team who lived nearby. They were working on a test that required daily check-ups, so he had arranged to be picked up and returned on both Saturday and Sunday. That gave Steven the car for the weekend.

"Okay," said Steven, "I'll meet you downstairs for breakfast and you can give me the rundown."

He wasn't buying this all yet, was he? If he saw Lucinda again, though, that would have to be it. He pulled himself together, got dressed and went downstairs.

Sara was already dressed and had forked an entire waffle, which she was waving around as she talked, dipping it into syrup periodically. Her mouth looked pretty sticky.

Steven poured himself a glass of orange juice and collapsed onto a kitchen chair with an "Okay, how much sloppier can you get?"

"Don't give me that look," said Sara. "I don't eat this way in front of anyone but you and Dad. We have more important things to discuss. Yes, you saw Lucinda and you'll see her again soon enough. I can tell you want this to go away, but it won't. She's here, as real as you and me, and I've already been out to visit her this morning. She's expecting both of us. I just want to go over everything first."

"All right," said Steven. "Let's have it. I can tell it's going to be really strange, so I won't even open my mouth once. Just shoot away."

And she did. She explained absolutely everything from start to finish. Steven broke his promise and got caught up in the story (he was still experiencing it as a story) and asked quite a few questions. Especially about the effect Lucinda was having on animals that caused them to be able to speak with each other. The car trip plan really threw him for a loop.

"Do you think Dad is actually going to buy this whole thing?" he asked. "I mean he'll probably think this is some kind of delayed response to Mom's death and his absence."

"Then you've noticed that he isn't around so much lately too?"

"Of course, Sara. I've been getting through this because I'm kind of moving off in my own direction now. I miss Mom a lot. It still hurts, not having her here, and I will miss her many times in the future—like when I have kids some day and they can't know their terrific Grandma. But I'm also excited about going off to college. I have

Lorraine and some good friends. Dad has been distant, and I miss him too. His work is his way of dealing with his grief. But I'm going to be okay. It's you, I think, who needs Dad most. You're going to be home several more years and I don't like to see you lonely."

Sara hugged Steven and he reciprocated.

"I wish you would have talked to me like this before, Steven. It means a lot that you understand how I've been feeling."

"I'm sorry, Sis. I guess we've all kind of withdrawn into our own worlds. Mine is my friends and future plans. Dad's is his work. And your's is this Lucinda. That's why I thought I'd dreamt the whole thing last night. But you're telling me it's real. She's real."

"Yes, absolutely."

"And that there are two squirrel brothers, Ekle and Apkin, who you communicate with through Lucinda and an owl called Owletta who is off on this mission to locate other Lucinda-like beings."

"Yes, exactly."

"Can you see why I'm having trouble with this?"

"Of course, but you did see her yesterday."

"Yes, I saw something strange. I'm not quite sure what right now."

"Well then you just need to have your disbelief removed again by coming out with me into the garden to meet her again."

"I don't know."

"What's there to know? All you have to do is meet

Lucinda, maybe a few times, and then you'll adjust. The same holds true for Dad. You'll see. Lucinda actually makes it quite easy for you to accept her. She's got a talent for putting people and animals at ease."

"It's kind of scary, Sara."

"It won't be, once you start spending time with her. Let's go. You've obviously got to speak with her again if we're going to make any progress."

"Okay, but let me give a quick call to Lorraine to postpone our drive till tomorrow. I think you need me right now."

"Thanks, Stevie," she used his nickname.

Steven made the call. They grabbed their jackets and stepped out into the fresh morning air. Lucinda was outside, sweeping up some leaves that had blown up in front of her door in a little pile. Ekle and Apkin were in attendance.

"Hi Steven, Sara," she called out to the two approaching humans.

"Hi, Lucinda," Sara called back.

Steven actually found himself rubbing his eyes like in the expression "*he thought he was dreaming so he rubbed his eyes.*"

Lucinda held out her unusual hand to Steven. Steven bent down and gave it a little shake. It felt real. A little cooler than a person's, a bit like peach fuzz, but definitely solid.

"Maybe I should pinch you," she said, giving his hand a bit of a squeeze. "Or maybe you need me to recite you your believing and seeing poem again?"

"No, that's okay Lucinda, I think I'll just have to find my own way to get the hang of this."

Then Ekle and Apkin came forward. They both gave a little bow in greeting.

"This must be Ekle and Apkin," said Steven. He was surprised at how normal his own voice sounded considering the bizarreness of what was happening.

"Yes, yes, it's us," they seemed to say. He let that one go and simply nodded back.

"Let Steven see your home," suggested Sara.

Lucinda cranked her door open and Steven peeked inside.

"Wow, it's really nice in here," he complimented sincerely. Seeing all the little homey touches made him feel a bit grounded. A little steadier. "I guess you really exist!"

Everyone laughed at this—the squirrels and Steven included. They all seemed to laugh and be aware that they were laughing. They decided to keep their visit outside. There simply wasn't enough room for everyone inside Lucinda's home. Then Apkin scurried forward and peered up at Lucinda.

"What's in your hair?"

"Is there something in my hair?" asked Lucinda.

Sara and Steven looked closer. Steven didn't know what he was looking for. Everything about Lucinda was new to him.

"There, there," continued Apkin with his usual impatience. He pointed with his right paw.

"Is he pointing?" asked Steven.

"Yes," said Lucinda. "Check my hair and find out what he means."

By now, Ekle and Sara knew to take Apkin's observations seriously, no matter how difficult they might be to understand. Ekle climbed the wall and took an aerial view of Lucinda's head. Sara started to finger through her leaf-like tresses carefully, looking for a bug or spider of some sort. Her fingers touched something warm and knobby and she jumped back.

"What is it?" Lucinda asked alarmed.

Sara parted the vines and looked closer.

"Lucinda, there are two green buds growing right out of your head near your hairline. And they're quite warm!"

"Really? I can't believe this! Unbelievable. My history banks tell me it is possible, but I never considered it. No wonder I've been so tired recently!"

"Oh, Lucinda," wailed Sara. "Is it serious? Are you going to die?"

"Oh for heaven's sake, no. It means I'm having babies. Twins. I'm having two little vinetropes of my very own!" and she reached up to pat the warm green knobs.

With everyone understanding each other quite well now, congratulations came spontaneously from everyone and everyone had to have a good look at this start of new life.

"Lucinda, you're going to be a mother," was all Sara could say.

Steven, now stable enough to think, had some questions. "How is this possible, Lucinda? I thought vinetropes

grew from seeds planted in the ground. And you don't even have a husband."

"A good question, Steven. This is a rare event, indeed. Only in times of great emergency can this happen, and only to a female glower. Not to a female vinetrope who isn't a glower. This insures the birth of additional glowers, when glowers are in great need. It also means that the mother can move about with her babies attached to her. They don't have to remain on the vine in a place that may have become dangerous. I guess this is a needy time for vinetropes. The less vinetropes there are, the more glowers they need!"

"This is wonderful!" said Apkin, with admiration in his voice.

"But I thought glowers were always born full adult size," Sara said.

"In normal times they are. Then only three or four glowers emerge in each generation. But under extreme conditions a glower born full size like me can generate more glowers by producing them quickly off of her own vine. And as I said, it allows the mother to move about for reasons of safety. The small glower buds are easy to carry until late in the process. In normal conditions, there would be a whole community to tend to the vine nurseries. But, like now, there is only me and my babies. I'm fortunate I have you all as my friends, or we would be all alone."

"And how long will it take for them to grow?" Steven continued.

"Glower babies mature more rapidly than non-glowing

vinetropes. And when they are mature enough they will snap off the vine and will grow even more rapidly. In two months from their separation from me, they will be my size and can begin to take on responsibilites."

"This is so exciting," said Sara.

"We're actually going to watch a rare form of vinetrope birth!" said Steven, enthused. Then he laughed, "Not that everything about vinetropes isn't rare these days."

"Yes," said Sara, "it's hard to tell what's normal for vinetropes or unususal, from our point of view."

The squirrels were ecstatic, running in circles and stopping to put their paws up on Lucinda's legs now and then, affectionately.

Right in the middle of their joy, a terrible thing happened. And it happened so quickly, no one had time to think. There was a sudden shadow, a screech, and then two claws had a hold of Lucinda by her dress and took off with her. It was a huge hawk-owl and it seemed to think Lucinda was its lunch.

"Do something! Do something!" screamed Sara in terror.

But they were all helpless. In a few seconds, Lucinda was a dot in the sky heading in the direction of the grammar school.

The squirrels ran back and forth making frantic squeaks. Apkin ran up a nearby tree and ran out on a branch, trying to keep Lucinda in sight.

"We have to do something!" commanded Sara. "Steven, I'm so afraid for her."

"We'll find her. She's smart, and she has a way with animals. This bird probably swooped her up to take to its nest and as soon as she starts talking to it, they'll probably become friends." Steven wasn't too sure about this theory, but he put up a brave front.

"Then you think she'll be all right?"

"I do. Let's all get in the car and go find her. I'll get the keys and lock up the house." He headed for the back door.

Ekle and Apkin looked miserable.

"We'll find her," was all Sara could say. She pet their heads and tried to comfort them. Sara felt cold and frightened and zipped her jacket shut. A day that had started out so happy was turning out so badly. She was sure glad that Steven was here to help.

In a short time, Steven was back. Sara opened the back door and the squirrels hopped in. She shut the door behind them.

"They better not scratch up Dad's car," Steven complained to no one in particular as he and Sara got into the front of the car.

"We won't," said Ekle, quite distinctly.

Sara and Steven turned around and looked at Ekle. He just sort of shrugged his shoulders.

"Steven, did you hear Ekle speak as clearly as I just did?"

"We'll focus on this later," said Steven. "I can't absorb so many peculiar things at once. Let's just get going."

Steven backed out of the garage, made a k-turn and pulled up the driveway into the street.

"Which way should we go first?"

Ekle was on the divider between the two front seats where their dad kept his CDs. He looked up at Steven and then lifted his right paw and pointed to the right.

"Last I saw them from the treetop, they were still going in this direction," he stated as clear as a radio announcer.

Steven made a right. " Yes, that's in the direction of the grammar school. We might be lucky, guys. There's the woods right behind the school. Maybe the hawk-owl has its nest there."

He headed straight for the school.

"Let's open all the windows," suggested Sara. "If she fell, or the nest is close enough to the street, she might be calling for help."

She and Steven opened their windows. Sara pressed the back window button and Ekle's window came down. Apkin immediately imitated her and opened his own window.

"And look out for any sign of glowing along the ground or up in the trees. It will be hard to notice in the daylight, so look carefully," Steven added to the instructions.

Ekle and Apkin both stood on their hind legs looking out. Their noses just made it over the bottom of the opened windows. They continued down Taylor Road, in the direction of the school.

"Maybe we shouldn't be in the car at all," said Sara, feeling another wave of panic. "She's got to be somewhere—in a backyard or wooded area. Not right along a street like this."

"Let's try and stay calm," said Steven. "The bird was moving at a fast clip. I still say it makes sense to go straight to the woods by the school. We'll be there in two minutes."

"I know, but I feel so helpless."

The squirrels kept a sharp lookout.

"Look, there, orange!" shouted Apkin.

Sara spotted it too.

"There, to the right, near the sewer," she said with excitement.

Steven pulled over slowly and came to a stop. They all got out and headed for the sewer.

"It's Lucinda's dress. It's her orangey rainbow skirt from her birth-dress." Sara was both excited and alarmed by the find. She picked it up. "I'd know this material anywhere." She stood looking at it as though she expected it to talk.

"Well, maybe this is a good sign. Maybe she struggled free and ripped right out of her dress," suggested Steven.

"And fell to the ground," said Sara. "She might be lying around here now, hurt or dead!"

"Let's do a full search right here," was Steven's answer to Sara's concern.

First they looked down the sewer as well as they could.

"We could use a flashlight," said Steven.

"Dad has one in the glove compartment."

Sara tucked the piece of dress into her jacket pocket and then ran to the car and returned quickly with the flashlight. Steven searched the sewer with the light, but Lucinda definitely wasn't anywhere in view.

Ekle and Apkin were doing their own thing. Using their skill as tree climbers, they could help survey the whole area more carefully than Steven or Sara could. Especially since it was possible that Lucinda was stuck up in a tree somewhere! Steven and Sara stepped off the street onto the grass and began a detailed search, calling out as they went. Taylor Road had big houses and big lawns and there didn't seem to be anyone home this Saturday morning. A beautiful setting, devoid of human life.

"It's kind of spooky, how quiet it is around here," said Sara.

"Um-humm, you'd think with some of these big houses you would have more activity. The bigger the house, the quieter," Steven observed.

They crossed a sweeping front lawn, passed a silent house, and had just approached the covered swimming pool in the owner's backyard when they heard a commotion overhead.

"It's Ekle and Apkin, I'm sure," said Sara.

Suddenly Ekle appeared on the grass in front of them. He chattered wildly, then turned and ran to the edge of a small wood at the back of the property. Here he waited until Sara and Steven caught up.

"We're coming," called Steven.

As they approached the woods, Ekle headed down a leaf strewn path that led out to the street that ran in back of the property. It was a wide yard and the wooded portion was deep. The ground smelled wet and mushroomy as they tore down the path. The trees were nearly bare. Sara looked up briefly through the charcoal branches into the autumn blue sky and said a prayer. "God, please let Lucinda be all right."

They reached the street at the end of the path and saw Apkin waiting for them. Ekle scampered up to Apkin and Steven and Sara arrived a second later. Ekle and Apkin stood at the edge of a sewer plate looking down. "In here!" said Ekle.

Sara and Steven peered down too, and they saw a distinct glow coming from the sewer.

"It's Lucinda!" gasped Sara.

"It's me all right," called a familiar voice.

"Are you okay?"

"I think so. But my right ankle hurts and I'm having trouble getting out."

Sara spotted Lucinda in the light of her own glow. She looked bedraggled, but her voice sounded strong.

"I've got an idea," said Steven. "I just need to get something from the car. I'll be right back."

He turned and ran back down the path through the wood.

"Just hold on, Lucinda. We'll get you out," reassured Sara.

The squirrels made their reassurances as well.

"Horrible!" said Apkin quite distinctly. "How could this have happened?"

"I'm so glad you found me. I'm sure I would have found a way out eventually, but right now I'm too exhausted and my ankle aches. How did you find me?"

Sara quickly explained their search and the discovery of her orange and rainbow colored skirt with the gold threads.

"Lucky it's a bright material and caught your attention. On the other hand, if it weren't so bright, it might not have caught Mr. Hawk Owl's attention either."

Steven returned with two blankets from the trunk of the car.

"You can tell me the whole story later," he said. "Let's get you out first."

"I'm for that!" said Lucinda.

Steven tied the two blankets together and then twisted a big knot at the bottom of one of them.

"Okay, Lucinda. I'm going to lower this blanket down. See if you can sit on the knot and I'll pull you up."

"Good plan, Steven."

Steven lowered the blanket and let the knot dangle just over Lucinda's head. Lucinda's arms were strong for her size and she grasped the knot while using all her remaining strength to hoist herself up onto it. Then she crossed her legs in front and gave the blanket a yank.

"Okay, I'm ready."

Steven pulled her up slowly. As soon as she reached the opening in the grating, she pulled herself out. Steven

carefully lifted her into his arms. Everyone gathered around. Apkin got up on his hind legs and put his paws on Steven's pants.

"Can you move your foot?" asked Steven.

Lucinda wiggled it. "Yes, it's just twisted a bit. I'll wrap it when I get home and get some rest."

"I guess you're okay," said Sara, crying a little now. "We were so worried."

"It was quite a scare. I think Mr. Hawk Owl had quite a scare himself. I started to glow like mad and yelled at him in hawk talk as fast as I could. I told him to put me down. I don't know what he thought I was, but he swooped low, almost to the ground. He might have been planning to put me down gently, but he had me by my skirt and the delicate fabric gave way and I fell. I was lucky he was on the way down or I might have been killed. I saw the sewer and I didn't want to take any chances. I wasn't positive he had become Mr. Friendly Hawk Owl, so I dove right into the sewer and out of sight. That's when I hurt my ankle! I don't even think he knew what happened to me or cared to find out, because he certainly didn't come looking for me. I limped for awhile underground and then, when I saw the light coming in above me, I decided to stop and try and climb out. I couldn't. You know the rest."

"Let's get you right home," said Steven. Steven cradled Lucinda gently in his right arm and Sara picked up the blanket. Then they headed back through the woods, past the pool and across the front yard. When they arrived back at the car, Sara spread out the blanket in the back seat and placed Lucinda in the middle. Ekle and Apkin took a place on either side of her. Lucinda looked tired and muddy, but in her what appeared to be silken tights (they must have grown along with her birth-dress) and her green hair, she managed to look dignified sitting on the back seat. With a squirrel courtier on either side of her, Sara thought she looked like an Elfin princess.

That's when Sara noticed the injury. One lovely green bud in Lucinda's hair was missing and there was a gash on the side of her head.

"Oh no," Sara gasped, her eyes widening.

"What is it?" asked Lucinda, but she instinctively guessed and reached for the hair near the forehead. She found what she feared most.

Steven was already back in the driver's seat and everyone turned to look at Lucinda.

"My bud, my baby, one broke off! She's gone!" Lucinda wailed. For the first time, Sara saw Lucinda cry in torrents. Her little body shook with grief.

"Oh, this is terrible." said Sara. "We'll find your bud, won't we everyone? We'll search until we find her, just like we searched for you."

Sara was crying now, too and everyone was trying to comfort Lucinda.

"It's no use," said Lucinda, wiping her face. "Once the bud is broken off it dies and withers almost instantly."

Steven drove them back and carried Lucinda to her home. He cranked open the door and climbed inside, almost filling up the room. He than placed Lucinda gently on her bed. Sara squeezed in behind Steven and gave Lucinda a drink of water and pulled the covers around her.

"Would you like something to eat?" asked Sara softly, while Steven got a fire going in the little fireplace.

"No thank you," said Lucinda, closing her eyes. I just need to be alone right now."

Steven stepped outside.

"We will keep a watch all night," said Ekle.

"If she needs something, we will get it for her," stated Apkin.

Sara leaned over and gave Lucinda a little kiss on her cheek and then left. Steven and Sara watched as the two squirrels managed to crank the door almost shut from the inside and then took positions outside on either side like guards.

Brother and sister walked back to their home. They didn't yet discuss the fact that they could both now understand the squirrels when they talked. They didn't say anything to each other. Steven took Sara's hand as they went up the back steps. Without saying anything, they felt closer than they had felt in a long time. They were there for each other.

CHAPTER TEN

Surprises All Around

Sunday morning, both Sara and Steven were eager to see how Lucinda was doing. They both woke up early, quickly dressed and headed out to the garden.

When they arrived at Lucinda's front door, they were pleased to see Lucinda up and about. Ekle and Apkin were nearby having a snack.

"How are you doing?" asked Sara gently.

"I'm just keeping myself busy. Losing the baby is disappointing and sad. But I have this other bud to think of. In another three or four weeks I'll begin to feel her move around in her pod. I have to keep busy and well for her and for the future. How are you both doing?" Lucinda

returned the question. "It was quite a day for all of us. Especially you Steven. We'd only met briefly the day before. So much has happened since our trick-or-treat outing. That seems like weeks ago."

"It is amazing, Lucinda. I feel like I've known you for such a long time," said Steven. "and the squirrels too. Talking with you boys seems natural. It's so weird and so normal at the same time. Was Halloween only two nights ago? Is that possible?"

"That's right, only two days ago," said Lucinda with sadness in her voice. "I feel like I was a child then compared to now."

"Too many things are happening," confirmed Apkin.

"Some good things, too," added Ekle. "Steven's our friend now and we can all talk to each other."

"Yes, I'm certainly glad you were there yesterday, Steven," agreed Lucinda. "If you weren't, things might have been much worse."

"And it is extraordinary that we can communicate so well," confirmed Sara.

"And that means we are more likely to find our mates," said Ekle.

"My darling," stated Apkin sighing. "How I miss her."

"That's so sweet, Apkin," said Sara, scratching a little behind his ears. He squinted and seemed to be smiling.

"And you are still going to have a baby," added Sara.

"I'm so grateful I didn't lose both. I wrote a poem about my feelings. It was harder to do than the others. I suppose because it came from my feelings and not from my programmed memories. Would you like to hear it?"

"Of course," Steven answered for everyone.

"Okay."

"In the summer
Deep summer
I forget and just live,
Time—it stands still
And the land—it just gives.
But then comes a moment,
Like a waking from dream,
When ripe is too ripe,
Life is not what it seems.

In the fall
There's an ending,
It has fire and style,
The decay is all hidden
In color and guile.
It's electric excitement
Lasts but a short while,
Like a squirrel I'm charged
To collect my nut pile.

In the depth of the winter
In a night with no moon,
There's a coldness
And darkness
I know will end soon,

And yet for the moment
I feel chilled by doom,
And words of kind comfort
Can't lessen the gloom.

In the spring there is pain
In the burst of each bud,
There is beauty
As life flows
Up from the mud.
Together—sweet-sadness
Is spring's second name,
A wound and a healing
A time for great change."

"That was beautiful," said Steven. "I think it says what you're feeling just perfectly."

"I hope so."

"It does," said Sara. "And the poem is a comfort, too. In the spring your baby will be born and you'll be busy with her and by then we'll have heard good news from Owletta, I'm sure."

"What good news will we be hearing?" asked the kids' father, coming up behind them.

"If there are other vinetropes in the world, of course …what? Whoa! It's you, Dad!"

"What the heck is a vinetrope?" their dad asked, coming between his kids with a puzzled look on his face.

"I'm a vinetrope!" announced Lucinda.

"Too many things are happening," said Apkin and he fainted.

"Apkin, are you all right?" asked Sara and ran over and picked him up, stroking his sides.

Sara's dad stared at these "happenings" with a bewitched and not too healthy look on his face.

"We'll explain everything," said Sara coming up to her dad with Apkin in her arms. Apkin started to wake up, but when he opened his eyes he was met by the dad's not too healthy expression and fainted again.

Meanwhile, Lucinda jumped on Steven's shoulder, so she could be at closer range to the tall man's face, presumably to make it easier to talk to him.

"Hi, I'm over here!" she waved to him, not sure he'd actually seen her because of the dazed expression on his face.

Sara's dad looked back and forth between the unconscious squirrel, and the "whatever-it-was," and seemed to get wobbly on his feet.

Steven leaned up against his dad to offer him support, bringing Lucinda in even closer.

"Let's get everyone inside," suggested Steven, starting to guide his dad back toward the house.

Sara, at a complete loss at what to do, simply followed her brother, carrying Apkin. Ekle followed behind. Just then Lorraine showed up. Her parents had dropped her off. Steven had forgotten to call her and change plans again. She came running over when she saw Steven helping his dad into the house.

"What happened?"

When she reached them, she saw Lucinda perched on Steven's shoulder between her boyfriend's and his father's face. She screamed. Lucinda screamed. Steven's dad screamed. Sara screamed and Apkin jumped from her arms and ran behind a bush. Then, finally, Steven started laughing. Lucinda started laughing and Lorraine fainted with Sara able to break her fall so that she didn't get hurt.

"I think we're going to have to start this all over again," said Lucinda, but she wasn't sure anyone was listening.

Steven and Sara managed to get both Lorraine and their dad into the house. Lucinda was still on Steven's shoulder and Apkin was rejuvenated and seemed to be enjoying the excitement now. The two squirrels followed right on in as though they'd been in a human's house many times before. In truth, everyone was so overwhelmed by the suddenness of this introduction, that nobody's responses seemed quite right.

Somebody had to do something, and not too surprisingly, Lucinda took the lead.

"I think it would be wise if we all went and sat down in that nice living room of yours," said Lucinda calmly. "We could have something to drink and maybe some chocolate chip cookies and talk," she added with practicality.

"A good idea," picked up Steven. He turned with Lucinda still on his shoulder and started into the living room. Everyone just followed behind him without protest. Lorraine and Mr. Umberland truly seemed dazed, almost in shock.

They walked like robots. In a few moments, everyone was seated in the living room. Lucinda took a pillow off the couch and placed it on the coffee table. She hoisted herself onto the pillow and sat facing Steven and the two new initiates who were sitting next to each other on the couch. Ekle and Apkin took a chair nearby together. Apkin, who loved comfort and pleasure, was carefully sliding the pads of his front feet over the chair's fabric and enjoying the texture.

"Very nice," he whispered to his brother.

Sara went running to the kitchen and came back a moment later with a platter of chocolate chip cookies and placed them on the coffee table next to Lucinda. Lucinda picked up a cookie and began to eat. Between bites, she spoke.

"Now everyone, just relax. I know I come as a shock. Let me tell you the whole story from the beginning. You don't have to say a thing. Just listen. Let me talk. .Have a cookie."

"Yeah, Lorraine, Dad, it's not as weird as it seems," Steven tried to console them. "It took me some time to adjust. The first time I met Lucinda, I just went blank. I mean it is weird, but the weirdness gets more normal feeling. When I saw Lucinda again, it all seemed much more real, almost natural. Now, it seems no more weird to talk to Lucinda or the squirrels than it does to talk to my friends Allen or Joe. Actually, it's pretty weird to talk to Allen. But that's beside the point. You'll find in no time that weird is all right and actually quite normal." He gave up and took a cookie.

"As I said," continued Lucinda, "it's probably best if I try and explain. Steven is very new at this, and although what he says is actually true, it doesn't make any sense when he tries to say it."

Sara, Ekle and Apkin started to laugh. Lorraine and Dad still looked dazed. But Dad looked worse. He had heard the squirrels laugh, whereas Lorraine could only hear Lucinda talk because she hadn't had enough exposure to the "language benefits."

"Did I hear laughter coming from two squirrels who are sitting on my living room chair?"

"Yes," confirmed Ekle. "Everything is getting so confusing there doesn't seem to be anything else to do but laugh."

"Nice seating you have here," added Apkin politely, giving the chair a pat.

Lorraine could tell that everyone else was acting like they were talking to the squirrels. She started to swoon again. Mr. Umberland got a kind of crooked smile on his face as though he was trying to participate in the amusement. It was not a natural smile. It definitely didn't look healthy.

"Okay, this is how it happened," started Lucinda. "I was born in your yard not too long ago on a beautiful moonlit night. I grew on a vine. I am an intelligent plant. My kind of being comes from the long distant past of earth. We thrived in great numbers before the Ice Age began. My seed survived through time, along with what might be others of my kind, under the ice and snow. Somehow, we think, some of our seeds surfaced in recent months and got transported to North Carolina. We haven't quite figured out that part yet. Oh Sara, Luv, would you get us some pecans for the boys and some drinks," Lucinda interrupted herself. "This is going to take a very long time, and my throat is getting dry already."

Sara jumped up, went to the kitchen and returned quickly, with a jar of apple juice and paper cups.

Lucinda took a sip of apple juice. "Now where was I? Oh yes, the night of my birth. Dear me, we have a long way to go, so I better get on with it."

And so, Lucinda did all the talking. And her power of language did its work. It both mesmerized and relaxed the newcomers. The veil of shock began to lift and they actually began to see Lucinda as a living being. The story she told, though incredible, began to make some sense. It had a kind of logic to it. At least it was an explanation of some sort. Lucinda's way with words and matter-of-fact attitude gave them the ability, at least while she was in front of them, to believe in what they were seeing. But for adults, even young adults, this was a great undertaking. It would surely leave some side effects, as it had with Steven, because of the effort it took to believe what should be impossible. Steven was making good progress, but had trouble expressing his progress. As for Sara, she was younger and adjusted completely. Indeed, she was completely at home with the situation, and Lucinda was both a friend and a mentor. Sometimes she was almost like a mother.

During this whole period—a couple hours or more —almost no one spoke but Lucinda. Ekle and Apkin fell asleep on the chair. Explaining this whole mess wasn't their job. But by the end of Lucinda's explanation, Mr. Umberland and Lorraine did at least seem to grasp the gist of her story. They even escorted Lucinda back to her home, with Ekle and Apkin joining, and peeked inside her house.

"Very pretty," said Lorraine, which pleased Lucinda.

"I'd like to study your habitat," said their father. It was the first thing he'd said all afternoon that sounded like him.

"Oh, don't worry about that, Mr. Umberland. You'll study it of course. But that's another whole part of the story."

"Why don't you call me Dad too," he suggested in a moment of tenderness. He didn't understand what was happening, but he knew nothing would be the same because of this little creature. And he knew somehow that it had already changed for the better.

"Okay, Dad. That would be very nice." She tucked at his pant leg and he bent over and received a kiss on his cheek as light as a dandalion puff.

To help them adjust to all these new and strange circumstances, Lucinda suggested that they all meet several times over the next few evenings. The reality of seeing her in a sequence, she felt, would help them sort things out. And when they returned to their house, Mr. Umberland was so exhausted, he just excused himself without a question.

"I'm really feeling quite bushed from all of this,

kids. I'm going to lay down for awhile."

"Sure Dad," said Sara and Steven simultaneously.

"Why don't we all go out for dinner later," he added, "I mean the humans."

Then he went upstairs.

Steven and Sara and Lorraine sat down at the kitchen table together.

"Do you still want to go for a ride?" Steven asked Lorraine.

"I think so."

"I think we should. We'll talk some more. It's best you don't tell anyone about this."

"I won't." She seemed spaced-out and too calm.

"Okay, Sara. We're going out for awhile. We'll be back in time for dinner."

"Fine, Stevie. I'll get my homework out of the way."

★★★★★

And with time, they did adjust. Lucinda became a regular part of their family life. So did Lorraine, who came over after school almost every day. The squirrels came by regularly too. They all looked forward to these nearly daily visits together and life became more cheerful for the Umberland family. Mr. Umberland delegated more responsibility to his staff where it was appropriate, and that meant he could be home for dinner three or four times a week. He made sure he was free every Sunday.

The squirrels were amazed at the way humans lived and they were given free range to explore, which they did constantly. A little door flap was built into the back door so they could have access. Everyone learned to play card games and Monopoly. Sara, Lucinda, and Lorraine took turns reading stories out loud every Sunday evening after dinner. If there wasn't much homework, they'd have a story time mid-week too.

The squirrels loved the stories, but didn't much like movies. Maybe their eyes weren't designed to translate the visual stimulus into recognizable experience. Whatever the reason, it bored them. Lucinda loved movies. But maybe that was because her eyes worked much like human eyes.

Some nights Lucinda even slept over. But most of the time, she preferred her own home, which she said suited a vinetrope better than the grand scale of human dwellings. She felt the outdoors was healthier for her in general. It was, after all, her natural habitat.

Sara's dad agreed that they must tell no one of Lucinda's existence at this point. Whenever they had guests over, Lucinda would return to her home. If they were going to be out in the garden with friends, they warned Lucinda. But the Umberland family was less sociable than they had been when Mrs. Umberland was alive and there were not many social gatherings planned. With colder weather arriving, there wasn't much reason to be outside with company anyway. The time they did have to just visit, they gave to each other. They had catching up to do.

"We used to have so many parties and family gatherings in this house," said Mr. Umberland one evening. "I think we should do that again. It would make your mom happy to know we carried on those family traditions. We just need to wait to resolve Lucinda's situation."

"And ours," emphasized Apkin.

"We can't make plans till Owletta returns," reminded Sara.

"Yes," picked up Lucinda. "There's no point till we know what and if Owletta succeeded. Otherwise I might as well stay here."

"Us too," said Ekle. "But what if she dosen't find vinetropes but she finds our mates?"

"We'll take you to your mates," promised Mr. Umberland. "You boys are like family too."

Sara's dad was especially anxious to get his hands on the glowing roots that Lucinda showed him. He wanted to start studying them. Finally, the trust having been established, she gave him some of the liquid from her watering vine and a few roots so he could get to work on his experiments. He would start this work quietly, by himself. Then, in the spring, when he had a harvest of roots, he would tell his colleagues that he had made a chance discovery of the glowing roots. He would tell them that from work he'd done so far he believed that the roots held great energy potential. Then he'd be sure to get permission to put his whole team to work on it. The watering fluid could be extracted from the roots and Lucinda could be left out of the picture for the moment.

"But Lucinda," he insisted, "there will come a time when you must step into the spotlight and be acknowledged for this great benefit you've brought to our world."

"I will. But first I must find out if my people exist

and if they do, what my responsibilities to them will be. I can't make any other commitments till I know what's happening."

This seemed a reasonable request.

CHAPTER ELEVEN

Owletta's Return

Time moved quickly. It was the day .before Thanksgiving. Their big concern was that Owletta had not yet returned. It had been over a month since she had left. But it had taken Owletta that long to accomplish her task and she had been on her way home with Hool accompanying her for the last two weeks.

Late Thanksgiving night, after everyone had gone home and all the lights in Sara's house were off, two remarkable things happened. One, it snowed! Just a light flurry, it's true, but the brown earth was sprinkled with fine flakes, like a chocolate cake dusted with confectioner sugar. This was an early and unexpected snow. But the second event was more important.

Owletta returned.

Lucinda had just stepped outside her front door to inspect the wintry night landscape, when she heard a woosh of wings overhead. Worried that it might be Mr. Hawk Owl back for a second try, she ducked inside her home and cranked the door shut in a hurry. A moment later there was a voice at her door.

"Lucinda, it's me. I'm back!"

"Owletta, is that you?" Lucinda gasped with excitement.

"It is. I'm back and I've brought a friend. We're exhausted. Let us in."

Lucinda cranked the door open as fast as she could and stared up into the faces of two tired owls—one familiar and one strange.

"Come in, come in," welcomed Lucinda, thrilled at the sight of her loyal friend. "Warm yourselves here by the fire, and let me get you something to eat. I'm overjoyed to see you."

"You will be more overjoyed when you hear the good news. There is a whole Vinetrope Nation in the making, Lucinda. And they need you. You are their Master Rhymer—their historian. But I'm too exhausted to explain everything now."

"Yes," spoke the other owl who was, of course, Hool, "the last few miles were rough flying. The wind and snow is much fiercer at higher altitudes, and a lot colder than I'm used to. We almost grounded ourselves south of here, but then Owletta began to recognize her surroundings, and we made the push to finish the journey."

Owletta collapsed on a log that Lucinda had placed in front of her fireplace to serve as a couch. Hool groaned himself into place next to her.

"I'm dizzy," said Owletta.

"Who's your friend?" asked Lucinda, trying to control her excitement. Owletta looked positively exhausted.

"His name is Hool Beechum. We are to be married in the spring," she added, shutting her eyes.

"Congratulations! So much news! I'm delighted to meet you, Hool."

But Hool had closed his eyes, too. The two owls, nestled together, looked like a heap of breathing feathers.

Lucinda was ecstatic. A Vinetrope Nation in the making and she was needed. She could hardly contain her excitement and curiosity, but she would have to. The two owls were in a deep sleep. Their journey must have been difficult. She didn't have the heart to wake them. Let them sleep. They were safe and the news was good. She would know everything soon enough.

Right now, she would prepare something gentle and nourishing for her friends to eat when they woke up. She prepared a soup made of healing herbs and roots, adding in several handfuls of ant eggs in respect for her friends' dietary needs. Soon the room filled with the scent of good food and the owls stirred in their sleep. They awoke for a few minutes, and ate a little.

"I'm sorry I'm so tired," said Owletta, her eyes closing again.

"That's all right. Just sleep. You're right here with me, safe and sound. You can tell me everything when you are rested."

It was doubtful that Owletta or Hool even heard her. They were asleep instantly.

Finally, on Friday, well past 10:00 a.m., the owls awoke and were rested enough to speak. Lucinda had only gotten up a short while before, herself. She had been up most of the night. The excitement of their return and what they had to tell made her sleep fitfully.

"Good morning," said Lucinda seeing them stretch their wings and widen their eyes. "I see you're awake."

"Awake, but stiff," said Owletta.

"Me too, my dear," added Hool, "My wings are aching."

"There's plenty of soup left over," said Lucinda. "I'll have it heated in no time."

Lucinda began to busy herself with another meal, but by now her excitement couldn't be contained. "A Vinetrope Nation, you say? They're expecting me? And you two are getting married!? Come now, tired or not, you must tell me everything!"

Soon they were seated at the table and as they ate, the owls talked and talked. When one grew tired, the other took over and gave the tired one a chance to eat. For the first time in Lucinda's short but full life, she was struck speechless. Not only was she not alone in her species, but there was a village of vinetropes—a nation forming! And she was already an integral part of it. She would join them

and instantly have her place, her work, her meaning. This was beyond all expectations.

"So you see," finished Owletta contentedly, "all we need to do is deliver you to your people and then we will make our wedding plans. Then you can come to the wedding."

It was now Lucinda's turn to speak. She pointed to the bud in her vines and explained to the owls about her baby-on-the-way. She had to tell them about what had happened with the hawk owl, and the retelling of her loss caused her some sadness. Then she had the good news. She had met Sara's family and they seemed to be adjusting well to the extraordinary circumstances. She also explained about vinetrope energy and how Sara's father might be able to figure out how to use it. Sara's whole family had agreed to help and to drive her to her people and the squirrels to their mates if Owletta was successful in the mission.

"And you were, my friend. More than successful. There is so much good news to share with our friends."

"My word! We almost forgot!" screeched Hool. "The squirrels!"

"My goodness. How could I be so forgetful?" added Owletta. "Call Ekle and Apkin immediately! We've found their mates!"

"What?" cried Lucinda. "How fantastic! I'll run and get them."

"I can't believe we left that part out of the story," said Owletta.

"We're just tired, my dear," reassured Hool.

In a moment, Lucinda was out of her house, a woven

milkweed shawl, as elegant as fine silk, thrown around her shoulders. In another minute there was a commotion at the front door and soon Lucinda's house was filled to the brim with friends.

The squirrels couldn't keep from chasing each other around the room they were so filled with joy. Finally, after everyone had settled down a bit, the whole story had to be told again—especially the details regarding Selena and Regata. Apkin had to be reassured that Selena had not found someone else to replace him. Lucinda decided that the Friday after the humans' Thanksgiving would always be her day of Thanksgiving.

Late Friday afternoon, Lucinda was expected at Sara's home to join the family in a dinner of leftovers. She rang the back door with her broom. She didn't want to use the back door flap for this occasion. Steven answered. When he opened the door his eyes widened. There, gathered on the back steps, was Lucinda, Ekle, Apkin, and two large owls.

"You're all here! This is fantastic! One of you must be Owletta. We've been waiting to meet you. Which of you is Owletta?"

"I am, young man. Don't tell me you can't tell the difference between a male and a female," said Owletta, insulted.

"Come, come," broke in Lucinda. "Let's don't get off to a bad start now that we're finally all here. You can't expect Steven to tell the difference. He has no experience with owls. He's a human." Suddenly, Lucinda did a double-take. "Wait a minute. You understood what he said?"

"Of course." Now it was Owletta's turn to be

shocked. "Oh my goodness, you're right, I did!"

"And I understood Owletta!" said Steven, even more incredulous.

Everyone's knowledge of each other's language had finally advanced to the point where there was no communication barrier at all. Humans, squirrels, owls and vinetropes, were on full speaking terms with each other. At least this particular group of their species.

Steven immediately invited everyone in and called his dad and Sara to join them.

"Now that we can all speak and understand each other," explained Ekle, "I feel even more confident about our plans."

"And soon we'll be with our mates," added Apkin.

They all sat down at the dining room table, and the owls filled in the humans on everything the squirrels and Lucinda had heard earlier. Hool remembered to inform them of Chantrek's discovery—that Vinetrope roots clean up polluted areas. So Vinetrope chemistry offered a solution to two major problems: it could clean up pollution as well as create a clean source of energy, so less pollution would be produced. Lucinda and Mr. Umberland explained that they were already on to that, but that this was wonderful additional evidence.

It's true that to an outsider, who hadn't yet had exposure to a vinetrope, Owletta's voice may have still sounded like a series of screeches and the squirrels may have sounded like a frantic series of squeaks, but to everyone at this table, all conversation was clear and easily understood.

This was an extraordinary historical event.

"I think we began to understand each other the day the hawk owl made off with Lucinda and we were worried for her life," said Steven to Ekle and Apkin. "Our joint concern seemed to speed up the process."

Ekle and Apkin agreed.

"We needed to understand each other," concluded Ekle.

"We needed to and so we did," added Apkin.

This unique group, gathered around the old walnut table made the most bizarre scene one could imagine. Sara and Steven ran around the house collecting pillows to prop up the seats for their smaller guests. Soon, eight "beings" were comfortably settled at the table. Only Lorraine wasn't present for this first round table gathering. "Beings" was the only way to describe this odd company. They looked very different from each other, as different as can be, but none the less, they all had intelligent minds.

And yet there was something natural about this gathering too. Natural in a larger definition of the word natural. These "beings" really cared for each other. And as they spoke, they graced the table top with wings, claws, hands and the elegant string-bean fingers of Lucinda. The sight was a marvel indeed. The room took on a soft glow and the mood of this special gathering felt both ancient and futuristic. It spoke of the past and things yet to come. This was definitely a first in history! At least on the Planet Earth.

The first thing to decide was when to make the trip to North Carolina. Mr. Umberland said that he needed to

set up a vacation in advance. He was finishing a project and just couldn't disappear from work right now. Lucinda was concerned about the impact of travel on her baby.

"I lost the one and I don't want to risk the other. I know how anxious you are to be returned to your mates, Ekle and Apkin, but I think it best if I wait until my baby is mature enough to be off the vine and in my arms."

"That sounds reasonable," said Mr. Umberland, "and it gives me time to set up a vacation."

"How long till her birth?" asked Sara.

"I would say the month you call March—in the middle somewhere."

"We can wait," said Ekle.

"But it will hurt a lot to wait," added Apkin, looking sullen.

"Well," said Owletta, "I told Chantek and the vintropes, as well as Selena and Regata, that it might take some time to return. I explained that we had to convince Sara's father to drive us, that bad weather might prolong our flight up here and that they should expect to be patient. I said that no matter what, I would get back to them by the spring when the weather was good for travel, and tell them where we stood."

"Then they don't expect us right away," said Ekle.

"We might as well wait to be safe for the baby," Apkin added, always choosing well in the end.

★★★★★

Before they knew it, the holidays had arrived. It was two days before Christmas. Lucinda was in the

kitchen with Sara helping her make a gingerbread house.

"This is a very clever idea," commented Lucinda, leaning against one side of the house on her knees, with her arms stretching around the two ends of the house to hold the walls in place. Sara frosted and placed the fourth wall into position.

"Okay, I think you can let go now," said Sara.

Lucinda stood up on the table, her feet a bit sticky. The cookie walls seemed to be holding.

"Lets get the roof up now," instructed Sara.

They each frosted the edges of a large rectangular gingerbread cookie and put them in place on top of the house. It looked good for one second and then the two pieces of roof began to slide off, causing the walls to become unsteady.

"Yikes! Avalanche!" shouted Lucinda.

"Quick, get the roof off, the whole house is coming apart!" shouted Sara.

They each pulled off their piece of roof and quickly pressed the walls together again. Lucinda took up her kneeling position on one side, and Sara held her side firm with both hands. They held for about thirty seconds, then Lucinda carefully let go and stood up.

"The walls seem to be holding again. I used to make one of these every holiday with my mom. One of my first memories of the holidays is watching Steven and Mom build a gingerbread house and my being too young to help. I guess I was three and Stevie was about nine. By the time I was five, Stevie wasn't interested in making them anymore and it was just me and Mom."

"It's a great tradition. Your mom would be happy you're making them again. I'm sure she hoped you'd be doing it with your kids some day."

"I know she would."

"But you don't have this roof part down quite right yet."

"Well, I'm working from memory. I think I might have made the roof too thick so it's too heavy."

"Hey, I've got an idea. Do you have any of those pretzels sticks around?"

"Yes, I think so."

"Take a look."

Sara went to the pantry and came back with a bag—the long kind that she preferred to the thin style.

"Here you go," she said, tearing open the bag and handing it to Lucinda.

Lucinda slid one out. It wasn't much shorter than she was.

"What does this remind you of?" Lucinda questioned.

"A pretzel?"

"Come on—in relationship to this gingerbread house."

"I don't know. A telephone pole. Wait—a log. We could frost them and use them to make a log roof!"

"Yup, I was reading about log cabins in your history book just yesterday."

"This is a great idea, Lucinda. They're just the right length and it gives it a whole new look. We can frost the

pretzel logs after we get them in place."

"And sprinkle them with these colored sugar seeds."

"Perfect."

Lucinda scooped a tablespoon into her pocket to use for planting.

Then she began to recite:

"We're making a cabin of
Cookies and cream
We want it to look like a
Child's sweetest dream.
We'll use ice cream cones
To make all the trees
And frost them points up
A green sure to please.
With sugar and egg whites
We'll whip up the cold
And frost up a world
Like the famous North Pole.
And inside the cabin
Place candles that glow
To cast winter shadows
Across the fake snow."

Everything had a new twist to it when Lucinda was around. The gingerbread log cabin, sitting in a snowy ice-cream cone forest, was a big success. They put the finished house, which was frosted onto a large serving tray, on the center of the dining room table.

Evening arrived. Evenings had become a tradition

among the new friends. They all got together for refreshments, conversation and storytelling after the day's responsibilities were done. The squirrels and owls arrived and complimented the gingerbread cabin. Sara had rummaged through the bookshelves earlier, looking for a story to read that night at the dinner table. She decided on "The Snow Queen," because she was very hopeful that it would snow that weekend in time for a white Christmas. There hadn't been a flake since Thanksgiving night. Sara brought her book of Hans Christian Andersen tales with her into the dining room and everyone took their accustomed seats—pillows already in place.

Sara's dad had made his wife's recipe for hot spiced apple cider. It was on the table, smelling wonderful, and there were plenty of gingerbread cookies left over from the "log cabin" project. A large bowl of mixed nuts finished off the table's refreshments.

"I don't understand," said Ekle with a little pile of nuts in front of him. "If you're going to drive us down to our mates, why don't you stay down there with us so we can be a family forever?"

"Well, first of all," said Steven, "I have to finish my senior year in highschool. I can't just pick up and leave. And there's Lorraine."

"Ah, yes, your mate," sighed Apkin.

"She's my girlfriend," snapped Steven. "Mate is going a bit too far."

"Also," picked up Mr. Umberland, "I have my work here. A very hard-to-come-by position in which I would have the power to lead a team on this energy project using vinetrope photosynthesis. It's an almost irreplaceable position and I would be jeopardizing the project and my family's financial security if I just picked up and left."

"I know it will be hard for us to go our different ways," said Lucinda. "But it will be necessary. Dad is right. I will need to spend concentrated time working with my people and will not have much time for anything else for quite some while."

"It is sad that we will be separated," Sara added, feeling the happy mood of their gathering slipping away.

"Quite sad," said Ekle.

"Not completely sad," added Apkin. "I will be with my Regata."

"But Sara," continued Lucinda, "we will work together in the future. I am sure of that. You will be the first human to see the vinetrope world. They are only allowing you to enter. And some day, when vinetropes are ready to make themselves known to your world, you will be the one to introduce us."

"Do you really think so?"

"Yes I do. So it is important that you return home and continue your own journey; as I will continue mine. We can't grow in each other's world until we gain some mastery of our own."

"Very wisely put," said Mr. Umberland.

"So we might as well enjoy each other now," added Steven.

"You're right, I know," said Sara, "but it's going to be real hard to say good-bye."

Christmas morning arrived and although it wasn't a white one, it was still wonderful. Amazingly, Lucinda's special birth dress had repaired itself. Each time she wore it, it grew back a little more. It was complete by Christmas morning. The animals arrived early to participate in the gift giving. Sara gave a wardrobe of doll clothes to Lucinda for her baby and the wooden doll cradle, stocked with a new mattress and several warm blankets. Lucinda was delighted. Lucinda's present to the family was an incredible collection of poems that she created and compiled on the computer. The collection came to 152 pages. She said she was now going to work on writing short stories. The squirrels didn't know what to bring, so they brought a lot of acorns and then ate them themselves. They were in a festive mood and their humorous antics were gifts enough. The owls each donated a "good-luck" feather to the family from their own wings. Sara's family gave the squirrels several bags of fancy mixed nuts in the shell, which thrilled them to no end. Then, for Owletta and Hool, there was a small hooked rug to make their nest cozy and a little water pot to hang outside their nest to collect rainwater.

The holidays came and went. Now came the slow

months of January, February and finally March. Lucinda's bud swelled and blossomed. The friends did as Lucinda hoped. They used these weeks together to increase their speaking skills and knowledge of each other. Spring was at hand. It was the season of change.

CHAPTER TWELVE

In Which the Baby is Born

Lucinda's baby-bud was huge by now, about the size of a tangerine, and many additional vines had grown into the gourd-like structure to give it support as it gained weight and to keep the baby hydrated. Then finally, on March 3, at 4:23 in the afternoon, it happened.

"It's time! It's time!" Lucinda called out to her squirrel and owl friends. They gathered at Sara's back door and rang the bell. In her excitement, Lucinda had forgotten to check if anyone besides the Umberlands were home. Fortunately, only Lorraine was over.

Sara opened the door and everyone piled in. Steven and Lorraine came in from the den. Mr. Umberland was not home yet from the lab and would be disappointed to have missed the actual event.

"What's all the commotion?" asked Sara as they filed in.

"It's almost time for the baby to be born," shouted Lucinda.

She seemed to be bursting with energy.

"You must have a poem for this occasion!" teased Steven.

"A poem, please!" said Ekle.

"Yes, I feel one getting itself together. Let me see—a journey to be made, seasons changing, birth—definitely time for a poem: *Springtime.*"

"In the spring I am moody
And I'm not sure quite why,
One minute I'm happy,
The next I might cry.
Sometimes I don't know
Who it is I'm to be
Then I'll chuckle and laugh
Well of course—I'll be me.

All around I see change,
While the ground seems to burst,
For change, I myself
Have developed a thirst.
Then just when I'm ready
It all seems too fast,
Why can't the old ways
Continue and last?

Well some things must change
There's nothing to do,
And some things stay constant
Like my friendship with you.
So please stay yourself
While you grow and you change
And I promise you, friends,
I'll do just the same."

Sara gave Lucinda a big hug. "I feel just like that. I'm afraid of all the changes ahead. I can't even bear the thought of saying good-bye to you. Yet it is exciting, wondering what lies in our future. It's like the mystery of our own lives."

"Yes, a mystery that will unravel itself as we live each day and probably give us more mysteries to solve as we go along."

"Selena, I'm coming!" said Apkin.

"It will be terribly sad when we part ways, Sara." Lucinda got teary-eyed. "But you know we will need to

come together in the not too distant future. When your dad gets a real understanding of how vinetrope energy works, we will have to all get together again and plan the next move. We have work ahead of us. Important work for the health of the world, and we all have a role to play in it. It's our destiny!"

Sara gave Lucinda another hug. "I'm so glad you decided to stay here to have the baby. I know how eager you must be to get to your people, but at least I'll get to see your baby."

"I wouldn't have had it any other way. And I will tell her all about you, Sara, so she will already know you well when she meets you again."

"And I'll take care of your house up here. Because you never know, someday vinetropes might want to live around here too!"

"You never know. Yes, keep my house for me, Sara. It would make me very happy to know that it is waiting here."

By now, everyone was teary-eyed. Hool wrapped his wings around Owletta, who was crying her eyes out. "There, there," said Hool. "Just think, by this time next year, we may be hatching a couple of little chicks of our own!"

Then it happened. The pod split with the feet pushing out first, just the opposite of the best way for humans. Feet first was the natural way for vinetropes. The kicking of the babies feet against the tight and drying pod was what usually caused the split to occur. Lucinda reached up with both hands and helped her daughter open the pod. She grasped her girl's tiny body firmly, for she was a little wet and slippery inside the pod, and removed her with a little twist and a snap. In a moment Lucinda held her baby in her arms.

"What a sweet little perfect vinetrope you are!" said Lucinda to her daughter who she examined from head to toe. "You are beautiful."

Her newborn answered her mother by sending out a faint glow.

"And you are a glower for sure!" continued Lucinda.

"She's beautiful, Lucinda," said Sara.

"I will name her Sarania Vinetrope after my best friend."

"After me?" exalted Sara.

"Yes, of course."

A moment later the pod fell from Lucinda's hair, dry on the outside and empty except for a little dampness. Lucinda instinctively reached for her watering vine, and placed the end of it in her newborn's mouth. The baby began to suck. Sarania nursed for a few seconds and then fell asleep.

"I think I'll return to my own home and take a little rest myself," said Lucinda.

They all escorted Lucinda back to her house and saw her inside, safe and sound.

Lucinda wrapped little Sarania in a doll blanket, and put her in the wooden doll cradle. Then she wrapped herself in a blanket and feeling very tired by now, curled up near her child and fell into a deep sleep.

The squirrels remained on duty for the rest of the day, and the owls stood watch by night. They just had to

make themselves useful.

Later that evening, everyone met again in front of Lucinda's to see how the new mom and baby were doing. Lucinda proudly showed off Sarania, who looked as though she had grown already.

"Oh, she probably has," confirmed Lucinda. "Remember, this is an unusual birth process for vinetropes, and glowers are normally born full size. So my little daughter will grow rapidly. She could be full size in three months and speaking a bit in a week. I'll only need to nurse her on the vine for a month or two—then she'll be on solids. My memory banks are explaining this all to me. I know just what to do! This is where the precoded data is especially useful."

"It's the most incredible growth process I've ever encountered," said Mr. Umberland, who came home early that evening to see Lucinda's baby himself.

"How are your experiments coming along?" asked Lucinda.

"I've made good progress. I can duplicate the biochemical compound of your special liquid, but it breaks down very rapidly. The "spirit" of it doesn't last, so its powers can only be harvested for a few moments. Yet the liquid you gave me has retained most its strength, as long as I keep it cool. It is breaking down though from its original strength. I've calculated that in two months it will have lost half its power. That is, if it continues to break down at the same rate."

"It is some progress, though."

"Yes, but I have so little of the compound at pure strength to work with."

"Don't worry," assured Lucinda. "My production is up with Sarania nursing, so I can give you a few viles more before we leave. When we get to my people, you will have plenty to bring home to your lab. You should bring some beakers with you and a cooler to transport it in. I will be able to send you home with an abundance of roots and liquid, donated by my people. I have no doubt. I will just have to explain the importance of you having it to them. I suspect they know its additional value already from what Owletta and Hool have told us. It's a question of my getting them to trust you."

"I think that will be possible," added Hool, "because they trust Owletta and me and we will back the importance of Mr. Umberland being able to continue his work."

"That will be wonderful!" said Mr. Umberland.

"And you do have a small harvest to work with in here," she gestured to her ceiling, which was now covered in a glowing white fuzz.

"Yes, I will tell my people I came across the roots in here. Their glowing behavior made me curious, and so I brought some down to the lab to examine. They needn't know any more for the time being."

"But if they come to investigate, which they will, how will you explain that the space looks a lot like a room?" asked Sara.

"She's right," said Steven and Lucinda simultaneously.

"Sara," said Lucinda unequivocally, "you will have to remove everything from here and destroy the chimney shoot and fireplace."

"Lucinda," Sara protested.

"There is no other solution."

"I understand," answered Sara. She knew it was the only way of keeping Lucinda and her people safe.

"Excellent."

"How long will the roots that are still in the earth last?" Mr. Umberland continued to question.

"Well, if you water it with some of the vinetrope water you'll be getting, let's say twice a week, you might keep it going for quite awhile. Maybe we can give you enough for six months growth. Hopefully, by then, you'll be producing your own."

"That makes the project much more doable. But how exactly should I water it?"

Lucinda laughed. "Just spray it evenly till it's nice and damp."

"With a plant sprayer I guess."

"You're right, you don't have a built in sprayer like I do! A plastic houseplant spray bottle would be perfect."

"Oh, that's no problem," said Steven, "I'll pick a couple up tomorrow."

"Could I spray them sometimes?" asked Lorraine with childlike excitement.

"Of course," said Mr. Umberland.

"Well, there's your solution," said Lucinda. "A fine mist over everything twice a week, should do the job."

Just then, Sarania woke up and put the foodvine in her mouth. She started to suck and then to glow very intensely.

"Wow!" said Apkin.

"She's dazzling," teased Ekle.

"Would you like to hold her, Sara?"

"I'd love to."

Lucinda undid her daughter from a tangle of hair and handed her up to Sara. Sara could hold the baby safely in the palm of her hand.

"She's so tiny and sweet."

The baby opened her eyes wide and looked Sara straight in the eyes. Everyone was delighted.

"Well, we leave in two weeks," said Sara's dad.

The squirrels began to whirl around in excitement.

"I'm not sure if I'm going to like travel by car," said Hool in a worried voice.

"Which reminds me," said Steven. "Dad, we will have to rig up some kind of safe seating arrangements for everyone."

"You're right, son. We'd better get to work on it."

"Remember our feathers when you're working on your plans," suggested Owletta.

"And tails!" added Apkin.

Everyone laughed. Steven, Lorraine and Mr. Umberland excused themselves.

"Sara, stay awhile," asked Lucinda.

"Of course. I don't get you to myself as often as I used to."

Owletta and Hool took this as a cue and left the two to themselves after encouraging the squirrel brothers to do the same. Sara handed Sarania back to Lucinda and the baby picked up the foodvine and put it in her mouth with great ease. Her eye-hand coordination was developing at an amazing speed.

"She's making fast progress," observed Sara.

"Yes, she may be saying a few words before we even leave on our southward journey. You know," continued Lucinda, "soon we will all be saying good-bye to you, Sara. We will all be staying down south, Owletta and Hool, Ekle and Apkin and myself and Sarania. You will be returning here without us."

"Oh Lucinda, all of you. I don't know how I'm going to stand it. I will miss you all so terribly. Especially you, Lucinda. I don't even want to think about it." Sara started to cry. "I lost my mother and thought I would never feel any happiness again. And then you came, Lucinda. We are a family. How can I give you up. What will I do?"

"But think about it, you must," said Lucinda. "You must be strong. We are all dear friends, but my family is with my people and Ekle's and Apkin's family is with their mates. Owletta and Hool will be married and may yet have children of their own. That's why we should prepare ourselves as well as we can now for this separation. I don't want you to feel left out or left behind, Sara. But think of what has happened in these few months. Think of how our lives have been changed. You have your father and brother back again too. I know your dad will never distance himself from you again. A healing is taking place. And you must remember the importance of your role in bringing your people and mine together. This is a responsibility I will place in your hands at some point in the future. Just because we will be separated for a time, doesn't mean we won't be working together again. Sooner than we may realize. Our friendship will withstand our time of separation and any other separations that our responsibilities may impose on us."

"But how will we keep in touch? Know when it's time to get together again?" questioned Sara.

"Yes, how? I will ask Hool and Owletta. They will have to be the messengers of that message to you."

Lucinda called out to her feathered friends. A perfect hooting. In moments the love birds arrived. Lucinda explained to them what she and Sara had been discussing.

"An excellent point," confirmed Owletta.

"We could fly back and forth as messengers every spring and keep you informed, Sara," suggested Hool. "You know, maybe even twice a year, see how your dad's work is coming along and let you know how the Vinetrope Nation is progressing."

"What an excellent idea!" said Owletta. "I'd love to."

"It's a wonderful plan," said Lucinda. "And generous, too."

"I think it will be quite romantic," said Owletta.

"Yes, my dear. We could make our first trip back this summer as our honeymoon."

"How lovely, Hool. We will find beautiful trees to stay in on our way up, and have my old home waiting for

us when we arrive."

"This is such a great idea," said Sara, dabbing at her tears with the sleeve of her jacket. "It gives me some comfort already, knowing that I'll see you both and have news of Lucinda."

Ekle and Apkin had made themselves present again when they saw their friends clustered around Lucinda's door.

"I don't want to leave Sara," Apkin started to wail. "I want Selena here!"

"Oh, Apkin, you're so sweet. I love you dearly," said Sara emotionally. She picked Apkin up like a cat and cuddled him. He allowed himself this indignity as a show of trust and affection.

"But it will be better for us to be home," said Ekle.

"I understand. Really, I think we've made excellent plans," Sara acquiesced.

"That's why it was important we had this talk, all of us," said Lucinda.

"Good-bye we must say
For there's work to be done
And the owls, our messengers,
Will make the long run.
The squirrels would love
To keep Sara glad
And if we're all honest
We all will feel sad.
The work we must do

Has made us a team,
Apart or together we'll
Build a great dream."

Everyone applauded. Here was history at work. It was obvious now. Lucinda converted all events into rhyme for storage, and her memory of her own life was being stored as a huge collection of rhymes that contained information to be passed into the future.

Sara picked right up on it. "Do you realize, Lucinda, that you convert everything that happens to us into rhyme?"

"Well, yes, that's how I remember everything."

"Of course. And when you tell us facts about your people, how does the information come to you?"

"Well, I hear a rhyme about the subject I'm focusing on, and then I simply convert it into conversation as we talk."

"Of course, Lucinda. Now I understand. That's why the vinetrope historian is always the Master Rhymer."

"How simple and clear, Sara. I never quite realized it. It just happens so naturally. But you are absolutely right. That's just how it works."

"To the Master Rhymer," Ekle bowed to Lucinda affectionately, tipping his head down.

"To the Master Rhymer," repeated Sara, and everyone gave a little bow.

"Oh stop this nonsense," said Lucinda modestly. "The rhymes come to me as easy as good bread to a good baker!"

" The baker has to bake!" said Owletta.

"And get up early," added Sara.

"And work very hard," added Ekle.

"I'm hungry!" Apkin concluded the conversation.

The squirrels took their leave for dinner. The owls flew off somewhere.

"Good night, Lucinda," said Sara. She kissed Lucinda and Sarania on her head. "We're doing okay, aren't we?"

"We're doing just fine," Lucinda confirmed.

CHAPTER THIRTEEN
Journey to Haw River

The two weeks passed so quickly it was mind boggling. Sara was busy with schoolwork. There were always a lot of tests and papers due just before the March vacation. This held true for Steven too, but he'd been accepted at a college he wanted to go to, so the pressure was off and he was in good spirits. Lorraine was still a Junior, so she had another year of high school left. More changes. Her parents were not about to let her go on a vacation with her boyfriend, so she would be staying behind. Sara's dad was putting in long hours again, temporarily, to prepare for the two weeks he'd be taking off from his work. This was his first vacation in three years, since his wife had taken ill and died. Now it was the day before departure. Five months of

planning were finally reaching the culmination point.

What an eccentric concoction of items went into the car! What an eccentric gathering of passengers for a trip! The excitement of preparations had been at a high pitch for the last two days. Ekle and Apkin were beside themselves with joy at the prospect of being reunited with their mates. They didn't have too much to pack themselves, but Sara's dad did put a litter box in the back of the car, under Sara's feet, for an emergency. The squirrels and owls were deeply insulted by this. They said they were quite in control of the situation, no different than any human, and that an occasional stop by the side of the road would be sufficient. Lucinda said the same would do for her. The litter box was removed.

Lucinda's luggage and supplies took up considerable space. She was bringing along all her dishes and pots, a small suitcase of her clothes and the baby's, as well as an assortment of gifts and toys. Of course, there was the cradle and bedding to fit in the trunk. The cradle was large enough for a grown vinetrope. All it needed was a few stones under the mattress, Lucinda said, and she might keep it for herself when Sarania grew up. That would be in a few weeks! Then they had to fit in the family luggage. They also rolled up the braided floor mat that Lucinda had worked so hard on. This way, she would have something to put down on the floor of her new home immediately. Sara included in Lucinda's supplies, ten bags of chocolate chip cookies, because it might be a long time before she had them again. Owletta and Hool didn't have much to pack either, just the rug and water dish they had received for Christmas.

"Thanks for the chocolate chip cookies," said Lucinda. "I must have done something wrong. My crop didn't grow."

"What do you mean?" asked Sara.

"Oh, I planted quite a few of the chips, but nothing seems to be sprouting."

"Lucinda, the chips aren't seeds," laughed Sara. "They're candy! They're made of processed plantlife—sugar and cocoa." She had to explain further.

"Well, that's a disppointment. I guess that means those colored sprinkles on the gingerbreadhouse won't sprout either?" She looked quite vexed.

"Nope, they won't." Sara held back her laughter.

They both looked at each other and then they both cracked up laughing.

"I guess I've still got a lot to learn," Lucinda concluded.

The big problem to be solved was transporting the animals and vinetropes safely. The solution to this problem took a lot of creative energy. Everyone brainstormed.

It was Steven and his dad who came up with the answer. Working with large chunks of dense foam rubber, an old baby-seat that used to be Sara's, and some rope, they were able to rig up some very clever travel arrangements for the squirrels and the mother and child. On the back windowsill of the car they secured a long piece of foam rubber that had two tunnels carved inside. The foam was not too high in the middle or it would block the view out the back window. As a result, the rubber was thicker at each end, thinner in the middle. The entries of the tunnels faced in toward the inside of the car. Each squirrel could climb into his tunnel from the back seat. Then they could move along the tunnel until it began to reach the middle of the window where it thinned out. Here Steven had cut out a little hole that allowed the boys to stick their heads out and peek out the back window as they moved along. If they wanted to speak with the others, they could just move back towards the entrance and put in their two cents. These rubber pieces were designed as safe travel seats and kept the boys well cushioned during movement and in case of sudden stops. At the same time it gave them some freedom of movement.

For Lucinda and her baby there was a similar, but more complex version of safety precautions. After all, with such a tiny baby, even the slightest jostling around could result in a catastrophe. What they did was fill up the entire baby-seat with a huge chunk of foam rubber. They then tied and stitched it into place. Then they carved two compartments. One was an indentation like a seat or pocket in the rubber. They left a sturdy strip of rubber intact across the indentation like the bar or guard you might find on a roller-coaster ride. All Lucinda had to do was climb in under the bar, turn around and slip her body into the pocket. Then she could make herself comfortable with her arms resting on the rubber bar. The other smaller indentation, was for Sarania. The whole car seat was put into place in the back between Sara and Steven. They tried it out and after a few minor adjustments, it was secure.

For the baby, the indentation was a cradle compartment. It went back into the rubber and down rather deep so that any unexpected jerks would still find baby Sarania safe inside her traveling nest. To further secure the opening, they created a flap using Velcro, which pulled over the opening and closed the hole but with air holes for sufficient ventilation. This made it almost impossible for the baby to fly out. This contraption also offered the darkness and sound cover necessary to insure Sarania's sleep. Lucinda could easily reach her child from her position in the seat, or drop the feeding vine down to her without removing her.

The men felt proud of their work and Lucinda seemed satisfied. To finish it off, they threw a small blanket in back, which could be draped over the whole baby-seat when they went through a tollbooth or had to stop to ask directions. People might own some strange pets, but Lucinda would not fit any known category.

Now it was the morning of their departure and they still hadn't devised a system of safe travel for the owls, who were not particularly cooperative.

"If you think I'm going to stuff myself into a piece of foam rubber," said Hool, "Forget it! I'd feel like one of those stuffed owls I've heard about."

"I don't think it would be too good for our wings," added Owletta, taking the rational approach. "It might damage them severely."

"We've got to come up with something," said Steven, shaking his head.

"Yup. We leave soon," reminded Apkin. "I don't want to be held up."

"Well, what would you be most comfortable sitting on?" Steven questioned gingerly. They had to start somewhere.

"A branch would be fine enough," said Hool a bit sharply.

"I think I'll take a break while you work on this one, Steve my boy" said Mr. Umberland, excusing himself.

"Where could we tie a branch?" questioned Sara.

They opened the car doors. Lucinda was taking a rest in her home with Sarania at the time, but the squirrels, the owls, Steven and Sara stood next to the opened doors staring inside.

"We can start by securing a strong branch to the side of the door as a perch," suggested Sara. "Then Owletta and Hool can have a nice view out the window as we go along."

The owls cheered at this plan.

"And they can be on my side," Sara continued.

Steven, along with the owls, scoured around the yard till they came up with a suitable branch for the job. Then Steven bolted into place, on the inside of the door, two simple handles. When secured, he slipped the branch into the handles like a curtain rod. With some rope and a few good knots, the perch was in place.

"Now we need some kind of safety feature," Steven said thinking out loud.

"No rubber. Please!" reminded Hool.

"Okay, just a simple restraint. How about I run a

wide ribbon of some kind?"

"We'll give it a try," said Hool.

So that's what they did. Steven bolted in place two smaller handles higher up on the door frame and stitched onto the end of one handle a wide ace bandage. This had a stretchable quality that would fit more snugly against the owls bodies than ribbon and yet not be as confining as elastic bands or a rubber pouch. He then had the owls get into place to determine the right length. He cut the bandage accordingly and stitched a clip-type hook to one end so it could be hooked and unhooked to the other handle as needed. The ace bandage worked and held the owls firmly but comfortably in place.

"It's livable," said Hool.

"It's fine, Steven," said Owletta. "Good work."

"Well then, we're done!" said Steven.

By 9:00 a.m. everyone was ready.

"I feel sad," said Ekle.

Apkin nodded. "And happy."

"Everything will be different now," Sara added wistfully.

They took their places and secured their posts. The house was locked. Steven would share the driving with his dad. Mr. Umberland was designated driver number One. He made a K-turn in the driveway and with one farewell wave by all they were on their way.

When they pulled out onto the highway and picked up speed, Lucinda was thrilled, but it took the others some getting used to.

"I'm seasick," said Ekle.

"How would you know?" questioned Hool. "You've never been on a boat. But I feel wind sick," he was quick to add.

"I'm getting dizzy looking out this back window," said Ekle.

"Shut your eyes," squeaked Apkin. "It's too much to take."

After a bit they began to adjust. Ekle and Apkin ate a few nuts in their tunnels and then poked their heads out to talk to each other. They still wouldn't look out the back window. Owletta and Hool made observations on what they saw to each other and Lucinda could easily reach in and pat her baby. The feeding vine reached easily into Sarania's little mouth. Furthermore, the driving seemed to make the baby drowsy and soon she was asleep. Things were going well.

"It will be a relief," added Hool, just before dozing off himself, "to get our sleeping patterns back in order. Working with people and squirrels has really confused my lifestyle. I'm not used to all these daytime excursions."

"You'll get used to it," teased Owletta. "I have."

So the first day of travel and the first night went smoothly. At night, the brothers and Owletta and Hool remained outside while the Umberlands and Lucinda and Sarania had motel rooms. They chose a meeting spot to pickup the furry and feathered friends in the morning.

Now the second travel day was approaching an end. They were in Virginia, close to the North Carolina border,

maybe a half an hour from Roanoke Rapids on Route 95.

"This car travel is very rapid" said Owletta as they came off the highway and began to look for a place to spend the night. "It took me so long to get here by wing. But it is more beautiful by wing," she added.

The squirrels could hardly contain their excitement.

"Tomorrow we see our mates, tomorrow we see our mates!" they sang joyously.

The sun began to set. They wanted to find a motel or bed-and-breakfast place before it got dark. Now, as twilight took over the world, they still hadn't found a place to stop.

About fifteen minutes later, after passing a huge willow that nearly stretched across the width of the road, they saw a sign for an inn. Set back from the road was a big old white colonial. They came to a stop in front of the open gate just past the willow. A sign was tacked on the gatepost.

"Willowgate Inn," read Sara out loud. "Vacancies."

The owls seemed to come out of a trance.

"We're stopping, we're here?" they both mumbled.

"We're not exactly sure," said Sara.

"Should we give it a try?" asked Mr. Umberland.

"Good trees," said Apkin.

"No problem for us," said Owletta. "Just let us out here and we'll become part of the scenery in a flash like last night."

"In fact, I could use a stretch" said Ekle. "We'll check out the outside while you check out the inside. If you park your car up there and don't come back, we'll know we're staying. If not, we'll meet you back by the willow tree and don't leave without us." Ekle was becoming quite an organizer.

Sara picked up the carry-on bag under her feet and put it on her lap. Inside were two apples, a bag of vanilla cookies and a wad of napkins.

"Okay, get in," said Sara, helping Lucinda out of her seat. Sara handed Lucinda the baby and then lifted them both into the bag. "We're ready," she said to her dad.

Steven opened the back door for a moment while the owls and squirrels got out. In seconds they blended into the outdoors. Then he shut the door and they drove slowly up the gravel road to the front of the inn.

Mr. Umberland went inside while Sara and Steven stretched their legs outside on the circular driveway.

"Neat old house," said Steven.

"Yeah—looks like there's a garden around back," said Sara.

"And an orchard of some kind, but it's getting dark and I can't tell for sure."

"It looks beautiful," said Sara. "Maybe we can take a walk back there if we stay."

"You'd might as well take that walk now," said her dad coming down the front steps and overhearing her. "We're staying. It's actually quite charming. They had two rooms available so Steven and I will take one and you get a room to yourself, Sara."

"Great."

"Not exactly alone," whispered Lucinda.

"Shhh..."

"There's only one other room open to guests right now and a mother and her daughter are staying in that room. They're doing renovation on the other four guest rooms. Dinner is at 7:00."

"Great! I'll do a little exploring out back, after we unload the car," said Sara. "Do you want to join me Stevie?"

"No, I don't think so. I'm tired and want to take a shower. We're not unloading that much, so why don't you just take a look around before it gets dark and I'll help dad with the bags." He took up a suitcase.

"Don't forget this one," said Sara, handing Steven the carry-on with Lucinda and Sarania inside.

Then Sara darted off. The gravel driveway continued around back to a patio area with several tables and wicker chairs. Beyond the patio was the garden. You entered through an arched arbor tangled with grapevines that were sprouting their bright green leaves in the early spring air.

The garden was planned around a double, circular walkway made out of brick. In the very center of the inner circle was a statue of a little boy with a bird perched in his upheld hand. Around the circle grew a large variety of herbs with little metal tags designating what they were. Sara could just make out the names in the fading sunlight. There were three kinds of thyme—kitchen thyme, English thyme, and French thyme, and there was also Rosemary, lemon verbena, sage, chives and dill. In the earth between the first walkway and the second larger walkway grew basil, curly parsley, Italian parsley, cilantro, and wintergreen.

At the far end of the garden lay another arbor that led

to an orchard. Steven had been right. As she entered the orchard, she heard someone talking.

"Ooh, you're so cute, aren't you, you little sweetie," a girl was crooning to someone.

"Hello," Sara called out.

From out behind a wheelbarrow, a girl stood up. She looked to be about Sara's age.

"Oh, hi," said the girl. "My name is Sandy. Are you staying here tonight, too?"

Then she turned and spoke to something in the bushes. "Don't run away you little cutey. You understand me, don't you?"

"My name is Sara. Yes, we're staying overnight—me, my dad and my brother. Who are you talking to?"

"Come here and see. I met the cutest little squirrel. He's so tame and smart and he loves these peanuts I was lucky enough to have in my jacket pocket."

Sara came around the other side of the wheelbarrow. Sure enough—it was Apkin—tempted by food once again.

Apkin made a squeak when he saw Sara.

"Isn't he darling," the girl named Sandy continued. "I swear, he'd actually make a great pet. He even let me pet him before—but don't tell my mom or she'll kill me."

"Oh, you shouldn't pet squirrels," said Sara, taking advantage of Sandy's words. She didn't like the idea of Apkin becoming a pet.

"Nonsense, look," and Sandy reached out and gave Apkin a little ruffle on the top of his head. "I've never seen anything like it."

Sara felt very angry at Apkin. How could he be so foolish as to take a risk like this for a few peanuts?

Just then, there was a rustle coming from the nearest of the fruit trees. Apkin made another squeak and darted into the orchard.

"Oh, no, I wonder what scared him away?"

"Who knows," said Sara. "Maybe his mate called to him. Doesn't like him talking to humans."

Sandy laughed.

"Well, we might as well go in. We'll have to get ready for dinner soon," said Sandy. "Where are you from, anyway?"

They began to walk back to the house, as Sara answered Sandy's friendly enough questions.

"And you?" asked Sara in return.

"Oh, my parents are divorced and we're visiting my grandma in Columbus, on my spring vacation. I sure wish I could have a pet," she said longingly. "That squirrel really seemed to like me."

"I think you'd be better off with a cat or a dog," suggested Sara. "He probably just liked those peanuts."

"Oh no, he really liked me. He seems smarter than any dog."

They made their way into the front hall and up the steps, and said they would see each other in the dining room later—maybe play a couple of board games after dinner on the porch. Sandy had spied a game table and a stack of games out there.

Sandy turned left at the top of the steps. She and her

mom were sharing a large room at the end of the hall. Sara turned right, toward the other two rooms.

Dinner turned out to be a rather grand affair. The room was filled to capacity with local clientele. The restaurant obviously had a following. The dining room was formal and authentic colonial, down to the pewter dishes. There was even a fire going in the fireplace. The food turned out to be excellent, but because it was an inn and not a hotel, they didn't feel comfortable asking for plates of food to bring up to their rooms afterwards.

They left Lucinda with the vanilla cookies and apples and said they would do what they could. Sara brought along her purse for the occasion and managed to slip in a roll, a biscuit, three carrots sticks from the relish tray, and a piece of roasted potato with rosemary and garlic. Mr. Umberland dropped a couple of chocolates into the pocket of his sports jacket. Steven swiped some packaged mints, but Sara said that didn't count because you were allowed to take those. They dumped the food on a towel on the bed in Sara's room and Lucinda nibbled a little of this and that. Then Sara went downstairs to meet Sandy for a few games out on the porch. Steven and his dad came downstairs for awhile too and had coffee with Sandy's mother. They all played a few card games with the girls and then called it a night.

The trouble didn't make itself known till morning. The family was packed and ready to leave by 8:00 a.m., but first they went downstairs to the dining room for some breakfast. Sara's dad paid the bill at the front desk and then joined them at the breakfast table. They had already put their luggage in the car, including Lucinda and Sarania. By 8:30 they were done with breakfast and ready to go.

Sara looked around the dining room for Sandy and her Mom, but they were nowhere in sight.

"Gee, I was hoping to say good-bye to Sandy. Do you think we could call up to her room before we leave?"

"Sure, hon, ask at the front desk," said her dad. "Meet us outside by the car."

Sara went to the front desk and asked if they could call up to the Petersons.

"Oh, I'm sorry young lady," said the young man at the desk. "They left already, about a half hour ago."

"Oh dear, that's right. Sandy did say something about leaving early. I guess Sandy didn't know how early or she would have said good-bye last night."

"Too bad," said the clerk.

Sara went out to the car and everyone got in.

"I didn't even take down her address. We were going to write," she added.

She placed the carry-on bag at her feet. They would wait till they came down the driveway to the willow tree to pick up the others and secure everyone in. They drove down and turned right onto the quiet country road, and came to a stop in front of the willow. Sara opened the door for the squirrels and owls to jump in while Lucinda got herself and Sarania into their seat. In a moment, the two owls and a frantic Ekle climbed into the car.

"They took him!" screamed Ekle, more upset than

they had ever seen him. "He's gone! Follow their car!"

"You mean Apkin?" asked Sara, not seeing him anywhere.

"Yes! Yes! Let's get going!"

"Who took him?" shouted everyone almost in unison.

"The horrible little girl! In a box! Tricked him with nuts—that stupid brother of mine. I warned him last night in the orchard! I don't know why Selena wants that stupid squirrel back!"

"It must be Sandy who has him," Sara realized. She quickly explained. "When I first met Sandy in the garden last night, she was feeding Apkin peanuts. Apkin was pretending to be a normal squirrel, but Sandy was very impressed with him. She was thrilled at how tame he seemed and said he'd make a great pet. But I never thought she'd actually take off with him. She said her mom would never even let her have a pet."

"Don't just talk. Let's get going!" said Ekle.

The owls and Ekle got into their places.

"Buckle up," said Lucinda.

With Sara's dad driving, they headed back as swiftly as they could to the highway.

"They're heading for Lumberton, in the southern part of the state," said Sara. "I'm glad that came up last night!"

"I know, I know," said her dad, "but we were to get off and head towards Raleigh. If we don't see them before we get to the Raleigh turn-off, we'll have to continue on."

"And they have a half hour head start," added Steven.

"I have a bad headache," added Ekle.

"It was a yellow volkswagon," remembered Steven, cars being something he noticed.

"That's right, with the new fancy grillwork. A bright yellow too," said Mr. Umberland.

"Now don't let's panic," said Lucinda, trying to bring a note of calmness to the situation. "We know the girl is delighted with Apkin. She wants him for a pet, for Heaven's sake, so he's in no danger."

"The danger is in never finding him!" shrieked Ekle again.

"Now, now, we'll find him," reassured Owletta. "Lucinda is right. He's in no danger. We may have to delay our arrival at Haw River, but we'll find him."

Two hours passed and they approached the turn-off for Raleigh with no sighting of a bright yellow car. They were closing in on their destination, but they would have to wait.

"We'll just have to continue south," said Sara's dad.

They increased their speed. Of course, they had no idea how fast Mrs. Peterson was driving.

"She could be a speed maniac!" informed Ekle, whose speech was developing further.

"I hope so," said Steven. "Then the police will be pulling her over and maybe we can catch up."

By now they were an hour south of their Raleigh turn-off. They had not even spotted a speck of yellow in

the distance and they were getting further and further away from their destination. At one point, they had to use the bathroom and luckily they saw a sign that said "Rest Area and Restaurant: 2 miles," so they decided to make a quick stop. As they pulled into the restaurant parking lot, they were welcomed by a beautiful sight. A bright yellow Volkswagon in the parking lot. And it was vacant! They pulled in alongside.

The Umberland family of three poured out of the car so quickly it seemed as swift as magic. Lucinda stayed in the car with Ekle and the owls and pulled the blanket over herself and the baby. Just as Sara, Steven, and their dad approached the front door of the restaurant, Sandy and her mother walked out.

"Sara, what a surprise! We didn't get to say good-bye," said Sandy.

"I thought you were headed towards Raleigh?" questioned Mrs. Peterson.

"We were, but then we had to follow you," said Sara.

"Whatever for?" Mrs. Peterson seemed alarmed.

"Because you have my pet squirrel!" Sara blurted out, not able to hold in her feelings.

"She's not your pet!" said Sandy, getting angry. "How could you say such a thing?"

"He is," confirmed Mr. Umberland. "Sara has had him since he was almost a newborn."

"That's ridiculous, Mom," said Sandy. "We both saw this squirrel in the garden last night. I was feeding him nuts and Sara said squirrels didn't make good pets. She never said little Missy was her pet. She just wants Missy for herself, because she saw how special she is!"

"He is my pet and he's not a she!" said Sara getting exasperated. "His name is Apkin."

"Can you prove it?" said Mrs. Peterson. "My daughter is so fond of this little squirrel. I never thought I would have agreed to a pet squirrel, but she does seem so tame and Sandy is so enthralled with her. I'm really quite impressed with her as well."

"Of course they can't prove it, Mom. The squirrel can't talk and I know they're lying. Let's just get in our car and drive away!"

"Now wait," interrupted Steven. "Just hold on a minute and I think we can prove the squirrel belongs with us."

"Yes," added Mr. Umberland, "Doesn't the fact that he's so tame with people show you that he probably grew up with them?"

"That is a reasonable point," responded Mrs. Peterson. "He is exceptionally tame or I never would have considered this."

"If he's yours," Sandy said sarcastically to Sara, "why didn't you say anything to me last night out in the garden?"

Sara had to think on her feet. A whole big explanation wasn't advisable at a time like this. "We were going to sneak the squirrels into our rooms after dark," she reached for an explanation. "We knew the manager wouldn't allow squirrels in the rooms, so we let them run free for awhile until we had a chance to sneak them in. We do it all the time when we travel."

"Oh, sure. Sounds like what everyone does with their pet squirrel."

"It does sound a bit far-fetched," said Mrs. Peterson.

"Well then, let us prove it to you," said Sara's dad. "Let's get his brother and show you. Sara, hon, go get Ekle," and he handed her the car keys.

Sara returned with Ekle in her arms and Mrs. Peterson and Sandy gasped.

"You see," said Sara. "This is Ekle, Apkin's brother, and he misses Apkin very much."

Mrs. Peterson nodded in acquiescence. "Yes, this certainly does prove it to me. It looks as though the squirrel does belong to this family," she said to her daughter.

"I don't care. I want her, I mean him. She has one and I have one. Let's just leave, Mom. What are they going to do? Chase us all the way to Grandma's and call the police?"

"We might very well do that if you don't see to reason," added Mr. Umberland with authority.

Mrs. Peterson seemed torn, but finally her better judgement took hold. "Let's see how Little Missy responds to them, Sandy. That should prove it once and for all."

She unlocked her car and took out Apkin who was lying quietly in a hat box. He opened his eyes. When he saw Sara with Ekle in her arms, he leaped up and was out the box and up on Sara's shoulder in a flash. Ekle and Apkin bumped noses in the joy of reunion.

"Well I guess that says it all," concluded Steven.

"There's no choice," Mrs. Peterson said with resolve

to her daughter. "The squirrel is theirs. I guess I couldn't offer to buy him or both of them from you?" added the mother.

"Not for a million dollars," said Sara.

"I didn't think so. Sandy, honey, let's go."

"Can I have a dog or a cat then?" asked Sandy, getting in the car without even saying good-bye.

"Well, I guess we'll have to get some kind of pet," they heard Mrs. Peterson say as she got into the driver's seat.

In a moment, behaving as though the Umberlands weren't standing there, the yellow Volkswagon pulled away and disappeared down the highway.

The family gave a sigh of relief and got back into their car. Of course, Lucinda had to invent a poem of joyous reunion. As they made their way back going north on 95, Lucinda began to recite:

"We lost our dear friend,
How? We'll try to explain,
He was picked up and boxed
And completely renamed,
From a he to a she
The kidnapper did title
Our Apkin the squirrel
Was now Missy—her idol!

For the culprit—a girl—
Made Apkin her pet

She lured like a spider,
Right into her net,
Then she loved him and pet him
Till he had to cry
'If I don't get away
Then from love I will die.'

I've been worshipped until
I can't take it at all
I feel so depressed
I'm curled into a ball,
She can coo me forever
But my love she won't claim
And I certainly won't answer
To 'Missy'—it's insane!

But for Apkin our friend
We would search till we dropped,
In our car we pursued them
Till they came to a stop.
Then we pressed them and argued
Till our point was full won,
We were lucky that thief
Had forgotten her gun!

We claimed him for ours
We proved him our own
We freed him from worship
And brought him back home."

CHAPTER FOURTEEN

The Homecoming

By late afternoon, they were closing in on their destination. As they approached their goal, the excitement between the friends grew and overpowered any sadness they would later feel at "good-bye" time. They sang and were merry. They had made a plan, stuck to it and would now reap the reward. By 4:30 p.m., they were off the highway and on the back roads heading for the edge of the Haw River.

"Does any of this look familiar?" Sara's dad asked

Owletta and Hool. Steven was in the driver's seat.

"Well, not yet," said Owletta.

"Doesn't look quite right to me," added Hool.

"But then, dear, what do you suggest?" Owletta questioned her fiancé. "I mean, this is your home territory. What feels right to you?"

"It feels to me like it's east of here. But flying is a lot different than driving. I can't quite get my bearings."

"Well I have an idea," interrupted Lucinda. "Why don't we concentrate on finding the river. It's got to be here, off to the right somewhere. We'll make our way down, Hool, and then you can get out and do a sweep of the area."

"Sounds sensible," said Sara's dad. "I'll make the first right I come to and we'll take it from there."

The opportunity arrived shortly. They made the turn onto a dirt road that cut between a field of tall grasses. There were many potholes and puddles in the road and the muddy water splashed up onto the sides of the car and even onto the windows. The road led them nowhere—only to a dead end with nothing in front of them but more brush and no river in sight.

"Boy, this really feels off the beaten track," commented Steven.

"Nice and peaceful," said Hool, seeing it somewhat differently.

"Maybe we should call it a day," suggested Mr. Umberland. "We can come back tomorrow and have all day to search."

This suggestion did not go over well with most of the passengers. Ekle and Apkin complained mercilessly, and Owletta and Hool insisted that they could find the way instantly, once they got to the river. Even the kids were anxious to push on. Lucinda remained calm, but her heart was beating wildly.

"Let's give it one more try," said Steven.He turned the car around carefully, avoiding the holes as much as possible. They made their way back up the mile of bad road to the paved road where they had turned. It was a good three miles before they came to another road that looked worth the risk.

"Okay, I'll give it another try," repeated Mr. Umberland, making his turn onto a road that looked very similar to the first.

"Here we go," said Sara as the car went over a big bump in the road and splashed some muddy water up on the windshield.

"What a mess!" observed Steven.

"Lots of mud," commented Apkin from the back window. He put his tongue on the glass and pretended to lick the mud.

The car went over another bump and now the road began to descend ever so slightly, weaving to the right and left. The landscape was dotted with trees, many of them willows, as they continued their descent. After one more sweep to the right the river came into view. A cheer went up in the car.

"Thar she blows!" cried Sara dramatically.

"Open the window," said Hool. "I want to get a sniff."

Sara pressed the button, down came the window and in came a splatter of dirty water as the car hit another puddle. Sara brushed a little dirty water off her cheek, as Hool and Owletta leaned out the window. They were moving slowly—down to a crawl.

"Smells like Vinetrope country," declared Hool and another shout of joy went up.

"I'll be to the river in another minute," calculated Mr. Umberland.

"Go carefully," said Lucinda, but you could hear the excitement in her voice.

The river was a wide, calm belt of late afternoon color. This was a soft and gentle river that didn't appear to be going anywhere in a hurry.

After a few more twists and turns, they reached the river's edge and Sara's father brought the car to a stop in a muddy clearing. They all got out and immediately their feet sank into the mud.

"Yuk," said Sara. "My sneakers are a wreck!"

Ekle, Apkin and the owls didn't pay much notice. In a moment they were all in a willow tree, stretching their legs and wings and commenting on the tranquillity of the spot. Lucinda, baby in arms, found a log down by the water to rest on.

"I'll circle around for a bit and get our location fixed," said Hool. In a moment he was gliding over the river.

"I'm exhausted," admitted Owletta. "All this driving is very tiring. My wings ache from being cramped almost as much as if I'd been flying."

"I hope we're almost there," said Ekle.

"Yes, yes—Selena—I'm almost home!" said Apkin joyously.

Sara, her dad and her brother went down to the moss covered log and joined Lucinda. They sat in a row facing the water. In truth, they were all feeling rather tired by now. Sara was just about to doze off against her dad's arm when Hool returned.

Hool seemed excited, but took a moment to catch his breath. "We're almost there! The Vinetrope village is only about a mile up river, but on the other side. We'll have to get back to the road, drive about two miles to a bridge, cross over and come back down the other side."

"Wonderful!" said Lucinda. "Did you stop in and speak to anyone?"

"Yes, Klent Abo, they are thrilled at your arrival, Lucinda. He also told me that Regata and Selena are at the old beech tree. Selena told Regata that you boys would be coming sometime in the next few months, so Regata moved into the beechnut tree with her. She's not afraid of vintropes anymore!"

"My Regata!"

"My Selena!"

"Yes, they're ecstatic too!" continued Hool. "And Cobcaw and Skitter are there as well, Owletta. They wanted to see how it all turns out. First we'll get Lucinda settled

and then we can head over to the beechnut. It's only a short ways from here by car."

"This is wonderful," said Lucinda. "What a wedding you will have my dear Owletta and Hool."

"Well then, let's get going," said Mr. Umberland.

Soon they were back in their seats and ready to go. Sara's dad took over, turned on the ignition, and put the car into reverse, but the car wouldn't back up. The wheels kept spinning uselessly, sinking into the mud.

"I was afraid this would happen!" he shouted.

He put the car into drive and the same thing happened.

"Steven, get in the driver's seat. I think I've got some kind of gizmo in the trunk to put under the wheels."

"Okay, Dad."

Steven got out of the back seat and took his place in the driver's, while his dad went around to the trunk. He had to pile half the luggage out of the trunk onto the grass in order to get to the supplies on the bottom. Along with the jack and a couple of flashlights, he found two rubber wedges—a device meant to overcome skidding by giving the wheels some traction.

"I found them," he said holding them up. "Okay, Steven, I'm going to put these things in place and when I give the word, put the car in reverse and go for it."

"Okay, Dad."

He placed the wedges in the most advantageous spot, stepped to the side and gave the word. "Okay. Give it a try!"

Steven turned on the motor, put the gears in reverse

and drove it hard. For a moment, it looked like it was going to work, but then the wedges themselves toppled over sideways and sank into the mud.

"Okay, stop," called Steven's dad. "This mud is awful. The more you stir it up, the worse it gets."

"Shall we try again?" Steven suggested.

"Okay, I'll set them up in front this time."

He placed the muddy wedges in front, but the mud was so deep and slippery, it was hard to keep them upright.

"Hon," he said to Sara, "maybe you should get out."

Sara got out and stepped to the side also.

Her dad again put the wedges in place, and with the help of a couple of stones, they looked pretty secure. He moved out of the way.

"Okay, hit the gas pedal!"

Steven gave it his best shot, but they were going nowhere.

"I'm afraid I'm just too small to be of any help," said Lucinda through the opened window.

"I wonder how far we are from the nearest gas station?" asked Steven.

"Pretty far, I would say," said Mr. Umberland.

"I wonder how far we are from anywhere?" said Steven.

"Well, we're close to the vinetrope village," said Sara.

"About three miles on foot for you walkers," said Hool, "if you walk to the bridge, cross over and then turn back down on the other side."

"Maybe the bridge gets some traffic and we'll meet

someone who can help," said Mr. Umberland.

"I think it makes sense for us to walk to my village," interrupted Lucinda, sticking her head out the car window. "If we happen to meet someone who can help us on the way, fine. But I'm sure once we get to my people, they'll be able to help you get your car out of the mud. We may be little, but as a group we can do a lot!"

"Well, I don't think we have a choice," said Sara's dad. "We're in the middle of nowhere on something that can barely be called a road. We could sit here till next March before anyone came along. I think you're right, Lucinda. We'll head for your village."

Everyone agreed. Ekle and Apkin seemed quite cheerful about the whole thing. They were glad to be on good old terra firma again. For Hool and Owletta the distance was no big thing. It was the humans who weren't too happy about walking three miles in the mud. Steven and his dad piled all the muddy luggage back in the trunk and locked it up. Sara decided to bring her trusty backpack and Lucinda, holding Sarania, hopped into it for the walk. Sara insisted.

The world was spring green and wet along the Haw River. After a half mile of irritation and complaints, the path became dryer and more pleasant. Everyone's spirits rose.

"You know," said Lucinda sounding quite elated, "It's kind of fitting that we walk the last mile. In all the great legends of vinetropes, the heroes and heroines are on foot making their way to their final destinations."

"That's true for human legends, too," Steven realized.

"Yes, just think of Bilbo in The Hobbit!" piped up Sara.

"Although I can't actually say I'm doing the walking," Lucinda observed.

"I love carrying you. This might be the last time for a long time, Lucinda."

"Someday we'll walk together again on an even bigger adventure," added Lucinda.

"If this adventure is as long as Tolkien's Lord of the Rings," teased Steven, "it'll go into the next generation!"

"Indeed it might!" confirmed Lucinda seriously.

Ekle and Apkin kept darting back and forth and Owletta and Hool patiently waited for them every few hundred yards, perched on some tree branch.

"Lucinda, this will be good-bye," said Sara sadly. "Somehow I didn't believe it was going to really happen."

They came to a turn in the river where many little pink flowers grew in the grass and the air smelled sweet. The sky was deepening into a melon color—that beautiful time of evening when day and night seem equal partners. Just then the party of friends heard the most beautiful music. It was the sound of pipes—an instrument that sounded like something between a flute and a clarinet.

"What's that wonderful music?" asked Sara.

"That's a glintlight pipe" exclaimed Lucinda with delight. "I've dreamt of this music, but I never thought I'd actually hear it."

"Then it must be a vinetrope playing it!" said Sara.

Lucinda was so excited, she climbed out of the knapsack and onto Sara's left shoulder with baby Sarania.

The music came closer as they continued to walk, and at the next turn, they came face to face with a young male vinetrope, playing an odd pipe that looked as though it were made of a dried pumpkin stem. He was dressed in a yellow tunic with brown leggings. He walked briskly, but the instant he saw them, he stopped in his tracks.

"Lucinda, our Master Rhymer, is this you?" He was looking up directly at Lucinda and grinning wildly. "Welcome! You don't know how excited we all are."

Lucinda motioned to Sara to put her down, and in a second, she was on the ground greeting the pipe player. They embraced in greeting and Sara could see that as good-natured as Lucinda had always seemed, she was not truly happy till this very moment.

"I am so happy to be home," were all the words Lucinda needed to say it all.

"And you have a child," noticed the piper. "A double blessing to our nation! But please, excuse me everyone. My name is Glintel Fernroote and I am the head musician of our growing population, with a number of talented young students already, I might boast."

"You seemed in a hurry," said Steven.

"Yes, to meet our Rhymer and her odd party of friends. When Hool arrived a little while ago, Klent Abo the Guide went straight to Chantrek, our Master Healer, and Chantrek sent me right out to meet you. I am known for my great gift of speed. That is why I am called Glintel,

because I dart as quickly as a ray of light glinting from one place to another—like a golden note."

"And your music sounds as clear as light," added Lucinda.

"Indeed. That is why it is called the glintlight pipe. Oh dear, I almost forgot my purpose. Chantrek has asked that only Lucinda, the owls and the human child Sara, be allowed to enter our world, as agreed upon. He hopes that the others do not take offense. Our days are new and we are vulnerable. Chantrek must think of our safety first."

"Dad, can I go? Please!"

"How long will she be with you?"

"Three or four hours will do," answered Glintel. "Chantrek wants the honor of meeting the human child, Sara, that Hool told us our Master Rhymer is so fond of."

Here Glintel made a bow to Sara. "I assume you are she?"

"Yes," said both Sara and Lucinda.

Then introductions went around. It was explained to Glintel that the car was stuck in the mud. It was decided that Glintel would leave with Lucinda, Sarania, and Sara and go straight to the vinetrope village. The owls would fly directly to Chantrek and explain to him about the car and where it was stuck. Chantrek could easily send some of his people by boat (boats much too small for humans) directly down the river to the car. Steven, Mr. Umberland and the squirrels should wait by the car for the boats. They would bring rolled mats made out of braided grass and they would use this matting to get the car free. It made an excellent traction device. Everyone would have to be patient. It made sense for the humans and the squirrels to go back to the car and stay put. Sara would be safe, visiting with the vinetropes. By the time she was done, the car would be free. Then they should first drive Ekle and Apkin close to their home at the beechnut and let them out. Then they should go directly to the bridge and wait for Sara. She would be accompanied back to them by the owls and Glintel.

"What about Lucinda?" asked Sara who suddenly didn't want to have to say good-bye.

"We will have said our good-byes already," said Lucinda softly, understanding the pain in Sara's voice. "Don't forget, it's not good-bye forever."

"I know," said Sara. "But it is good-bye for now."

"How will we get all of Lucinda's supplies to the village?" Steven remembered to ask.

"Yes, Lucinda, and the supplies you promised to me for the energy experiments. We can't forget that," added Mr. Umberland.

"We can easily transport all Lucinda's possessions with us back on the boats," explained Glintel. "But I don't know anything about these other supplies you refer to."

"Of course not," said Lucinda. "I will explain it to Chantrek and my people when I arrive". Then she turned to Sara's dad. "Just make sure you put all your specimen bottles on the boats along with my belongings. I will take care of everything else. It will delay your wait at the river."

"Then it will just have to," said Mr. Umberland.

"It will give Sara a little more time with us," Lucinda realized.

"Yes," said Glintel. "We will time bringing Sara to you at the bridge after we get you these "specimens" that you need."

Now was the first sad parting. Lucinda had to say good-bye to Steven and Mr. Umberland. The squirrels and the owls she would still see with some frequency.

"We've had some great times, haven't we, Steven!"

"I'll never forget the night I met you, Lucinda—sticking out of the trick-or-treat bag like a lit-up pumpkin!"

"Or how you rescued me from the sewer."

Steven bent down and gave Lucinda a kiss on the forehead.

"Take good care of that little girl of yours. She looks twice the size already."

"I will. In another couple of months she'll be able to start helping her people."

Mr. Umberland bent down to say good-bye now. His eyes were moist and he shook Lucinda's fuzzy hand and gave the baby a gentle hug with his thumb and forefinger. Lucinda and Sara got teary-eyed.

"I'll get you those supplies," said Lucinda to Mr. Umberland.

He nodded. "I'm very hopeful about the outcome."

For the first time in history, at least that we are aware of, squirrels shed tears. It was time for Ekle and Apkin to say good-bye to Sara, and later the rest of the Umberland family.

"I'll miss you fellows so much!" said Sara, giving them each a little head rubbing.

"I'll miss human fingers," said Ekle.

"You won't be meeting our mates," added Apkin with disappointment in his voice.

"Oh, that's right," said Sara.

"It's best for now," explained Lucinda. "We can only do so much at a time."

"Yes," agreed Ekle. "Regata may have accepted vinetropes by now, but she's had no time to learn human ways."

"Selena would be scared too," agreed Apkin.

"And I don't want to make them anxious at a time when you should all be rejoicing," Sara said with understanding.

"And you'll miss our wedding," realized Owletta.

"We will," said Sara, feeling another loss.

"But we can tell you every detail when we come up to visit," remembered Owletta.

"And we will," Hool promised.

"That's enough," said Sara. "I can't take this anymore, let's get going."

"Come," said Glintel. "Let's be on our way. Our people are impatient for your arrival."

Mr. Umberland and Steven left with the squirrels to return to the car. Lucinda and Sarania got back into Sara's backpack and Glintel led the way. Owletta and Hool headed straight for the village to explain about the car.

Sara had to walk quickly to keep up with Glintel,

who walked twice the speed of the average human even though he was so much smaller. As they came across the bridge, it was nearly dark. They entered a thicket, and then a wooded area. Now both Glintel and Lucinda turned up their glow, so they could see into the darkness.

"I'm so excited!" Lucinda whispered into Sara's right ear, leaning out the side of the pack. "It all seems too wonderful to be true. Remember when I thought I was the only vinetrope in the world?"

"Of course I do. You didn't show it, but you must have felt terribly lonely to think you were the only one of your kind in existence."

"You made me much less lonely, Sara. If it weren't for you, and how you accepted and befriended me, I think I might have withered. Why you made me feel extraordinary—almost magical."

"But to me, you are extraordinary and magical!" said Sara.

"Not so extraordinary. Just a vinetrope. A glower, true, but even glowers are normal for my species. It's you who seem extraordinary to me, Sara. So full of life and interested in everything around you."

Glintel's music led them further into the wild.

"Doesn't he play beautifully?" said Lucinda dreamily.

"Yes."

"I've heard music like this a hundred times in my dreams and now I'm really hearing it. He's kind of cute, that Glintel, don't you think?" Lucinda whispered.

"Another wedding?" teased Sara.

Lucinda chuckled. "Time will tell, but I do have a feeling about that boy."

After about fifteen minutes of steady walking and winding, Sara and Lucinda began to notice a soft light in the distance. It would disappear and then begin again, like dense fog catching the light emanating from a lantern.

"Just a short ways to go," called Glintel over his shoulder.

The ground felt particularly soft and spongy under Sara's feet, and where the glow from the vinetropes touched the ground, the grass looked a brilliant green. The terrain became hilly, with gentle slopes, and had opened up from a wild thicket into a grassy field with occasional groups of trees. Everything smelled clean and spicy. The ground seemed warm under Sara's feet.

"Yum! It smells like home," said Lucinda.

Directly in front of them loomed the largest willow tree Sara had ever seen. It was to the side of this tree that the occasional glow seemed to be coming from.

Glintel came to a stop by the willow and Sara could see that a hill rose up beyond the tree. A mass of vines tumbled down the hill. Owletta and Hool were waiting for them near the vines.

"The boats are on their way," confirmed Hool.

They stood quietly next to Glintel and a spray of vines was pulled to the side to reveal a smiling face and a glowing entrance.

"I turned up the glow a couple times to let you know the coast was clear," said the smiling face.

"This is Klent Abo," introduced Glintel.

"Lucinda, I'm overjoyed to have you with us!" said Klent Abo to Lucinda, bowing and smiling. They both embraced. "And you must be Sara," he bowed to Sara as well. "Step inside quickly and watch your head, Sara. It gets higher once we're in the hall, but the entrance is a tight fit for a being your size."

Sara ducked inside and her eyes widened with wonder. With her head bent down, she ran down the little incline and then was able to stand upright in the glowing hallway with just a few inches to spare over her head. The walls and ceiling seemed alive with light. Owletta and Hool followed her in.

"It's beautiful!" said Sara.

"It's wonderful and beautiful and home!" said Lucinda.

"I'll stay at the entrance and keep my watch," said Klent Abo.

Glintel nodded.

"Put me down now," said Lucinda. "I want to enter my village on my own two feet."

In a split second, Lucinda was standing on her own turf with baby Sarania nuzzled against her. The baby was wide-eyed and kept sniffing the air.

"Follow me," said Glintel, heading onward, playing his music once again. He slowed up a bit so Lucinda could keep at his pace. This gave Sara time to gaze about in wonder as they walked. She took in all the same amazing details that Owletta had mentioned on her visit. Now this was an adventure! Sara asked many questions. She noticed all the details—the variety of colors that the roots glowed in, the intricate details and patterns the vinetropes were able to sculpt them into, the warmth of the air, the breezes that blew through the hall, the wonderful fresh smell. All of it delighted Sara and delighted Lucinda even more.

"It's just right, it's just perfect," Lucinda kept saying.

Then they heard music up ahead.

"Something I composed in your honor, Lucinda," Glintel turned to say. Then he stepped forward and his piping blended with the music up ahead. The melody soared. It was a sound so moving and splendid that Lucinda began to cry with joy and Sara felt so much that she thought she would burst.

They arrived in the Great Hall, in a wave of music, with all the town there to greet them. Chantrek came forward and Lucinda stepped ahead of Sara to greet him. They embraced, and the crowd gave a cheer of such welcome that Lucinda began to positively sob.

"My vinetropes, my vinetropes. I can't begin to tell you how happy I am to be here. And I wouldn't have had the courage or the ability, if it wasn't for my dear friend, Sara."

"To Sara, to Lucinda and her newborn daughter!" cheered the crowd, lifting glasses into the air while the musicians played. Sara and Lucinda were offered glasses filled with a pale green liquid.

"Our village is now complete! A nation in the making!" announced Chantrek to his people. "May we grow

and prosper and find our place in this world. Let us drink to our Master Rhymer, who will give us our history and make us our legends so that we can live with meaning."

"And let us also drink to our first human friend, the child Sara, whom we have named Sara the Connector—for when the time is right, we believe she will be the link between her world and ours."

A cheer went up and everyone toasted the two friends. The drink tasted at once cool, sweet, spicy and rich. Sara found it impossible to describe to her family afterwards.

"Do you accept your Vinetrope name, Sara the Connector, and all it might mean?" asked Chantrek.

"In Vinetropese," explained Lucinda, "your name would be pronounced Sara Kroenda."

"I accept," said Sara, too overwhelmed to fully understand the implications.

"To Sara Kroenda," cheered the crowd.

"I already have a job for Sara to do," announced Lucinda.

Sara was surprised. "What?"

"I think I must first explain to my people some of the problems this world holds for all of us," said Lucinda, "and how our own natural energy supply could help greatly to solve some of these problems."

"We know that our watering system cleans up spoiled earth," said Chantrek. "And we know that some day we will need to share this helpful tool with humans. But what is this energy supply you speak of, Lucinda?"

Then Lucinda explained to her people that humans, who had created so many wonderful inventions, also, unknowingly at first, used an energy source that was unclean and unhealthy for the planet. They couldn't run their world without this energy. She explained that she had given Sara's dad, who was a scientist, some of her watering liquid and roots to study. That if he could learn to manufacture vinetrope energy, it would not only clean up the earth, but keep it running clean from then on. The vinetropes were thrilled to know that they could offer so much help to the world and agreed unanimously to do so. They would fill the jars for Sara's father that would be arriving with Lucinda's belongings. Then they would transport them back to the car.

"But we need a safe plan to go about helping the humans," warned Chantrek. "How can we know they won't misuse us? How can we know who to trust?"

"And that's where Sara's help will be needed first," Lucinda answered. "We must hold off making ourselves known for awhile. Sara's father will simply say he discovered the roots. We need time to deal with our own growing population. But we cannot hide forever."

Everyone pretty much agreed, and because they were going to remain unexposed for a still unknown amount of time, they had time to work out any of their concerns.

"I know that if intelligent plant life and intelligent animal life work together, we can solve many problems," continued Lucinda. "It will be Sara's job when she is older to introduce me to her world. I will be the first Vinetrope humans will meet because I have the most experience and knowledge of them."

"Lucinda, how long have you realized this?" asked Sara.

"It didn't form fully in my mind until today, when I knew I would have to say good-bye to you. Do you accept the challenge?"

"Do you think I'm the right person?"

"Definitely and absolutely. We're in this together."

"Than I accept."

Owletta and Hool cooed and clucked. They were as proud of their two friends as if they were their own children.

"Let us sing a song of beginnings in our ancient tongue," suggested Chantrek. He turned to Lucinda. "Will you recite your first rhyme to your people in Vinetropese?"

"You have a language?" Sara asked, feeling foolish after she asked it.

"Of course, Sara. I think I did mention it to you once. You've never heard it because I had no one to speak it with," she smiled, her eyes moist with feeling. "Now let me think." She closed her eyes and spoke:

"Saranda ve Vinetrope
Ata woodnet je vine,
A tamba ty ut tamb
Ki te Kindtrope
Eh Vinetrope

Metateta krone vine.
Kanta te Vinetrope
Ehmoorranndra eh
Klowt ut at lite
Metatata
Je Vinda
Te kronda
Eh keet fiir
Ata Nite."

Lucinda finished. Everyone held silent for a moment and then began the applause. Many vinetropes were crying.

"Let me translate for my friend Sara," said Lucinda.

"Let there come
New Growth
From new wood
To last through
All time—
So that Old Growth
And New Growth
Will make a strong vine.

Let the vine grow
And spread out and
Touch all with light
And chase away fears
That may trouble our nights."

This time Sara hugged Lucinda and everyone again applauded.

"Then vinetrope means new growth?" said Sara, picking up enough through the translation to catch that meaning. Her new name as "Sara the Connector" began to take on greater weight. New growth and old growth, twined together, connected, to make a stronger world. She had a lot to think about.

"Yes, my dear, vinetrope means new growth, like the new growth of vines, or to put it another way—it means beginnings."

"It seems that in the short time our Master Rhymer has been here, many of the questions we've had about our future have already been answered," said Chantrek.

Everyone toasted Lucinda and seemed excited to know that they all would play a role in helping the world.

Lucinda then went on to explain some of their history to them. She told them about the Ice Age and how their people must have foreseen their end and buried many of their seeds with the hope that some day the world would warm and once again vinetropes could flourish.

"But there is one mystery that I can't explain myself," said Lucinda, "even though I'm your historian. The answer is not built into my memory, because it obviously happened after my seed was made. Can any of you tell me how our seeds got here, to North Carolina, so far away from where they were originally buried?"

"That's right," said Sara. "We know that Lucinda's seed got stuck in Ekle's foot before he and Apkin were

locked in the pecan barrels and shipped up north. That's how her seed got in my garden. When Ekle and Apkin escaped the barrels, they made their home in my yard. Lucinda was obviously originally part of your seed pile. But we never figured out how all of you arrived here."

"I may have a partial answer," said Chantrek. "I was the first to be born, along with three regular babies. Thank goodness I was a glower and was there to take care of them. We grew on a vine near a large rock with many holes in it. The rock was on the edge of what I believe you call a yard, Sara. The giants, humans, lived in this place in an extremely large house. Their size and strangeness worried me."

"Then that's why you all speak English!" Sara realized, interrupting. "I'm so used to Lucinda speaking to me it didn't occur to me till now that I shouldn't have expected that you would."

"Exactly," said Lucinda. "I've been a bit overwhelmed myself."

"Yes," continued Chantrek. "Many of us here sprouted near humans. I observed what I still thought to be giants from behind the rock. That's when I noticed something shimmering in one of the holes in the rock. When I looked closer I realized what it was—a pile of vinetrope seeds. I didn't have to be a Master Rhymer to figure out what they were. At the edge of the rock had sprouted many other vines with eighteen pods. Two had orange flowers on it and one a green flower. That meant three glowers to help me in my task."

"How exciting," said Hool.

"What did you do?" asked Lucinda.

"I was afraid that the bright flowers might draw the attention of the humans. I also knew I must move the seeds and pods to a safer, more remote place. I braided a mat and secured the babies to the mat, uprooted the pods properly for transplanting, and put the seeds in my pocket. Then, dragging the babies and pod plantings behind me, I headed into the countryside until I found a spot that seemed safe. Here!"

"My goodness, Chantrek, you had so much more to do than me!" said Lucinda with admiration.

"Well, I had help. The flowers became Setalia, and Rousemira, and Glintel, whom you've met, so right away things became easier. Setalia and Rousemira, where are you?"

Two young women vinetropes stepped forward and waved.

"We planted a few seeds at a time, not wanting to overburden ourselves, as we already had a large nursery of babies to take care of. All the pods but two matured safely after they were transplanted and the babies were born two weeks later within days of each other."

"How fantastic," said Lucinda. "You thought it out so well."

"How many Vinetropes did the seeds produce?" asked Owletta. "The seeds you put in your pocket."

"We grew fifty babies and ten Glowers from the original seeds."

"But since then," continued Chantrek, "we've

matured and there has been quite a few marriages and new seeds made."

"And so we're in the world again!" Lucinda proclaimed.

"I wonder where the rock came from?" asked Sara. "Were there others like it in the yard?"

"No. After we were settled, I came back to check, just for that purpose. I came at night to see if there were more seeds scattered anywhere else. The humans had many unusual rocks all over their yard, but every one of them was different. There wasn't another one like the rock that held our seeds. I checked them all, anyway. There were so many. One was purple and glittered. There was one that looked like it was made out of silver and one black and so shiny it reflected the moon."

"What color was your rock?" asked Sara. She was seeing something in all these rocks.

"It was a deep red, filled with holes, and lighter than the other rocks. I could move it quite easily and checked to see if any seeds had fallen underneath."

"That's it," said Sara, delighted at her detective skills.

"What?" several members asked at once.

"The rock sounds like a piece of volcanic rock. There is volcanic rock in Iceland—a very likely place for your seeds to have been buried with the coming of the Ice Age. Over time the seeds must have been exposed. A lot of people go to Iceland now to go glacier skiing and stuff, and scientists study in places that are more remote. I think the owner of this yard likes to bring home geological samples from the places he has traveled to. He decorates his yard with rocks from around the world. One of his trips must have been to a place like Iceland, and he brought the rock with your seeds in it, home to North Carolina, where the warm air allowed you to sprout!"

"Sara, you've done it again!" said Lucinda. "What fine thinking. Your theory makes good sense. I'm certain it is right. Do you see, everyone, how much we can solve if humans and vinetropes work together?"

"But what took you so long to sprout, Lucinda?" asked Hool. "This village has been growing for some time and the squirrels brought you up north only a year ago."

"Well, we can only guess that my seed was not moved with Chantrek's migration," said Lucinda.

"You could have been lost in a suitcase or packing box," said Sara.

"Exactly, and got dumped out at some later point in time for Ekle to step on me."

"We'll never know all the details," said Chantrek.

"But we know enough to make some sense of our continuing history," concluded Lucinda. "And Sara has been a great friend and good thinker for us."

Everyone cheered and toasted to a future in which intelligent plant life and animal life would share the world in harmony.

"Let us drink to the health of our Rhymer and our Connector," said Chantrek. "May we tell their story to our children, and to theirs from this time on. And may we add richly to this story so that it will become a great legend from which we may all gain strength—humans and vinetropes and animals alike." With this, Chantrek took a sip from his glass and everyone followed with cheers and cries of good will.

Sara was seated at a banquet table and given delicious things to eat—some salty and some sweet. There was dancing to the wonderful music, more toasts and good conversation and then, all too quickly, it was time for her to leave.

"Come," said Owletta gently, "It is time for us to go."

Sara took Chantrek's hand and said good-bye. She waved to the crowd who cheered to her—"Sara the Connector, Sara Kroenda! We will see you again! To the future, to the past, to the present—to our history!"

Sara dropped to her knees and gave Lucinda a big hug and baby Sarania a little kiss on the cheek. Then she could contain her sadness no longer, nor could Lucinda, and they both had a good cry.

"Bye-bye, Sara," said a tiny voice.

"Did you hear that everyone! My baby just spoke her first words. And they were to you Sara," she said, smiling through her tears. "She knows your name is Sara."

Sara returned a teary smile.

"Be happy for me," said Lucinda. "I am home."

"I am," answered Sara, finding it difficult to talk.

They hugged once more and then Sara stood up and followed Glintel, Hool and Owletta out of the big hall and into the passageway from which they had entered. Just before losing the view of the Great Hall, Sara turned back one last time. There danced Lucinda, happy and at home with her people, her baby being fussed over by a crowd of vinetropes. Yes, this was the way it must be. She took a long look. It might be a long time before she saw Lucinda like this again. Then she turned and left quickly, catching up to the sound of Glintel's pipe.

Fred Ross
1994

EPILOGUE

It was a warm June evening and Sara sat alone on the very wall where she had first met Lucinda nine months before. Her feet dangled next to Lucinda's front door. She had done as she promised and removed all traces of Lucinda's chimney and pulleys—all signs of civilization. She just left the roots. She missed her friends Ekle and Apkin and Owletta and Hool. She kept expecting the other squirrels or birds to talk to her, but they didn't. She wondered why. After all, many of them had been around while Lucinda was here. It was obvious—some animals were pre-disposed to the incredible changes that had occurred in her friends, most were not. She wondered if that would be true for people as well. If so, that was a problem she could start thinking about now. And what of those giants and goblin-like-beings Lucinda had told her about. If they were sentient plant life too, wasn't it possible that they also might have seeds sprouting somewhere at this very moment? She would let the implications of so many possibilities ripen. These were major questions and she didn't know if she was up to the task. She certainly couldn't answer them alone. But then, she wouldn't have to be alone. She had family and friends.

School would be out in four days and before she knew it, Owletta and Hool would be up for their visit with news of Lucinda. She hoped so. Yes, it would happen. Her dad was working on the experiments with his whole team and was very excited. She and her dad talked about things all the time now. He called her his "thinker." Steven was going on an official "dig" in Arizona next week, and he would be getting credit for it for college. Then he would be leaving for Boston at the end of August. Dad was proud of Stevie too. He had won a scholarship. Lorraine would be entering her last year of high school. She had promised to call and visit and when she got her driver's license they could go shopping together. Summer was officially only two days away and she was going to spend two weeks at the shore with Rona, who had turned out to be a good friend, although she could not confide in Rona about vinetropes.

Yet, despite all these good things, Sara was feeling sad. But then feeling sad was unavoidable. It was simply that she missed Lucinda so much. But it wasn't a terrible sadness, not like the loss she felt for so long after her mom died. That was a sadness that no one should ever have to know. But it was one that many do know. And if she could survive a loss like that, she could manage missing Lucinda.

Just then, as evening deepened into night, Sara caught the flicker of a firefly. It was close by, below her, right in front of Lucinda's old home. Then, further away in the dark bushes, several more blinked in the stillness.

"Lucinda's stupid cousins," she giggled out loud.

She felt a little better. It was a beautiful night. "Enjoy it," she thought. She couldn't spend her whole childhood waiting to see Lucinda again. Lucinda definitely wouldn't approve. A time would come when they would be together. But right now she was almost twelve and the whole summer lay ahead of her. There was so much to discover. Even without Lucinda.

S. LAZARUS ROSS

Closing Poem

So it unfolds,
This tale of new birth,
This story of life
Coming up from the earth.
A story of growth
With both sweetness and pain
Where two beings meet
But things don't stay the same.

The leaves spread out green
And cover our heads
While too many tears
I hope were not shed.
For to tell a good tale
The heart I must pull,
I hope that your heart
Is now feeling full.

We will all take a rest
While our two friends still grow,
When it's time to resume
I am certain I'll know.
For they both live inside me,
They'll know what to do
And I promise, my friends
To share it with you.

Sherry L. Ross has a background in arts and writing. She attended the Arts Student League in Manhattan for three semesters, studying with Robert Schultz and Nathan Cabot Hale. She also worked in the fashion industry for two years as a designer for a trimmings and applique′ manufacturer. Ross worked with Marguerite Young at Seton Hall University in the seventies and with the poet David Ignatow for three semesters at the 92nd St. Y in Manhattan in the early '80s. In the '90s she won two awards from POET magazine for two chapbooks of poetry. *Seeds of the Pomegranate* is her published book-length version of one of these chapbooks.

The Light of Lucinda is Sherry's first published novel. It is a fantasy/adventure for children and a dream-come-true for the author. *The Light of Lucinda* combines many of Sherry's interests. It is a novel in which the main character spontaneously speaks in rhyme and because of this technique this book is a wonderful introduction to poetry for children. In these poems, which are woven into the prose as dialogue, she implements the use of rhyme and meter to make the poems delightful for the young reader and refreshing for the adult who hasn't read rhyme in quite some time. All the black and white drawings are her work, and the beautiful cover illustration and interior color plates are her husband Fred's work.

The author and her husband have a son and a daughter. They live in NJ with their teenage daughter and their three Abyssinian cats.